THE SMUGGLER'S DAUGHTER

CLAIRE MATTURRO

Unlocking New Worlds

The Smuggler's Daughter
Red Adept Publishing, LLC
104 Bugenfield Court
Garner, NC 27529
http://RedAdeptPublishing.com/

This is a work of fiction. Names, characters, places, and incidents either are the product of the author's imagination or are used fictitiously, and any resemblance to locales, events, business establishments, or actual persons—living or dead—is entirely coincidental.

1.   http://StreetlightGraphics.com

To William D. Hamner, the best brother ever

Prologue

Dolphin Cove Fishing Village, Gulf Coast of Florida, Summer, 1959

Tank Pettus was sweating in his backyard, trying to fix the torn webbing in one of his nets, when his daughter, Kitty, and her best friends, CeCe and Nicky, came running around the side of the house.

Kitty threw herself at him in a hug that made the beer in Tank's hand slosh. He put the can down and hugged her back.

"Daddy, you forgot to give me a dime for the collection plate, but Nicky gave me his to put in." Kitty pulled out of the hug.

"I'll give you both two dimes for next Sunday," he said, smiling. "Now, run inside and change and get something to drink." Walking back from church had to have left them hot and thirsty.

The children dashed toward the back door. They were such pretty kids. Kitty was dark-skinned like her mom, while CeCe and Nicky were blond twins, all three of them long-legged and skinny.

He'd barely sipped another swallow of his warming beer when the kids rushed back to him.

"Daddy." Kitty's high voice held a hint of a whine. "What are we supposed to do? We can't get in, and we got on our Sunday school clothes." She tilted her pixie head to look up at him, a frown creasing her tanned forehead.

"I'm hungry," Nicky said.

Tank laughed. Nicky was always hungry. He turned to CeCe, who seemed to be the steady one in the group. "What's the matter?"

1

"Kitty's mom locked the doors. We're all shut out of the house." CeCe brushed at her pink skirt as if already worrying about getting it dirty.

"She must be feeling poorly then." *Again.* "Go play. And don't get your clothes dirty." If his wife didn't get up by nightfall and let them all in, he could break into the house by prying open the back window. He'd try to give her as much quiet as he could, but hungry six- and eight-year-olds wouldn't be put off long.

He couldn't run them off to CeCe and Nicky's house. Their folks were out trying to get enough mullet, even if it was a Sunday, to keep paying off the banknote on their boat. The Lord would have to understand a working man sometimes had to work on a Sunday.

"I'll take y'all to the Burger Barn if she don't get up soon. Play quiet while I finish with my nets."

Kitty, CeCe, and Nicky wandered away. He forgot about them for a bit, working on his beer and his net and his grievances. After a while, hungry himself and with the sun too hot in the midday even with the muggy breeze off the mangroves, Tank went around to the front to check on the kids. They were play-acting a wedding, of all things.

CeCe pretended to be the preacher. "You, Kitty, and you, Nicky, are married. You can kiss now."

Kitty and Nicky pecked at each other's faces, then they all giggled.

Tank chuckled. "Come on. As father of the bride, I reckon the wedding dinner's on me." He hoped he had enough money to buy them all a burger and a shake.

They piled into Tank's pickup and headed east through the mangrove wetlands and occasional tomato fields toward the town of Concordia. The humidity blew in the open windows, making their faces shiny and sticky. Wind whipped the girls' hair around their heads. Tank drove with Kitty smashed against him, then Nicky and CeCe. Boy, girl, boy, girl.

He did have enough cash. Barely.

On the way back to Dolphin Cove, he turned off on rutted Mariscos Bay Street, a road paved in the Florida land boom of the 1920s then abandoned after the bust to the salt spray, sun, and hard summer rains. Old shell-and-limestone corner markers showed where somebody who'd come to Florida with plans of easy money had laid out a subdivision. The names on the shell markers had worn off long ago. The road, now more shell and sand than asphalt, was barely passable in places.

He parked the truck at a point where the land jutted out into Mariscos Bay. On the other side of the bay, Dauphine Island rose out of the bright water in a strand of thick green mangroves. Small fiddler crabs scurried away in front of them as the kids and Tank spilled out of the truck and started down the shell and sand pathway.

"Right here." Tank pointed to a high spot in the land where the broken pieces of a tabby foundation made of lime, sand, and crushed coquina shells was visible. "This was my great-granddaddy's place. And my granddaddy's. Him, I remember."

Tank walked over to the only section of the tabby foundation that still looked like part of a house and ran his fingers over it. "Course this weren't their first house." *No, sir, it took them a while to work up to a real house like this one.* He wasn't sure if he remembered the house or had just heard his granddaddy talk about it so much he might as well have remembered it. They'd sold it for a big price in the land boom and bought another place and a couple more boats in nearby Dolphin Cove and took to fishing for a living.

"They came out of Alabama during the Reconstruction, looking for a place where they could have a fair shake at living. I've been right here in Florida all my life so far, 'cept for the Navy and the big war.

I was older than most of them boys in the war, but I knew boats so good the Navy was glad to take me."

Tank looked back at the kids. They were listening. He loved them, all three of them. He hoped the Lord would forgive him for coveting Nicky like he was his own son.

"They got a penny a pound for mullet when I started fishing as a boy in Dolphin Cove, two cents for mackerel, and six cents for pompano. Took the boat out of Dolphin Cove in the mornings, waters 'round here full of mullet. Dusk, coming back in, we'd see a deer sometimes swimming across from Mariscos Bay to Dauphine. Had a place out there on the island we called Hunter's Point, where we could always find something to shoot for supper that didn't come out of the Gulf." Tank pointed across the mangroves and bay toward the island. "Didn't have a bridge to Dauphine when I was a boy." *No, sir, and we didn't need one.*

"Nothing but sand and shell roads, what roads we had, 'fore the boom. Daddy and his daddy used the boat to get around." Tank squinted and watched as a mullet jumped, its wet scales catching the sun and bouncing the bright light right at Tank's sunburned face.

"Course, by the time of the big war, we'd fished all the mullet out of the bay. Same for the scallops. Folks that didn't go to the war had to make do with bait shrimp and boat building." He looked back at the three children. "I want you kids to remember that. You can't take too much out of the bay or off the land without ruining it good for you and what comes after you. Got to give old Momma Nature a chance to take care of things, and just take what you need to get by. Y'all understand what I mean?"

The children nodded.

Nicky came up beside Tank and asked, "You rather live then or now?"

"Oh hell, boy, *now.* I didn't have you kids back then, did I?" Tank ran his hand over the boy's white-blond hair, thinking what pretty children Nicky and Kitty would have when they were all grown up. "I tell you what, boy. When you and Kitty tie the knot for real, and I mean y'all oughta wait till you're both out of high school, I'll give you part interest in my boat, and we'll be partners."

"I'd sure like that. Yes, sir." Nicky spoke in a serious tone, then his face burst open with a big grin.

They tramped around the old trails until they were all welted by mosquitoes and the kids' Sunday clothes were crusty and damp. The beer lost its hold on Tank, and he decided they'd better get on back to the house.

They were still locked out when they got home, so they sat out in the backyard and watched the sun shoot shards of bright colors off the water while they waited for the cool night to drop over them.

She would get up and let them in sooner or later. Tank was sure he would give Nicky part interest in his boat once Kitty married that boy. They would keep the fishing in the family, like with his granddad and his dad and him.

Part I
Gulf Coast of Florida, Spring, 1992

Chapter One

K ate Garcia's feet hit Dauphine Key beach with a steady slap, slap as waves pooled and eddied in the wet sand beneath her. Her dark hair, captured in a long ponytail, snapped against her tanned shoulders as she ran. She kept her eyes straight ahead, ignoring the sunset and dodging the other runners, joggers, and shell gatherers. Her narrow face was sticky with sweat, her arms pumped at her sides, and her mouth hung open as she gasped in the heavy salt air.

Across from CeCe's Bed and Breakfast, she paused long enough to study the crowd gathered on the deck. CeCe, her white-blond hair blowing across her face in the gulf breeze, floated from guest to guest.

Still breathing hard, Kate wiped her face on her sleeve and turned away. She crossed the two-lane road that divided the beaches on the Gulf of Mexico side of Dauphine Key from the bay side with its restaurants and T-shirt shops. On the bay side, she walked down the city pier. Bleached gray by years of sun and salt, the pier was deserted as the beachgoers crowded the other side of the island to watch the sunset.

At the end of the pier, Kate stopped and stared out across the bay at the mangrove shoreline of Dolphin Cove Fishing Village. The fetid, fishy smell of low tide and trapped trash rose with the almost visible humidity. She took off her sunglasses and gazed at the dark green of the land's edge.

Squinting, she could just make out the house across the bay where she had grown up. CeCe's house had been on the same block, but it was gone, not even rubble left to mark its place. Kate snorted and shook her head, flinging beads of sweat off her face. It was 1992, and she was two decades gone from the Cove. *No point in looking back.*

Beneath her, the bay waters hit the pilings of the pier with the same persistence as the waves on the beach. In the lapping, she heard her dead father's voice.

"Go, gal. Get out of here. Run."

Kate rubbed her eyes, turned, and walked back down the pier. Once across the street, she headed toward the beach. Inhaling a lungful of the salt air, she resumed running. She intended to go the two miles back to her car as flat out as she could stand.

———◦———

CARTER RUSSELL TUGGED at the tie he rarely wore and looked around at the clock on the wall between the six-point buck's head and a painting of the crucifixion of Christ. He turned back to the small crowd in the side room of the Riverside church and rubbed his damp hands on his best pair of dress pants. The muscles in the back of his neck throbbed. More people had shown up at the gathering to discuss how to stop the proposed phosphate mine than he'd expected, but he had to leave.

"Meeting's over. I've got to go now." He hurried toward the door as people shifted in their folding chairs and started to rise.

Outside, he went over to stand in the fading light under an ancient live oak. He lit a cigarette and drew the smoke in deeply.

A man in a frayed cotton shirt hurried over to him. "Glad you came, partner. You really know your stuff about phosphate," the man said. "But I got to ask. How come you hate those mines?"

Carter blew the smoke out slowly before he answered. "Those mines tore up my childhood, ruined my granddaddy's farm, and killed my daddy with lung cancer from inhaling toxic shit from digging up the stuff."

Carter could have ranted some more, but he needed to leave if he were to make his late meeting with Alton Weaver, the state attorney, at the Calusa County courthouse. Waving the man off, Carter hopped into his car. He slipped out of Riverside in a few minutes and was soon in the country. The golden glare of the setting sun blurred his vision as he drove west, his shoulders tense. Hot, damp air blew in through the windows, smelling of orange blossoms from some nearby grove.

He was humming to the song on the radio when a pickup came up behind him, already running its headlights in the dimming day. Carter slowed, waiting for the vehicle to pass, but the driver of the truck braked too. Carter sped up, hitting the gas harder than he meant to.

The pickup rushed Carter's back bumper then swung wide and passed him. The driver swerved in front of Carter before slamming to a stop. Carter braked hard and veered off to the right. The front of his car left the roadway, dug into the dirt and brush along the road, and spun. His vehicle clipped a tree and came to a stop just off the pavement, in a clump of palmettos and mud. The seat belt jerked Carter back, snapping his neck as the pickup continued up the road and disappeared around a curve.

Carter unsnapped his seat belt, leaned over, and opened the glove compartment. He reached in for his .38, but the gun wasn't there. Dread hummed inside his brain. He rifled through the glove compartment, pulling everything out and scattering the accumulated detritus on the floorboard. Next, he bent over and felt around under the passenger seat. Nothing.

Sweat pooled over his upper lip, and steam clouded the corners of his glasses. He sat back up behind the wheel, hoping to get back on the road and away from the isolated spot. His tires spun as he tried to steer out of the soft dirt off the shoulder. He got out of the car and looked up and down the two-lane road. No pickup.

He weighed his options. Walking beside the road made sense as long as the pickup didn't return. The other choice was the scrublands and cypress swamp around the watershed of the Calusa River, which wasn't a place he wanted to walk in at dusk, wearing only loafers and having no weapon. He glanced to the left. Silhouettes of cypress trees trailing gray moss loomed above the sharp blades of the palmetto thickets. To the right, the landscape was less dense but still filled with the palmetto shrubs that were favorites of rattlesnakes.

Carter started walking down the road. Minutes later, as he stumbled on some loose gravel, the pickup came back, rounding the curve and heading straight toward him. The bright headlights caught Carter in his eyes with such a flash that he dove into the ditch beside the road. Slipping in the mud, he tried to find traction with his feet so he could be ready to flee.

The pickup stopped when it reached Carter's car resting in the brush. A broad man with dark hair crawled out of the cab, a rifle swinging at his side.

Carter ran. He ignored all the advice he'd learned growing up about where one did and didn't put one's feet when traveling through the scrublands, swamps, and hammocks of Florida. *Don't pick up firewood. Don't put your foot down on the other side of a log without looking first. Stay out of ditches. Don't stick your hands down gopher tortoise holes. Don't go into the woods or the swamps alone. Don't go at dusk without a good gun. Don't. Don't. Don't.* The litany repeated in Carter's mind in an odd rhythm, almost like a forgotten mantra, as he stumbled and thrashed like any amateur alone and scared in a cypress swamp.

With barely enough light left to see by, Carter slowed and glanced back to see if he was being followed.

He was.

With the rifle still swinging at his side, the man strode through the thickening undergrowth, carefully stepping on the spots of dry leaves and matted fiber, leaving no obvious trace, unlike the wild steps Carter took.

Just as recognition struggled out of his subconscious, Carter tripped over a decaying log and fell into a patch of dank moss. As he put his hand down under the outer ledge of the log to push himself up, he heard the rustle of leaves and a hiss.

Carter flailed and jerked back as fangs sank deep into his right hand. A burning jab hit him as he started rolling away from the snake. Even in the failing light, Carter couldn't mistake the rows of diamond-shaped brown markings outlined against the cream-colored scales. He was close enough to see the white oblique stripes on the side of the rattler's face.

Lie quiet. Don't move. That much of the childhood lessons came back to him. Already his hand was swelling with pain that leapfrogged up his arm. *Be still. Don't provoke it.*

The man with the rifle stepped up and stopped a few feet away. Carter waited for the bullet.

The man snickered. "Damn if this isn't working out even better than I planned. I thought I was going to have to shoot your ass, but maybe now I won't. I can let that snake do my killing for me."

Carter didn't move, even when vomit filled his mouth.

"Yes, sir. A fine mess. Now an eastern diamondback'll sure hold its ground and strike if you piss it off. It can even bite you twice if you rile it again. But you know that, don't you, being an old Florida cracker?" The man's boots, camouflage military-style, heavy and thick soled, eased into Carter's field of vision. "So I reckon the trick here is to not piss off that big snake. And I got to tell you, it's a beaut. Must be four feet."

Carter's hand and arm were on fire, the pain streaking through his whole body as his heart pounded too fast. *Keep still. Slow the heart rate.* The faster his heart beat, the quicker the venom would spread through his body.

"I got to say, I admire how quiet you're lying there." The man stepped closer. "So if you're not going to piss off the snake again, I guess I will." He raised the rifle and held it out at arm's length. With the tip of the barrel, he nudged the log by the snake's head, shaking it until the snake coiled into a striking position. "Got you."

Carter barely heard the words before the diamondback sank its fangs into the side of his cheek below his left eye. He screamed, vomited, and jerked away.

The man chuckled. "Ain't true a rattler got to rattle, is it? That one sure didn't bother. Makes you think the ones that don't rattle don't get found and killed and live to get bigger. You think on that a while, boy, in the time you got left." The man walked off, humming.

Get back to the car. But then what? I'm forty-five minutes from the nearest hospital. Even if a car comes by and stops. But forty-five minutes is enough time. Get up. Get to the car.

He moaned as he tried but failed to sit up. A shadow, like a ghost, hovered in front of him. It was the girl, the one with a sprinkle of freckles on her pale face and the long white-blond hair. "CeCe," he whispered.

Chapter Two

Raymond Slaverson sat on the weight bench in his spare bedroom, breathing deeply and preparing for his next set. Sweat dripped down his wide face, and a lock of his thick graying hair stuck to his broad forehead. The phone rang, and brushing his hair back with one hand, he tugged his wet T-shirt away from his chest and answered, hoping it was Kate with an invitation to come right over. He thought of the engagement ring he'd bought. *Maybe I'll ask her later tonight.*

"Hello."

"I'm not Kate. Sorry," Luke Latham said.

Ray grunted, running his free hand over the barbells as he sat back on the weight bench. He knew he wouldn't get to the next set. He and Luke had been friends for what seemed like forever, both of them long-time officers with the Concordia Police Department. Recently, they'd become partners in the detective squad.

"We got a big one," Luke said. "I need your help."

Running his tongue over his teeth and his hand over his face, Ray hoped he'd have time to shower and shave. "Who is it?"

Behind Luke's breathing on the phone, he could hear other voices. Somebody cussed at somebody, and the talking got louder.

"Alton Weaver. Mr. State Attorney himself." The judicial circuit's boss prosecutor and a man Ray and Luke had both worked with over the years.

"Damn. Where?"

"In his office. Once in the head. Nice and neat. Efficient."

"Okay, I'm on my way."

UNIFORMED AND PLAINCLOTHES officers milled around in the hallway, keeping the press and the curious out of the way. Ray eased through the officers with only a few head nods and stepped inside the state attorney's office.

Alton Weaver was slumped over in his red leather chair, his head on his desk. A crime-scene technician was snapping photographs at various angles, while Luke crawled around on the carpet, looking under Weaver's desk with a flashlight.

In a corner, as far out of the way as he could get, a man in a blue polo shirt and khaki pants stood with a uniformed officer. The man was pallid and kept wiping his hands on his pants, but he was watching everything with a sharp interest.

Standing in the doorway, Ray took in the scene, studying the office he'd been in countless times as if he were seeing it for the first time. Then he ambled around the outer perimeter of the room, listening to the comments being made but not speaking or greeting anyone.

He made mental notes. No dust on the windowsill. No dust on the file drawers, the couch, the coffee table, or the credenza with the books and the stylish coffee maker. Nothing seemed out of place. He wondered if Weaver ran such a tight ship that everything in his office at the end of the week would appear so neat. He realized the answer was yes, and that gave Ray a moment of hope. Anything out of order should jump out at him.

Ignoring the body behind the desk, Ray navigated around the room slowly in ever-smaller circles, studying but not touching a thing. At the end of his gradually constricting orbit, he finally stood in front of Weaver's body. He took a long look at the man's head, which lay in a pool of congealed blood. Ray hadn't liked Weaver, and Weaver hadn't liked him. But over the last few years, Weaver had made a good state attorney, and that was something Ray respected.

He thought it too bad that Weaver had never respected him in return. Not that it mattered any longer.

Ray bent down until he could see Luke, who was still crawling around on the floor with his white-gloved hands. "So tell me what you've got so far."

Luke stood up, rubbed his back, and shook his head. His fading chestnut hair stood up in odd tufts like hackles raised on the back of an angry dog, but his sunburned face was calm, his expression oddly pleasant. Deep lines crossed around and under his blue eyes, and his lips were all but hidden by the thick droop of a mustache. "Lawyer guy there"—he pointed at the man in the blue shirt—"comes in here around ten to pick up a file he was going to work on over the weekend. He sees Weaver's light on and thinks he'll brownnose a bit. Finds Weaver dead. Gives up on brownnosing."

Ray looked over at the man, who jammed his hands in his pockets and stared right back at them. "I've never seen him before. Any reason to be concerned about him?"

"None I know of. Name's Richard Constantia. He's the new lawyer in Weaver's office. Just started last week. Believe this? That guy just got out of law school. Must be our age, second career and all. I talked to him, but he claims he didn't see or hear anything. I got a feeling he's not going to be much help. But I want you and me to talk to him again now that he's calmed down."

"In a minute. What else you got?"

Luke rubbed his back again. "Nothing yet. Not a damned thing. Shot in the temple. Sitting at his desk. No sign of a struggle. No mess. No forced entry. No appointments on the book for a Friday night at the office. Paperwork on year-end stats laid out on his desk like he was looking at them but no notes or anything on them in his handwriting."

"Stats? He wouldn't be working on those. His staff gathers all that."

"Looks to me like Weaver was just passing time while he waited for somebody. Like he was expecting a visitor." When he said "visitor," Luke looked across the room at Constantia.

Constantia, who was still huddled in the corner, glared back. Ray thought there was something hostile in his look, or maybe the guy was just nervous.

"Okay, so Weaver's waiting for somebody," Ray said, turning back to Luke. "Then that somebody just walks into his office and shoots him in the head?"

"That's about all we have to start with."

"We better check that Constantia guy's hands for gunpowder," Ray said, even though he was pretty sure Luke would be a step ahead of him on that one.

"Yep. He's already agreed, and we'll get his fingerprints too. Meanwhile, here you go." Luke pulled an extra pair of latex gloves out of his pocket and handed them to Ray. "The medical examiner himself's on the way. No assistants for this one. Let's you and me take a closer look. Oh, and thanks for coming in. Nothing against Dayton, but I didn't wanna be partnering up with only him on this one."

"Where is Dayton?"

"I sent him out with some uniforms to canvass the building and the neighborhood, like we'd be lucky enough that they'd find anybody who saw or heard anything unusual. Still, it's pretty late, so anybody left around would be kind of interesting to talk to."

"So, a way to keep Dayton useful and out of your way, huh?"

"For now. If he gets done too early, we'll send him out for beer and peanuts, then after that, sleeping bags and teddy bears. Lets me think without his jabbering."

Ray worked the gloves over his fingers before he stepped toward what was left of Alton Weaver. Bending over, he took a closer look.

He hadn't touched a thing when James Gilroy, a tall, slender black man, stepped into the office. Ray straightened and nodded.

"James," Ray said. "Why don't we step outside?" As the highest-ranking assistant state attorney and probably Alton's replacement, James had a right to be there, but Ray didn't like amateurs polluting the crime scene.

James took a long, hard look at Alton before he acknowledged Ray and returned to the hallway.

"What have you got?" James asked as soon as Ray joined him.

"Nothing yet."

"You keep me in the loop. Everything, no matter how trivial it might seem." James glared at him. "I mean it."

"Yes, sir," Ray said, clipping his voice at the last moment to soften the sarcasm.

"I'll be taking over the Rollinson murder trial," James said. "You and I will have to get together and go over your testimony. No reason to ask for a continuance."

Ray thought it might be a little early and a lot cold that James was already assuming authority and moving ahead. But the man had always struck Ray as overly ambitious. And the Rollinson trial, which involved a particularly nasty murder of a real estate agent at an open house, was coming up quickly. "The week before the trial soon enough?" Ray asked, eager to get rid of James and get back into Alton's office.

"Call me first thing Monday, and we'll set up a time." James turned away and pushed through the growing crowd. He stopped beside a TV reporter with a photographer.

Yeah, you do that. You put your face out there. Ray shook his head and stepped back inside the office.

Guess it won't be a good night to propose to Kate after all.

Chapter Three

R ay nursed his coffee and watched Kate. Her dark hair streamed about her narrow face, and in the shadow of it, her hazel-green eyes looked black.

Kate squinted at the newspaper print. "Those people are outrageous."

"What people?" He was waiting for her to finish the A section of the Saturday *Herald-Tribune* so he could read what they had to say about the state attorney's murder, but he knew better than to rush her.

"The phosphate people. Big plans to mine phosphate in Calusa County, up in the eastern corner where it and the other counties come together, there on Cattleguard Creek. The creek would run right through the center of the mine."

"They're mining nearby already, aren't they?"

"But they've never mined in this county before. And Cattleguard Creek runs right into the Calusa River, and that's where the south county gets their drinking water. You want to drink phosphate runoff and all that phosphogypsum?"

Phosphogypsum, the by-product of phosphate mining, was radioactive, and the industry had a bad track record on containing it. Kate could go for hours if she got started. Ray didn't know if he had enough coffee in him to handle a classic Kate rant so early in the morning. "No." *Answer simply and hope it passes.*

"Somebody ought to do something." Kate smacked the paper on the table as if she were swatting a fly.

"Then you should do something about it." Even as he said it, Ray realized he shouldn't encourage her.

"Yes, I think maybe I'll see about that. Nobody should be mining phosphate in the watershed of the Calusa River."

Ray cleared his throat. *Here it comes.*

As if reading his mind, Kate nudged his foot under the table. "Not too much on Weaver but some basic obit-type stuff. Good photo."

Ray slumped a bit in relief as she slid the paper over to him. Picking it up, he was momentarily startled by the large photo of the man whose body he'd so carefully and futilely studied last night.

Kate stood up and moved toward the kitchen counter. She grazed the back of his neck with her fingers as she passed behind him. At the slight sound of the bag of bread being opened, Maggie, her pet pug, darted into the kitchen. Kate bent down and picked up the dog, telling her she would have to wait a few minutes before the toast and eggs would be ready. After putting the animal down, Kate washed her hands and went back to fixing breakfast while Maggie danced around the kitchen.

Ray couldn't help but smile. He wondered where Maggie the cat was but didn't think on it too long. The fact that Kate had named both her pets "Maggie" still tickled him.

He remembered when Kate had first invited him inside her small house. In those early days together, Kate had struck him as the kind of woman who would have cats, each with complex literary names befitting her job as a librarian.

"Maggie," she'd said that first time, pointing at the black cat who arched its back and hissed at Ray. Maggie the cat had then turned and coolly left the room.

The cat still ignored him. He returned the favor.

The dog was something else. The first time he met the dog, she came dashing up to Kate in a hysterical burst of speed and noise that startled Ray.

"Maggie," Kate had said, holding the wiggling dog out to Ray.

"What is it?" Ray asked, looking at its pushed-in dark face, pop-eyes, and short, thick body with a stub of a curly tail. The dog snorted and squirmed and licked the air with a tongue that seemed entirely too long for so flat a face.

"A pug."

"They're both named Maggie?"

"Sure. Doesn't matter." Kate grinned. "Neither of them answers when they're called."

That had been over a year ago. They'd been together now long enough to have their own rituals, their little truces of habit. Long enough to make it permanent, Ray hoped. He wondered what living with her full time with a ring on his finger would be like as she fixed the dog a plate of eggs and a piece of toast before she made plates for the humans.

At least the dog didn't eat on the table like the cat sometimes did. Having a strict fundamentalist upbringing in which his father barely tolerated the kids inside the house, let alone a dog or cat, Ray often struggled to hide his annoyance with Kate's indulgent ways with the Maggies. "Stop being so rigid" was what his ex-wife had yelled at him. He was trying. And he had to admit, in a crazy way, he'd ended up fond of the hyper little dog.

After breakfast, he said, "Look, I've got to meet Luke and Weaver's secretary at the state attorney's office at ten to go over Weaver's files, appointment calendar, and stuff like that. Then I've got to talk to the ME's office. With a case like this, Luke and I need to attend the autopsy. The state attorney's office'll probably send somebody too."

"Sure."

"I don't have time to cut your grass like I promised."

"You don't need to." She stood and gathered the dishes. "It doesn't grow much now that it's stopped raining."

He followed her and kissed her at the kitchen sink. Her night-gown hung off one shoulder in a way that could be suggestive—or sloppy. With Kate, he could never read the signals. He rubbed his palm lightly against her small breasts under the thin cotton, and her nipples hardened. She pressed against him, raising her face for a second kiss, as she wrapped her arms around his waist.

He eased back enough to start lifting her gown.

She rubbed against him then sighed. "You don't have time." But she tightened her hold around him and rested her face against his chest as if she were listening to his heartbeat.

"Tonight then. It's a date." He brushed her hair with his lips, inhaling the fresh apple smell of her shampoo.

"We've got Luke's to go to. Supper with his family." She touched his cheek with the tip of her finger. "Remember?"

"I'll do my damnedest to get away from work and come home—come *here*, I mean—in time."

"Just be careful out there, okay?" She let go of him and picked up a dishrag. "I met Weaver once. He preened a bit but was basically nice."

He leaned against the kitchen counter. *Preened. Yes, that would be Weaver all right.* "When did you meet him?"

"At the library on Thursday. He came into the reference section, needing some help threading the microfiche."

The day before he was killed. Ray straightened. "What was he looking at?"

She hesitated then shrugged. "I don't really remember. Old newspapers."

"You don't remember, or you won't tell me?"

She washed a dish and put it in the drain tray.

"Kate? Which is it? Can't or won't?"

"Both, I guess. You know libraries can't give out that information. Patrons have a statutory right to privacy about anything they research or check out."

Ray knew that because as soon as he'd learned she was the head reference librarian at the county's library and she'd learned he was a cop, they'd had a long discussion about a popular movie where the police solved the crime by obtaining a list of reading materials a patron had checked out at a public library. Wouldn't happen, they'd agreed. "But would that privacy right still matter? I mean, he's dead now. And if it has anything to do with his murder, you should tell me."

"How could it? He was looking up old newspapers, really old ones. Forget I mentioned it."

"How old?"

She slapped down the dish rag and turned around to face him. "Historic old. Don't press it."

"Okay." He swayed close enough to kiss her again and made a mental note to send Dayton over to check at the library during Kate's off hours. Dayton with his puppy-dog good looks might sneak some information out of one of her assistants.

Chapter Four

Wyman Greenstreet made a list of his debts so he could decide which ones he would pay off first. He smiled as he jotted numbers and sipped a very fine, costly Hawaiian coffee he'd read about in a connoisseur column in the local newspaper. He'd been saving the beans to impress someone with his good taste and knowledge, probably a date or a client. But what the heck. He'd laughed and ground the beans just for himself.

Finally, he would have some money, *big* money. Of course, he already lived like he had money. But what he had was debt.

All those trial attorneys who'd looked down their noses at his tame legal practice and those plaintiff's attorneys who'd cast about for the next big class action while sniggering at Wyman closing on condo sales could all go to hell.

His decision to expand his safe but not yet fully lucrative real estate practice to include land use and environmental issues had paid off. All it had required was a small ad in the newspaper, advertising that he was now handling environmental issues as well as real estate. And a few discreet inquiries among the single-issue environmental groups in Concordia had gotten the ball rolling. Wyman had planned to offer cut rates in exchange for some on-the-job training. He would learn environmental law while the client paid him a modest hourly rate to do so, then he could claim he was an environmental lawyer.

Wyman had found one taker. That was all he'd needed.

Wyman took a big mouthful of coffee and gleefully scratched another debt off his list. *Hot damn.* Nineteen ninety-two was the year he was finally taking off into the big time. And he wasn't even going to have to go into a courtroom, something that had terrified him since law school.

Being afraid of judges had put a certain chink in his plans for conspicuous success, but he had known the drill since his first year in Concordia. To be a rich, successful lawyer, he needed to *look* like a rich, successful lawyer. The clients with the real money weren't going to those little law offices sandwiched between the delis and the auto parts stores. And they didn't want a lawyer whose best suit came from JCPenney. Having the right home address was paramount with the ultimate goal being beachfront property. But canal-front or bayfront was an acceptable step. And his car had to be expensive and imported.

Wyman mentally checked off what he already had: the car, the address, the clothes, and a growing real estate practice. If the bank and the credit card people weren't so pushy, he'd have made it the old-fashioned way with hard work and a slightly above-average intelligence. But he was running out of time. The cargo of his debt pulled at him unrelentingly. The first phone call from a collection agency had terrified him almost as much as the thought of being in a courtroom. But he was going to dump that debt.

He stood up, danced over to his phone, and dialed the number for Annette, his secretary. He'd already promised her a raise, which she deserved, so he didn't feel guilty about reminding her she was to meet him in the office at nine this morning. He didn't care that it was Saturday. He had a lot of work to do.

After he hung up with Annette, Wyman made a short to-do list while finishing his coffee. He wrote "Call James" at the top.

He added the list to the papers in his briefcase and headed out to his garage. He locked the inside door between the garage and the house and turned to the Lexus. He frowned. The side door of the garage was standing wide open. He knew he'd left it closed and locked.

Wyman stopped, a small squirm of fear catching him off guard. *Damn crackheads.* Though his house was bayfront, it was also close to US 41, the infamous Tamiami Trail with its trade of whores and drugs. Break-ins were common in his neighborhood.

Wyman scanned the garage but saw no one and no obvious damage. He squinted at the open side door and thought the knob looked mangled. It was hard to tell without his glasses, and he didn't want to stop and put them on.

He debated over going back in the house to call 911 or sprinting for the car, driving away, and calling 911 from the car phone. Someone could be crouched behind his high-end treadmill, which had been abandoned before it was even paid for, or hiding on the other side of the Lexus. He stifled the urge to bend down and look under the car for feet on the other side.

He shook his head. It was probably just some punk who broke open the side door but couldn't get through the state-of-the-art dead bolt on the inside door. *It's okay. Go on to work.*

Just as he took a step toward his car, he heard a clinking sound. His heart rate sped up. He heard a shifting type of noise, like rough fabric against fabric, then a dragging noise, like shoes on concrete.

He dropped the briefcase and dashed back toward the door. He tried to pull it open, but the dead bolt stopped him. He fumbled for the key with shaking hands.

When he heard the distinct sound of someone charging at his back, he started to turn to face his attacker, but a volley of pain crashed through his head. He heard an odd splintering sound and felt warm liquid wash down his neck. Another wave of pain echoed the first.

No, not now. Not yet.

Chapter Five

Ray let Luke take the lead with Miriam Calvert, Weaver's administrative assistant. The three of them sat around a small table in Weaver's office, Luke and Miriam side by side, and Ray across from her.

Luke had a soothing quality about him that Ray admired but couldn't duplicate. Maybe Luke's mom and all his aunts had taught him something that Ray hadn't learned from his own mother, a French war bride silenced by her years in occupied France, her own shy nature, and her husband's haranguing.

Luke had called Miriam last night and asked if he and Ray could stop by her condominium. By the time they'd gotten there, she knew Weaver was dead because she'd seen the news bulletin on TV. Luke told her he was sorry he hadn't been able to tell her in person as he had planned. Ray had been relieved she already knew but ashamed that he felt that way.

Ray leaned back in the chair and studied Miriam while Luke played grief counselor as a prelude to their own version of twenty questions. Probably well into her fifties, she was a handsome woman with perfect carriage and a wardrobe that even Ray's untrained eyes could tell was expensive. She was perfectly made up and coiffed, bearing the look of the women from the million-dollar-plus beachfront homes on Dauphine Key. He wondered why such a woman was working at a state employee's pay rate.

"Thank you, Mr. Latham, for understanding." She put her thin, tanned hand on top of Luke's as if they were more to each other than they were. Her eyes were swollen and red.

"Luke, ma'am. Please call me Luke."

Miriam took her hand away and turned to Ray. After acknowledging him with a short nod, she handed some papers to Luke. "These are the lists I've made so far this morning. I couldn't remember everything you asked for last night, but I've listed the names of all Mr. Weaver's active cases, the names of the defense attorneys involved, the statuses of the cases, names of the defendants, and crimes committed. You can look at any of the files, of course, but this gives you some idea."

She must have been there at the crack of dawn to have pulled that much information together. It was not the first time Ray had admired her efficiency.

"You can take that copy," she said. "I made it for the investigation. You told me you took his appointment calendar last night, so I'll go through old files and start a similar list. What else do you need?"

Luke took the papers, still wearing his sympathetic face. "You knew him best, I'd bet. Been with him for years. What was going on? Why would anyone want to kill him?"

Miriam shook her head. "I just don't know. I thought about it all last night. Any of those criminals he prosecuted, I guess, but..." She paused so long Ray leaned toward her again, hoping for something beyond that first obvious observation. "I simply can't think of anything *personal*. You do know what I mean, do you not?"

"Yes," Luke said, nodding slightly.

"How would somebody get in on a Friday night?" Ray asked, assuming whoever shot Weaver hadn't simply come into the public building when it was wide open during business hours then hidden until everyone except Weaver left.

"Well, all of us have the access code for the back door. After five thirty, all the doors to the building should have been locked. Mr. Weaver was not a careless man, so I'm sure when he came back in, he locked the door behind him. In fact, he probably came in the back door, and it locks automatically. The front door has a key, but nobody who works here actually uses it."

"But it could be left unlocked? That is, somebody could come in and leave the door unlocked behind them?"

"Oh yes. If you wanted to, one could leave the front door unlocked. But Mr. Weaver would never have been so careless."

Ray wondered who else had been in the building after five thirty. They would have to compile another mind-numbing list of people who had keys and go office to office on Monday, asking the same questions over and over. "How often do they change the access codes?"

"Once a month or after somebody leaves."

"And the front door keys?"

"Well, that I just do not know. But only certain people have keys. The rank and file do not have keys. And when an attorney leaves, he has to give the key back."

"Do you have a key?"

"Oh no." She looked straight at Ray when she answered but then turned back to Luke.

"Last night," Ray said, "you told us you were sure Mr. Weaver had left and gone home, that he must have come back to his office later. Explain that to us again, please."

"Well, yes, as I said last night when we spoke, Mr. Weaver left around five fifteen. I watched him walk out, then I closed up and left. Like I told you, it was just a second or two after five forty-five when I went to my car to go home, and Weaver's parking spot was empty." She glanced at the door as if wishing she could leave, then she closed her eyes and took in a deep breath, struggling to compose herself.

Ray wished he had some words of comfort and started to offer his mother's favorite platitude but decided against it. Somehow "*Dominus dedit et Dominus abstulit*"—the Lord gives, and the Lord takes away—didn't sound consoling.

She opened her eyes and said, "The next thing I heard about him was the news bulletin just before you arrived."

"Was it unusual for Mr. Weaver to work late on a Friday night?" Luke asked.

"Friday night, yes. He often worked on Saturday mornings, but he rarely worked on Friday or Saturday nights unless it was right before an important trial."

"He had the Rollinson trial coming up. Might he have been planning to work on that?" Ray asked.

"No. He'd made sure I cleared off his calendar the whole week before." Miriam gazed up at Ray. "And he had a note that I was to call you and arrange an appointment to review your notes and rehearse your testimony."

Rehearse, yeah. That was Weaver, not willing to trust Ray had enough sense to offer input or insight or even answer a question without the attorney's script.

"He wouldn't have been working on the Rollinson case Friday, then, to my knowledge. But usually..." She hesitated.

"Usually what?" Ray prompted.

"Oh, you didn't know Mr. Weaver that well, did you? You just knew him professionally. All those times you testified in his trials, I guess you didn't know about his personal life." Miriam looked uncomfortable.

Ray shook his head. "No. I didn't really know him."

"What are you trying to tell us?" Luke asked, his voice very soft.

"Well, you see, Mr. Weaver was quite the..." She stopped again and studied her hands, which were folded in front of her on the table.

"Quite the what?" Luke prodded gently.

Still looking at her hands, she muttered, "He was quite popular. Friday and Saturday nights were important to him, and..." When she raised her head, her face had a pink blush.

"What exactly are you saying?" Luke asked.

"He... he was..." Her cheeks reddened even more as if she'd suddenly applied rouge. "He was... oh, he was very good-looking and charming, and so he always had a... a date on Friday nights." She took a deep breath and looked at Luke. "Well, the question was whether he normally would be in here late on a Friday night, wasn't it? No, he wouldn't be."

"We aren't even completely sure of the time of death yet," Ray said.

Full rigor mortis had set in, so Weaver had been dead at least a few hours when he and Luke examined the body. The autopsy could possibly be more precise, depending on what the medical examiner found in Weaver's stomach and intestines and if the detectives could determine when Weaver had last eaten. A few other things could be factors as well, things he didn't want to spell out while talking with Miriam.

Still, they had a framework, imprecise as it was. Weaver had been found around ten p.m. He'd left the office around five fifteen then returned after Miriam left at five forty-five, so the time of his death could have been as early as six p.m. or as late as eight p.m. That information was most likely more accurate at setting his time of death than anything the postmortem could show.

Ray cleared his throat. "It could have been around six or seven, so he could have been planning a date later, after catching up on some paperwork. Would you know if he had a date? And with who?"

"No. I didn't keep his personal calendar, just his professional one."

"Who might know?" Luke asked.

Miriam shook her head. "I don't know."

There was a knock on the door, then Dayton stepped in without waiting to be asked. Ray looked up, ready to snap at him, but the man's expression stopped him.

"We got another one," Dayton said, panting a little as if he'd run to get there. "Another lawyer. Bashed-in head, brain matter—"

"All right, Dayton, we got a lady here," Luke said, pushing his chair back.

"Sorry, ma'am." Dayton's face turned bright red. "Real sorry."

"If you will excuse us, ma'am, we better get going." Luke patted Miriam's hand then strode toward the door, Dayton right behind him.

Ray stood up and hurried after Dayton and Luke. *What the hell is this? Two dead lawyers in twenty-four hours?*

Chapter Six

No matter how Ray tried to figure it, nothing about Wyman Greenstreet added up to a bashed-in skull and the tantrum of papers tossed around in his garage and house. When Greenstreet hadn't shown up at work or answered his phone, his secretary sent the office runner to the house to check on him. The runner, a high school kid, had to be sedated after what he'd found.

Greenstreet, Ray and Luke soon learned, had been a lawyer who rarely set foot in a courtroom. His cases didn't make the evening news. He shared his two-man law office with a harried partner and a young secretary, who was nearly hysterical from the news of Greenstreet's murder. With two ex-wives, a bayfront home on a heavily treed lot, and a lot of debt, he was the kind of lawyer people dealt with once or twice, paid, and forgot. His practice focused on real estate—with condominiums as a specialty—some contracts, and a few simple wills.

Nothing about his career should have led to the pulp and gray matter that was once his brain leaking out on the floor of his garage.

For once, Luke and Ray abandoned their pet theory that the first suspect was the other spouse or the ex-spouse. Greenstreet's first ex-wife was a schoolteacher he had married the summer before he started law school and divorced the summer after he graduated. Greenstreet had her phone number in his cell phone contacts even though she'd long since moved away from Concordia and claimed to have had no contact with him in recent years.

Still, she'd had a surprised and sad response over the phone when given the news of his death. "He was a nice guy really. He just worked too hard. I wanted somebody I'd be able to, you know, actually do things with." She hadn't had a clue as to why someone might murder him.

The second ex-wife still lived in Concordia. She let them inside her small, tidy house with only a worried glance at their IDs. Her first question, before either Ray or Luke spoke, was whether her two children were all right. After they assured her they were not there because of her kids, she relaxed. Then, as if it were an afterthought, she asked about her husband. Luke finally got a word in and gave her the news.

A small woman, almost fragile looking, she cried, and kept saying, "Oh, poor Wyman."

When they asked, she told them she left him because she wanted a baby.

"He didn't?" Ray asked.

"No, he just said he didn't care one way or the other." She glanced at the mantel, which held a series of framed school photos of a couple of children that bore a striking similarity to her. "I wanted my babies to have a father who cared, who wanted them. You see?" She started crying again.

"I know what you mean." Luke pulled out a photo of his two children and his grandson and another one of his daughter holding her baby with Luke Junior grimacing beside them. The ex-wife showed him the most recent photographs of her two children.

Ray fidgeted until the photo exchange was over. They had all the information they were going to get from the woman, and none of it was useful, except to paint in the picture of the man Wyman Greenstreet had been, a nice enough guy who worked too much. And as petite as she was, she couldn't have smashed in her ex-husband's head.

Once they were back in the car, Ray said, "She could've hired someone to do it, but I don't think so. You?"

Luke shook his head, "Naw. She's not behind this."

With the ex-wives out of the way, that left clients, robbery, or random happenstance violence. They went to Greenstreet's office, where the law partner was waiting for them.

With the awkward pleasantries quickly out of the way, the partner told them about an ex-client, Stuart Ledbetter, who'd hired Greenstreet to handle a complicated land deal. When the deal went sour, the man sued Greenstreet for malpractice.

"Spurious suit, waste of time and money," the partner said. "Wyman won on a summary judgment, which the man appealed. Wyman won the appeal, and that was probably the end of it. But I have to say, the client was angry, very angry."

"Mad enough to knock in the back of Mr. Greenstreet's head?" Luke asked.

"I don't know," the law partner said, looking over his shoulder as if someone might be listening. "Maybe. But don't tell him I told you about him."

Ray and Luke left Greenstreet's office and headed to the address the partner pulled out of the file for them.

Old Florida cracker boy was Ray's immediate assessment as Stuart Ledbetter shouted, "What do you want?" at them through the hooked screened door of his old house trailer, which sat on a piece of low land in the eastern side of the county. An angry-sounding pack of dogs barked and growled behind the man in the doorway.

Ray had dealt with hundreds of men like Ledbetter, native stock struggling to hang on in the new Florida that didn't have much room for their back-country rural ways anymore. Most of them were not nearly as irate as Ledbetter though.

After showing him their badges, Luke asked, "Do you know a lawyer by the name of Wyman Greenstreet?"

Ledbetter sputtered and turned red in the face. "Hell yeah. He's this sorry-ass attorney I hired once. I had to sue the son-a-bitch. I had me one sweet deal here, finally about to make me some money. Some real good money."

Luke nodded with a sympathetic expression that Ray admired. His partner knew how to relate to folks no matter who—or what—they were.

"Only trouble is the son-a-bitch who owns the front piece, the one between my piece and the highway. He won't let me have a paved road through so somebody can build something on mine." Ledbetter slapped his palm against the screen, and dust and rust flakes flew off it. "I bought this piece a while back. Knew this county was gonna take off. Can you believe the land prices now? I got this place pretty cheap, and I been holding it, waiting for the money to come this way."

Ray and Luke turned to look around the place. The land was low enough to flood in the heavy summer rains and had a marshy look to the back part, which would be buggy, and so far inland the Gulf breezes wouldn't reach to cool the area.

It wasn't prime property, not even close. But even the poor plots of open land in Concordia County were selling and turning into residential and commercial developments quicker than anyone could track. Locals talked about the phenomena like the weather. "Hot enough for you? You see that new development going in out on Cattleman's Road?" Ray figured it wouldn't stop until all the orange groves and cow pastures were paved over and built up.

Ray turned back to Ledbetter, who wouldn't unlatch the outer screened door. Maybe that was a good thing, given the increased growling of the dog pack behind him. The man was thinned-lipped and reedy with shaggy dark hair. He was maybe in his forties but already had an old-man slouch about him.

"Can't put in any apartments, duplexes, or houses, nothing but this little trailer I got," Ledbetter said, a hint of a whine in his voice. "I can come and go, but nobody else. That's the deal. Could cut a road through all that shit in back of us if you got the time and money and could get the asshole owner to agree, and you could sue that son-a-bitch that owns the piece 'tween me and the highway in the front. Try to get a court make him let a road come in. So it's not like it can't be fixed. But as it sits now, can't do squat here."

"You mean your property is landlocked?" Ray asked. "No ingress and egress."

"Yeah, I guess those is as good a words as any. Got me an easement so I can come and go like I please. But Mr. Know-it-all Greenstreet says it ain't an easement that I can sell so's the buyer could put in the kind of roads the county's got to have so somebody can sell houses on the damned place. Had some long name for it. Easement a-put-ture or something. I got a headache listening to that man."

Ray thought maybe Mr. Ledbetter should have asked a few more questions before he bought the piece of land. "So how was this Mr. Greenstreet's fault?"

"Damn fool told my buyer. That's why it's his fault."

"You mean you sued him because he told the buyer that you couldn't guarantee him ingress and egress to develop the property? Didn't you or Mr. Greenstreet have a legal or ethical duty to inform the buyer?" Ray remembered filling out a standard real estate form listing everything he could think of that was wrong with his old house before he sold it. His realtor had explained that he had a legal duty to disclose known defects. "Buyer beware" had been legislated out of practice in a state where real estate, land speculation, and development were prime businesses.

"You sound like a damn lawyer."

"Aren't you even curious why we're here, asking you about Greenstreet?" Ray asked.

"Hell no. I don't give a good crap."

Ray was already tired of the man. "Maybe you *should* care. He's dead."

"Good. Thanks for telling me. Now get the hell off my land, or I'll put my dogs on you." Ledbetter slammed the metal trailer door behind the screen door.

Without any warrant or any legal reason to bring him into the station, that ended the interview. But Stuart Ledbetter had put himself squarely on their radar. Ledbetter struck Ray as the kind of man who could break open a garage door lock and a man's head and then take the crowbar he'd used home with him and toss it back into his toolbox. But they didn't have enough for a warrant.

Back at the police department, Ray climbed out of the car and stood beside it, letting the sun beat down on his face and wishing he was with Kate. Ready to quit for the day but not quite able to shut his mind down, Ray asked, "Think we got a serial killer here, somebody specializing in lawyers?"

Luke cocked his head. "You mean like somebody took too seriously all those skid-mark, bottom-of-the-ocean, and shark jokes?"

"Something like that."

Luke shook his head. "Naw, that'd be too easy. What we got here is one big job to connect the dots between that dead real estate lawyer guy and the dead state attorney. We're going to have to figure out what these two lawyer guys had in common that got them both killed."

"Why do you think there's a connection?" Ray asked.

"Because I'm smarter than you." Luke grinned so big the fillings in his back molars showed for a half second.

Ray laughed. It was an old joke between them. And the thing was, Ray figured it was probably true.

"Naw, but to get serious..." Luke's grin dropped off his tired face. "Two dead lawyers, one right after the other. It's not like Concordia's a big enough city for that to be a coincidence. What do you reckon the odds of two lawyers killed that close together would be and them not be tied in somehow? They're not drug dealers, where a high casualty rate's not too unusual. There's damn sure a connection."

"Probably. Unless their murders didn't have anything to do with them being lawyers." Ray thought idly that he might ask Kate to find some stats about how many lawyers had been murdered in Florida so far in the last couple of years to see if it was more common than Luke expected.

"Think how much time we're going to spend next few days, comparing these guys' cases, appointment books, phone records, and stuff like that, looking for a connection."

"Let's keep Dayton with us then," Ray said. "He loves that kind of stuff. Never knew anybody to like looking at lists of things so much."

"Must've been something kinky in his upbringing, you reckon?"

"Could be." Ray thought about what a crappy Saturday it'd been so far. At least he and Kate had tonight at Luke's to look forward to. He hoped no more lawyers got killed before then. But he had that queasy feeling he got sometimes that told him the whole mess was only going to get worse.

Chapter Seven

Ray tripped over a pile of shiny parts that looked like a dissected roller skate but caught himself before he fell. Kate snickered, offering him an arm. Straightening, he laughed. He knew better than to walk blindly into Luke's house, especially on a Saturday night.

"Careful there," Luke said before turning his attention back to Duke, a large determined dog. "Get back in the garage, Duke." He grabbed for the dog's collar but chuckled as the dog evaded him with a graceful lunge.

Luke and Aleyna's youngest child and only son, LB—his full name was Luke Boyd, the Boyd after his grandfather—waved Ray and Kate farther into the house. "Head for the living room," the ten-year-old said and scooted off after the escaped dog.

Their grandson squealed in protest from the playpen in the middle of the living room, holding out his arms for rescue. A puppy was simultaneously gnawing on and growling at the coffee table leg, the television volume was turned up even though no one was watching it, and from the far back of the house, music escaped under a bedroom door. Aleyna came out of the kitchen, grinned at Kate and Ray, and grabbed for the shepherd at the same time Luke did. Duke made a dive through them and ran up to Ray, growling and wagging his tail at the same time. LB snatched the dog's collar, and Duke dropped at the boy's feet.

"He's just playing," LB said as if Ray had never been to their house before.

Kate bent over, cupped the dog's jaw in one hand, and looked him straight in the eyes. "Don't jump, okay?" She squared her shoulders and, edging around LB and the dog, went to greet Aleyna.

LB led the dog to the garage and ran back into the living room. A moment later, winking back at Ray, Kate followed Aleyna into the kitchen. LB launched into a monologue about why his Little League team was actually better than their record. The shepherd scratched at the garage door and barked twice. Then, apparently satisfied he'd protested enough, he quieted.

Before Ray got comfortable on the couch, Aleyna and Kate carried in bottles of beer, glasses, and a tray with crackers, cheese, and sour cream dip. Ray took a beer, ignored the cross-eyed look Kate gave him, and opened it. When he realized there weren't enough glasses on the tray—no doubt Kate and Aleyna's idea to save him from drinking too much—he sipped from the bottle. *One beer. That's it.*

Luke and LB exhausted local baseball as a topic and started warming up on professional baseball. Aleyna lifted the baby out of the playpen and set him down on the floor, where he lunged for the puppy, who gave up on the coffee table leg and played with the baby.

Luke popped a piece of cheese in his mouth, and the puppy paused in its play to sniff. Rising up on its long legs, the animal advanced on the cheese while the baby, holding on to its back for balance, toddled along with it. Just as the puppy lunged for the cheese plate, Luke raised the plate out of reach without missing a word in his sentence. Aleyna deftly scooped up the baby a moment before he would have tripped face-first into the sour cream dip.

"Got his daddy's coordination," Luke said with a snort of contempt.

"Yes, but he's got his momma's good looks," Ray said, thinking of Lilliana, the child's mother. Luke and Aleyna's daughter was married with a baby and not even nineteen. A good-looking, dark-haired girl with her mother's chocolate eyes and sassy tongue, she had enough spunk that Ray figured she'd do just fine, no matter what.

"I have a favor to ask." Aleyna leaned closer to Kate. "If you aren't busy, could you maybe watch LB some tomorrow? I've got a church committee meeting, and Luke is going to be tied up working." She cast her eyes at Luke and sighed.

"Hey, I don't need a babysitter. I'm almost eleven." LB protested further by standing up as if to show how tall he was.

"Nobody thinks you need a babysitter," Kate said and smiled. "But you could help me out some tomorrow at the library and keep me company."

"The library?" The boy didn't sound enthusiastic. "Isn't it closed on Sundays?"

"Yes, but I've got the key. Benefits of high rank and all that. Best time to be in the library is when nobody else is there to bother you."

"Yeah?" LB sounded like he might be warming up to the idea. "What'll we do?"

"I'm going to find out all about that phosphate company and what permitting steps they have to go through. But you can be my test market. See, I've got some new videos and some games, and we like to check them out before we put them out for the kids. They're mostly educational stuff, but some of them look fun."

"Educational, huh?" LB eyed his dad as if hoping for a better offer.

Luke clapped his son on the back. "Like your momma said, Ray and me got to work tomorrow, son. No fishing for us. Sunday don't matter when somebody like the state attorney gets killed." Luke showed his good sense not to spoil the evening by explaining that they would be at Weaver's autopsy.

"It's a date then. I'll come pick you up right after church."

Ray smiled, content for a rare moment as he looked at Kate and his friends. Then the old anxiety gut-kicked him. He wondered if it could ever last, this thing with Kate.

Chapter Eight

At the library on Sunday, Kate got LB settled in with the new video games, not at all surprised by how quickly he'd figured them out. "I'll be in my office or in the microfiche room if you need me. All right?"

When he nodded, Kate went to the microfiche storage room, where she unlocked the Staff Only door. She hoped to find the film Weaver was looking at before his murder. Library patrons were never allowed to refile the microfiche, because if they did it incorrectly, the films were as good as destroyed. The process was simple: a patron would make a written request for the film, someone on the staff retrieved it, then the patron dropped the film in a refile box beside the microfiche reader when finished.

After three days, Weaver's form would have long since been shredded. Jenny, a twenty-year-old Calusa Community College student, normally filed the films in the afternoons, but she had been filling in at the information desk, so she might not have had the time to do it. Kate was hoping the film would still be sitting in the refile box.

Off and on all day Saturday, she'd been thinking of her brief encounter with Weaver that Thursday afternoon. He'd been sheepish when asking for help, but he couldn't get the film to thread through the machine.

"Been college since I've used one of these," he said then asked for her name. He flirted a little, making an elaborate showing of a simple handshake and introduction.

Kate was flattered and flirted back. "Oh, I *know* who you are," she said, slipping her glasses off and running her fingers through her hair to pull it out of her face.

When she leaned a little too close over his shoulder, inhaling a sandalwood-and-spice cologne too expensive for her to name, she saw that he was looking at an issue of the *Tallahassee Democrat* from 1972. That was the year after she'd graduated from high school, the year she'd hoped to spend in college but hadn't.

She didn't catch the day or month, because when Weaver heard her almost involuntarily whisper the date, he'd laughed and said that had been a very good year for him, his senior year in law school. She'd wished him well with his research and left the room, a bad mood settling in on her for the rest of the day.

That was Thursday afternoon. By Friday night, Weaver was dead.

The odds that the film had anything to do with his murder were remote, but Kate saw no reason not to look through the microfiche to see if she could find the right date. After a few minutes of checking the films, Kate retrieved the only 1972 film of the *Democrat* in the box. It was from the third week of January. She carefully threaded the film into the machine. Since she had no idea what she was looking for, or even what day Weaver might have viewed, she decided to scan the whole thing.

She found articles on Nixon and Vietnam, Nixon and McGovern, college campus unrest, and Florida State University funding problems, as well as local stories about politics in the state capital and the Sunday features. None of them seemed to have any connection to Weaver. Kate had been looking for something that might have Weaver's name in it, but that, as Luke was fond of saying, would have been too easy.

On her second pass, a story on the bottom of page one of the A section in the Tuesday paper made her pause. With a sense of having somehow been ambushed, she read about a teenage girl and a young man found dead on an isolated jut of land called Alligator Point, not far off US 98. A fisherman had discovered the decomposing bodies on the eastern tip, at a place the locals called Bald Point.

Bald Point. Kate ran her fingers through her hair, pulling the feathered bangs out of her eyes for a second before they fell back again. She took off her reading glasses and rubbed her eyes, already sorry she'd started her little foray in being a detective.

According to the news story, the girl was shot in the back while running away. The boy had taken a bullet in the face from someone standing close. The police had no leads or suspects, but a few bales of marijuana had been floating just offshore, and the favorite theory was that the couple had surprised some drug runners on the beach. The coast through that area and into Alabama and Louisiana, with their miles of remote beaches and inlets, was popular for offloading drugs brought by boat from Mexico through the Gulf of Mexico or up from South America through the Caribbean. From the Gulf Coast, the drugs could be smuggled through the ports at Mobile, Pensacola, or New Orleans.

Kate knew the stretches of those beaches, full of dunes and sea oats with miles of gulls, terns, and sandpipers. She remembered how US 98 near the turnoff to Alligator Point rose like a ridge of asphalt through the salt marshes and Spartina grasses with stands of pines just off the shore, pines that adapted to salt spray, frequent hurricanes, and the year-round rigors of a hot, bright sun.

Alligator Point, with its reptile-shaped peninsular thrust of beach, was just one slice of the coastal shoreline that ran more or less along US 98 from the Florida panhandle into Alabama. In 1972, the eastern tip of the point had been undeveloped and usually deserted, with the western tip home for not much more than a marina and a few concrete-block houses. High school kids favored the empty coastal beaches and dunes all along the area for making out, smoking dope, drinking Boone's Farm strawberry wine, and just being teenagers out on their own.

Kate rewound the microfiche and turned off the machine. Instead of taking the film back to the collection box, she held it a mo-

ment, wondering if she should hide it. She shrugged. She was the only person still living who knew Weaver had looked at the film, and
she was not volunteering any information. She dropped the film back
in a tray by the filing cabinet, figuring somebody would eventually
refile it.

Kate went to check on LB. She stood for a long time in the doorway of the children's library, watching him frantically working some
sort of game that apparently required him to grunt and shout over
the existing sound effects.

"God save you from being in the wrong place at the wrong time,"
she whispered then headed to the reference materials to see what she
could find out about the Antaeus Mining Company, Inc. If that company wanted to mine in the creek that fed the Calusa River, Kate
aimed to at least try to stop them.

"The Calusa River," Kate whispered, thinking how the words
made it sound sacred as it was named for one of Florida's lost tribes.

She'd canoed that river with Ray on many a Sunday—more recently with Luke, LB, and Aleyna joining them in a second canoe
and stopping on a bank to picnic and let LB run off his energy. For
reasons she didn't fully understand, the river made Ray moody, but
he always wanted to go back on it. The Calusa River drew him in in
an almost mystic way with its tepid, tannin-rich waters banked with
live oak and cypress trees that housed small worlds of hidden wildlife
in their roots and branches.

Ray wasn't much of an activist. But Kate figured if she could convince him the Calusa River was at risk, she could pull him on board
to fight AMCI's plans.

They have to be stopped. No matter what. And Ray can help.

Chapter Nine

L uke cut his eyes up from the pile of crap on his desk and tried not to glare at Dayton Whitfield as the younger detective thunked down more files and papers on the already crowded desk.

"Nothing, I tell you. No connection. None. *Nada.* Get it?" Dayton, twenty-seven and with the blue-eyed face of a kid still in school, sounded defensive even before Luke could respond.

"I tell you, there's some way or another those two guys connect." Luke pushed his glasses up on his nose and rifled through the papers Dayton dropped in front of him. "Did you—"

"Yeah, I did. I told you yesterday, and I told you the day before that. I took all this home, studied it, and made charts and lists of my own. They're right there on top. Nothing in their case files or their calendars. Nothing. All right? They don't have anything in common, not even the same doctor or dentist."

"Did you check their memberships? Things like Kiwanis and committees of the local bar or the Florida Bar or—"

"Like, duh."

Luke snapped his eyes up from the pile of paper. *Like, duh?* That was the way Lilliana, his eighteen-year-old daughter, talked. Luke frowned at Dayton over his bifocals. He'd sometimes seen Dayton and Lilliana chatting outside the police department in the evenings while the rank and file from the neighboring office where Lilliana worked pulled away in their secondhand cars, heading east to little concrete Florida ranch houses. Luke hadn't thought much about it. Dayton had spent a lot of time over at their house this last year, and he and Lilliana were friends of a sort. But Lilliana was also a married woman.

Like, duh, huh?

Trying to ignore his sudden nagging worry, Luke shot Dayton a hard look. "So is that a yes or what?"

"I checked all that. Like I told you, I checked everything. That Greenstreet fella didn't join anything, didn't even go to church. Nothing."

"So we're back to having nothing and one less shot in the dark to follow." Luke eyed the stacks of paper and guessed he'd better go through them himself or maybe split it with Ray and not tell Dayton. "Chief'll be down here, sticking his finger in our eyes again. And that James Gilroy, already acting like he's the new boss man, calls us regularly like he doesn't trust us to let him know what's going on."

Luke glanced at Dayton, who glared right back but didn't say a word. Luke understood Dayton was sensitive to suggestions that he didn't know what he was doing. He was young to be a detective, and he'd been shot his first year on the job.

While working the Officer Friendly beat at an elementary school, Dayton had saved a first grader from being dragged into a car by a convicted pedophile. In the fight that followed, the pedophile shot Dayton. By then, the little girl was running back toward the school. Dayton managed, even with a bullet in him, to shoot the pedophile's car as the man fled, causing the guy to wreck.

The girl's father was rich and influential, and the police chief was nothing if not political, so both took an interest in promoting Dayton once he healed. After all, he was a hero, though he often acted, even yet, like someone one day out of the police academy.

"All right. Thanks then," Luke said, forcing the image of a bleeding Dayton on the pavement out of his mind. "Find out anything about Ms. Miriam Calvert?"

"She's married to some retired rich guy, and they live out in one of those expensive condos on the Gulf. She worked for Weaver for eight years. Seems like a real nice lady. Efficient as hell. Real fond of Weaver."

That much I know. "What else?"

"What do you mean, what else? She a suspect? Classy lady like her?"

"No. Not a suspect. There's just something Ray and I can't put a finger on. Why don't you take her some flowers for pulling all that paperwork together for you, spend some time with her, talk to her. Listen real good. And listen real good to what she's *not* saying." *Let's see what Dayton's got for instincts.* Still, Luke knew he'd spend some more time with Miriam himself. "See what kind of read you get off her, all right?"

"Yeah. I mean, yes, sir." Dayton grinned. "Thank you."

Well, he is a likable guy. Luke watched the younger detective walk back to his desk, practically skipping with the delight of being trusted by Luke with something that wasn't just checking paper against paper.

THAT AFTERNOON, RAY went to Weaver's funeral. Dressed in his best suit, he arrived early to watch the people who came into the chapel for the service as well as those who just signed the guest book, shook a few hands, and left. The day before, he and Luke had divided up the hours of the visitation between them and studied the people who came.

Ray worked his way through the crowd to the display of flowers surrounding the casket. As he took in all the floral arrangements, Luke and Dayton ambled up to him, each of them wearing a gray suit with a maroon tie and looking strangely alike. Ray had never noticed the resemblance before, but now he was struck by it.

"Keeping your eyes open, I reckon," Luke said, glancing around the room.

Ray didn't bother to answer. As more people shuffled into the chapel, he looked down at Weaver's birth and death dates on the laminated memorial cards the funeral home was giving out. "Pretty short ride, 1948 to 1992."

Dayton pushed closer to Ray and Luke. "So, like, what is it we're looking for? I mean, besides somebody with a guilty look on their face when they come in."

"Girlfriends, for one thing," Luke said, as he went over to read the cards on the abundance of flowers scattered around near the coffin. "Seems he had a date of some kind Friday night, and I would like to talk to her." He plucked a card off an arrangement of lilies, then he folded the card in half and slipped it into his pocket.

Ray caught Luke's sleight of hand as he pocketed the card and opened his mouth to ask what was on it, but one of Weaver's assistants pressed close to Ray, maybe listening. He moved away from Luke and the flowers and stepped toward the open casket.

"Man, I hate looking at dead bodies." Dayton jammed his hands into his pants pockets and jangled his keys.

"Well, danged if you didn't pick the right profession then," Luke said, rolling his eyes.

Dayton looked like he was going to say something back but thought better of it.

Ray couldn't seem to take his eyes off the body in the casket. "It's amazing what the undertaker was able to do. I mean, he looks all right."

"Yep, for a dead man that had his head shot up," Luke said, "and then cut off in the autopsy."

The ME had sliced across the top of Weaver's scalp and pulled a flap of skin down over his face so he could get to the skull easily. As bad as that was to watch, especially when he knew the man with the tag on his toe and the Y-shaped incision in his torso, the worst part was still to come when the ME sawed open the skull and removed the brain for inspection. Ray had attended autopsies before, and every time it got to that part, he almost lost it.

In the end, the autopsy hadn't told them much that they didn't already know. The cause of death was a .38-caliber bullet, which was still lodged in Weaver's brain. The pattern of burn marks around the wound indicated the shooter was probably four or five feet away when the shot was fired. There were no rips, tears, or scrapings on Weaver's hands nor any puncture marks or other wounds on his body. He was muscular with minimal body fat. He had a partially digested meal of tuna and romaine lettuce in his stomach, and his lungs, stomach, and heart had all been in healthy condition.

Weaver had been an unusually healthy example of a forty-four-year-old man, the ME had observed. Except for the bullet in his head, Luke had added.

The same ME had examined Weaver's body at the scene before it had been moved, and based upon the rigor mortis, lividity, and algor mortis, he'd estimated the time of death at about eight p.m. Nothing during the autopsy changed his opinion. So Ray and Luke were looking for anyone who might have been around the state attorney's office at eight p.m. on Friday, but Ray had given up thinking somebody would show up who'd seen or heard something.

With the autopsy still plaguing him, Ray felt a tinge of regret when he glanced down at Weaver's head in the casket. He wished he had tried harder to get along with the man. As he stepped away, he wondered who would come to his funeral if he were shot tomorrow.

"Having people come stare at you when you're dead is not right." Dayton turned and started toward the back of the chapel, walking slowly through the gathering crowd of those who'd come to pay their last respects to Weaver. "I don't care what people say. I am not having an open casket. No way."

"Me neither." Luke nodded toward Ray and followed Dayton.

Ray joined him, patting his shirt pocket as if checking for a pack of cigarettes. "I didn't get to study the guest book much," he muttered.

"All right. We'll get the guest book after the funeral and run down everybody's name on it. You and me and Dayton here," Luke said as they caught up to Dayton. "I'm going to call everybody on that list till we find somebody who knows who Weaver was planning to spend Friday night with."

"Why's that so important?" Dayton asked, slumping against the back wall.

"Jeez, stand up straight, will you? You're going to embarrass us in front of all these bigwigs." Luke poked Dayton's arm hard enough that the young detective winced.

Dayton straightened, massaging the top of his right arm with his left hand. "All right, clue me in here. Why's his date important?"

"Maybe it's not. We won't know till we've found out. But maybe some little gal will say, 'I had a date with Alton, but he called and said he had to meet somebody at the office and he'd be late.' And maybe, if the gods are with us, she's even going to say, 'He said he was going to meet Mr. Who's'it.' And then we go get Mr. Who's'it. See?"

"Well, sure. But I mean—" Dayton stopped as Miriam came in the side door to the chapel, and they all watched her for a moment. Her husband was not with her. "Y'all excuse me a minute." Dayton eased into the aisle next to Miriam and took her arm as carefully as if he were the best man ushering the mother of the bride to her seat.

"Getting all sensitive on me, isn't he?" Luke watched Dayton for a moment. "Well, hell, the date thing's a long shot. That's all we got on this is long shots."

Before Ray could respond, the low murmur of voices picked up, and he turned to look back at the door. James Gilroy, followed by his entourage from the state attorney's office, entered. Most people moved aside for them, but a couple of local politicians reached out to shake James's hand.

"Don't guess there's much doubt now, huh?" Luke eyed the group as they moved toward the front. "The governor is likely to be announcing it any day now: James Gilroy, our new state attorney."

"He's a good prosecutor. Why not?" Ray wasn't particularly interested at the moment.

"No reason. Lord knows, that man's worked his butt off these last years."

"So, what's on the card you pilfered?" Ray asked.

"Oh hell, man. You got eyes in the back of your head or what?"

"Some days. What's on it?"

Luke pulled out the card and shoved it into his partner's hand. Ray turned it over, read it, and put it in his pocket without saying a word. *Cindy Lu.*

That was a long time ago. He was over Cindy, and he loved Kate now. But he still couldn't deny that thump in his chest at seeing Cindy's name on the card. She was in the wind, having disappeared the morning before a warrant for her arrest for embezzling was to be served. Ray told anybody who asked that there were a lot of ways Cindy could have known her arrest was coming, but he knew most folks thought he had tipped her off because he was so blatantly in love with her. Internal affairs eventually cleared him, but his chances for future promotions were gone. As far as he could tell, Luke was the only cop on the force who believed Ray hadn't helped her run.

He found it odd that Cindy would send flowers to the funeral of the man who'd tried to have her arrested, but she'd once worked for Weaver, back before the gambling ruined her life. Maybe it was a way to say she was sorry. Maybe it was just a way to taunt him for never finding her.

Ray glared straight ahead, a hint of a headache beginning to trouble him. He wondered if Cindy would have sent flowers to his funeral if he were the dead man in the casket.

Constantia walked over, dressed in an expensive-looking black suit, and offered his hand. He greeted Ray smoothly, as if he were running for state attorney along with James. Ray didn't like the glad-handing and had half a mind to ignore the proffered hand, but he shook it and responded with a barely polite "Hello."

Constantia turned to Luke, shook hands, and offered condolences as if Luke were family. That bugged Ray even more. Something was off about the man.

"When this is over"—Ray kept his voice low and his eyes on Constantia—"why don't you come back to the police department so we can set up a time for a lie detector test?"

"For who?" Constantia asked, his expression puzzled.

Ray glared at him. "For you."

Luke stepped closer. "Not the best timing, but Ray here is right. We've been meaning to get back in touch with you about—"

"Those are not admissible evidence. Surely even you two cops know that."

"Somebody might have mentioned that," Luke said, pushing between Ray and Constantia. "Nonetheless, we want you to come by and schedule a lie detector test. I'm sure you want to help us catch who killed your boss."

"This is harassment and bullshit. Just because you can't find the killer, you're threatening me. Stand back, or I'll sue you both."

"Please go ahead and sue us." Ray spoke with a forced calmness to cover his anger. "Then we can depose you under oath."

"I'm invoking my right to silence," Constantia said, backing away from Ray. "Now get out of my face."

Ray's hands curled into fists at his sides, but he made himself grin. "I wonder how the brand-new state attorney would feel about his brand-new assistant invoking his rights against self-incrimination."

Constantia stomped off.

"Well, that worked out good, didn't it?" Luke said. "Come on. The music's started. Let's get a seat for the service."

Chapter Ten

With their funeral jackets wrinkling beside them, Luke sat next to Ray on a concrete bench on the pier across from the library, looking out at the Calusa River. The breeze off the river kept the bugs off his face, and the smell of frying fish drifted down from the restaurant on the pier, making him suddenly hungry. A few feet away, a homeless man eased into the cover of a thick bush and curled around a jacket on the ground.

"Hang on," Ray said and rose from the bench. He headed over to the man.

Luke squinted in that direction, though he knew what Ray was going to do. A second later, Ray pulled out his billfold and handed the man some folding money. They exchanged a few words, then Ray reached down to shake the man's hand.

As Ray returned, his step had just that hint of a limp he got when he was worn out. A souvenir from Vietnam, the old wound in his hip explained why Ray gave homeless vets money when he saw them on the streets. Ray sat back on the bench without a word and aimed his eyes out at the river as if daring Luke to say something.

Luke shifted his weight, seeking a more comfortable position for his aching back. *Maybe this is a young man's job after all.*

The gold-and-pink glow of the setting sun ricocheted from the west to settle on the water in front of them. Out on the beach, it must have been a glorious sight, but even if they couldn't see the real sunset on the Gulf of Mexico, they could absorb the reflected colors of the evening.

"Well, damn," Luke said. "We're getting down to the wild hairs."

"I'll dig around some more in Constantia's life. Something's off with him, but still, I can't see that guy doing it. You don't shoot your boss then call 911 and stand around and wait."

"Not unless you figure that's a kind of smoke screen or alibi or something. Like everyone would think you'd never call in a murder you did yourself."

"Maybe." Ray didn't think that was it, but there was something there they didn't know despite all the background checking and investigating they'd already done on the late-blooming attorney.

Miriam had vouched for him in her own way. "A bit of an overachiever. I guess he's trying to make up for lost time, starting a legal career so late. He doesn't listen to instructions well, but he's a nice enough man," she had said. "Yes, he got along fine with Mr. Weaver. In fact, Mr. Weaver took a special interest in him."

The night Weaver was shot, Constantia had agreed to the gunshot-residue test without any hesitation. Luke had watched while the technician swabbed the dilute nitric acid solution over Constantia's hands, paying careful attention to the webbed area between the thumb and the forefinger. Negative. Unless the man had been wearing gloves or used a gun so well made it didn't leak any residue, he hadn't recently fired a weapon.

After the gunpowder test, with modest encouragement, Constantia had even let Ray and Luke walk through his apartment, and they'd found nothing except the usual mess of a guy living alone.

They'd asked him several different times and several different ways why a man would start law school at the age of forty-four. Constantia gave them what they figured was his official party line: He'd grown up in Steinhatchee on the nature coast of Florida, run a successful stereo business in Tallahassee, and even started franchising. But he'd wanted to do something more challenging and more worthwhile.

"I'd been kind of a useless and wild man when I was young, and maybe I just wanted to balance my karma some," he said. "That's why I particularly wanted to work in the state attorney's office. Balance my karma in that direction."

Luke figured Constantia's sheepish smile when he talked about his karma was just part of the show. He and Ray had joked about it.

"That'd be a line to use on the young ladies at the frat parties when you got twenty years on the competition, don't you reckon?" Luke had asked.

They'd started calling him the Karma guy. Even so, there hadn't seemed to be any reason to suspect he'd shot Weaver or otherwise been involved until today at the funeral.

"The lie detector test thing bugs me," Ray said. "I can't figure out why he'd get so pissed off."

"Maybe he figured enough's enough. And bringing it up at the funeral might not have been our best move."

"Maybe. But if he's scared of a polygraph, he's got something he's hiding. Might not mean a damned thing to us or have anything to do with the murders, but if he's scared of a polygraph, something's there."

"Well, he did come out of the Big Bend part of Florida, and he would've been about the right age to have been a dope smuggler. Remember the Steinhatchee Seven?"

Luke chuckled. The story was legend. Seven good old boys had tried to smuggle in fifteen tons of marijuana only to get trapped by low tide. "I think they arrested all of them, though." He sounded disappointed, almost as if he wished they'd gotten away with it.

Luke leaned back on the bench, glad to be hashing things out with Ray and glad his friend and partner was stone-cold sober after a long, hard afternoon. In the old days, they would have been someplace with Ray tossing back beer after beer while they tried to piece together little threads of this and that, looking for the big picture.

If they went fishing, Ray would be drinking the hard stuff, a bad habit he'd picked up in Vietnam and brought home with him, like the wounded hip. If they went out after work, Ray would be drinking. If Ray came over for dinner, he would bring a bottle of whiskey. When Luke went home to Aleyna and their kids, Ray would skulk through the bars, boozing and looking for women.

He hadn't liked that part of Ray, the heavy drinking and barhopping. But Luke didn't know much about picking up women. He'd married the first woman he fell in love with and was still married to her. He counted it one of God's great blessings the day he sat down at a counter in Aleyna's parents' Cuban deli and she served him the daily special. They fell for each other right there over the black beans and rice, neither of them yet twenty-one. So he'd never had to troll the bars for dates.

That was where Ray had met Cindy Lu—in a bar. Ray was a good-looking, strong-jawed man who moved with a clear message of physical prowess. Drinking or not, he worked out with weights, ran, punched the bag, and stayed in shape. His thick, curly black hair had grayed some over the years, and he'd never recognized that suit jacket lapels changed with the fashions, but he had big sad dark eyes and never had any trouble picking up women.

However, he had a problem keeping them. His two ex-wives came from marriages of less than a year. His girlfriends were numbered by the weeks. Luke never knew what the problem was and didn't ask, but he remembered Cindy once screaming at Ray that he'd better stop interrogating her like she was a suspect. She'd also called him a sanctimonious choirboy. So Luke suspected that Ray had never learned the essential lesson that compromise and forgiveness were as important as love in a long-term relationship. But Luke kept his nose out of it. If Ray wanted advice on women, he would have asked, and he hadn't.

At first, Luke hoped Cindy would be different and that she and Ray could somehow make it together. She was smart and beautiful, and beneath it all, she had a tough central core. But it all turned into a giant clusterfuck faster than any of them could have expected when her gambling addiction led to her embezzling, and she'd skipped town minutes before arrest. After she was gone, Ray took to drinking in his own backyard, deep into the night, steady, unrelenting, solitary.

"She was just a damn gambler," Ray had said about Cindy one night. "Just a damn gambler," he slurred.

Luke and Ray had been sitting out in Ray's backyard in cheap little plastic chairs from a discount store when Ray said that. The night was hot for February, with the smell of the last of the orange blossoms coming at them off Ray's trees in sweet swells on the night breeze.

"You reckon that's much different than being a damn drunk?" Luke had asked.

That was the first thing Luke ever said directly to Ray about his drinking, but it got through. Ray stopped the steady drinking. Not immediately and not smoothly or easily, but he got it done. By the time Ray met Kate at a small grocery store on Main Street, he was down to one ritual beer with Luke on the weekends, usually on a small boat in the Intercoastal, fishing rod in one hand, warming beer in the other.

"You were one hog's breath away from being a full-fledged drunk," Luke had said to him one dusk as they were dragging the boat up the landing. "I'm real proud of you."

That was all Luke had ever said to Ray about the way he quit being a drunk.

So instead of drinking while they recapped the day's efforts and the funeral, they sat empty-handed on a bench by the river, taking in the twilight.

"It'll go down. You'll see. We always put 'em down," Luke said, standing and stretching.

"I owe Weaver," Ray said, brushing his empty hand through his thick hair.

"We owe them all, Ray."

Chapter Eleven

Luke stirred the fried okra in the iron skillet and wondered if he'd put enough salt in the cornmeal batter. He liked it salty, even if the doc thought that was a bad habit. Aleyna, bless her Cuban heart, never did learn the knack of frying okra the way he liked it.

When the telephone rang, he stepped away from the stove and picked up the phone on the kitchen wall. He kept his eyes on the skillet. Okra could burn in a split second. "Hello."

"Daddy, put Momma on the phone, okay?"

"Lilliana, hello to you too." Luke grinned. He liked that his daughter and her mother were close, but he sometimes wished she would call just to talk to him.

"Hey, Daddy. Sorry, I'm just in a rush."

"Okay. I'll get your momma on the phone."

He turned down the heat on the stove and went looking for Aleyna. He found her watching a yoga video while sitting on the floor, legs stretched out in front of her.

"Think we could learn to do that?" she asked, tilting her head at the screen, which showed a young woman twisted in a triangle shape on a mat. "They say it helps with sore backs."

Luke shook his head. "Not for me. Lilliana's on the phone."

Aleyna hopped up and went to grab the phone in the den, while Luke returned to the kitchen.

As he reached to hang up the receiver, he heard Lilliana ask, "Can you set a Pyrex dish on fire?" That got him curious, so he listened.

"Lilliana, what in the world are you talking about? Why would you want to set a Pyrex dish on fire?" Aleyna's voice had that edge it got when the kids did stupid stuff.

Luke stretched the phone cord so that he could reach the stove and turned up the heat under the skillet.

"'Cause I want to make cherries jubilee for dessert. And I need to set a dish on fire to do that."

"*¡Los santos nos preservan!* Why do this?"

"Dayton's fixing to come to dinner tonight, and it's got to be something special."

Dayton? Uh-oh. Luke didn't like the way that sounded one bit.

"Why is Dayton coming to dinner?" Aleyna's kids-doing-stupid-stuff tone of voice got sharper.

"Like, because I asked him to, okay? Now can I set the Pyrex on fire or not? The recipe book says I need a fireproof bowl, and—"

"Lilliana, do not let that husband of yours near a lighter and any brandy. You remember what happened last time?"

Luke stifled a chuckle. He remembered when Stevie nearly burned off all his facial hair lighting the backyard grill. Fortunately, he wasn't hurt.

"I do not believe how you marry a boy so... *desmañado.*"

"Aw, Mom. Stevie's not that clumsy. Besides, I'm the one cooking dinner."

"No excuses. That baby is your responsibility, and you shouldn't be setting fire to things with your son around. That child's your number one priority."

"Like, duh, okay? I'll do it, and I won't have the baby anywhere near the kitchen. Now I got to know about the Pyrex."

"You come here. Bring the baby and leave him with me. Then you go to Winn Dixie and buy a pound cake. Now why did you invite Dayton to your place?"

Luke wondered the same thing as he stirred the okra, which was popping in the grease.

"I thought he and Stevie might get along."

"Lilliana, you want somebody to play with Stevie while you cook, invite Little LB over."

Soon after that, they hung up. Luke replaced the receiver in the phone cradle, wondering if eavesdropping on his wife and daughter had been a good idea. He hadn't gotten the okra dumped on a serving plate before Aleyna stormed into the kitchen and wanted to know what was going on between Dayton and Lilliana that their daughter wanted to set her good dishes on fire to impress him.

"Damned if I know," he said.

RAY SAT OUTSIDE IN the cool night air. The funeral had depressed him. Or maybe it was seeing Cindy's name on that damn card. Either way, he wanted a drink. He wanted a cigarette. He wanted to be twenty again, with enough time in front of him that he could afford mistakes. Even thirty. Thirty still gave you the luxury of a lot of time to waste. But forty—and he was already halfway to fifty—didn't have the safety net of plenty of time. And damn it all, hardly any margin of error was left at fifty.

Ray envied what Luke had with Aleyna, and he wanted one more chance at finding that. Maybe it wouldn't matter that he still thought of Cindy, especially late in the night when he fought off the old urges. Maybe it didn't matter that he had two failed marriages that had started and ended before he was thirty. He was a lot more together now.

Trying not to admit how much he wanted a drink, Ray took a shower and put on a white dress shirt and his best pair of gray pants. That would make Kate suspicious right off, yet that was all right. He wanted her to pay attention. It was past ten, but that would be okay too. Kate never went to bed before midnight.

He dug the ring out from under his T-shirts in the dresser drawer. He would be paying on it for a while, but Kate was worth it.

Twenty minutes later, he knocked on Kate's door. Waiting for her to answer, he fingered the felt-covered jewelry box jammed in his pants pocket.

She opened the door, and they gave each other the usual perfunctory greetings. She didn't ask why he was there, though she'd eyed his dress shirt. He followed her out to the back porch, the pug darting between them, snorting and tripping over her own energy. She offered him some guava juice from the Cuban grocery store, though he saw she had a half-empty glass of wine beside her chair. When he declined, she sat down and took a drink of her wine.

He walked over, pulled out the jewelry box, and handed it to her. "This isn't how I meant it to go, but I was hoping... that is, I *am* hoping, you'll marry me."

She took the box. "Bad funeral, I take it. Poor Weaver." She closed her hand around the box as she spoke, her voice flat.

"This isn't about that." He eyed her wine.

She looked down at the box then back up at Ray, following his eyes to her drink. "I'll pour you a glass. Or bring you a beer. But no hard stuff." She'd laid that rule down early on.

He licked his lips but shook his head. He wasn't sure she would make a good homicide detective's wife, but he was sure he wanted to be her husband. He'd lost the last woman he'd loved in part because he was a cop. He wasn't going to make the same mistake again. "I'm going to retire. Soon as this one's over. I owe it to Alton Weaver to finish this one though. Then I'll quit. I swear. I'll find something else to do."

Kate rose from her chair in a fluid unraveling of legs and long floral skirt. She pulled Ray into an embrace. Her tongue touched his, and he slipped one hand under her blouse. She wasn't wearing a bra, and his fingers found the hard tip of her breast. He eased his other hand under the waistband of her skirt and rubbed the smooth skin above the top of her panties.

"Say yes, and come to bed." He squeezed her nipple but not too hard. Unlike Cindy, Kate didn't like it rough. Ray had learned to slow down and go softly with her.

One of Kate's hands inched to his chest, and her fingers found their way to the exposed triangle of hair at the top of his shirt. She traced a path across his skin before she pulled her hand free and headed toward her bedroom. Ray followed.

The next morning, as he was leaving Kate's house, he realized she'd never answered his proposal.

Chapter Twelve

Kate ripped out a story from the *Herald-Tribune* about a group of citizens in Riverside who were organizing to fight AMCI's plans to mine phosphate in the corner of land adjoining Concordia. They had a grassroots movement already going, and Kate wanted to join their group and also start one in Concordia. She planned to look up phone numbers that day and give them a call. After she let the Maggies finish their breakfasts, she headed into work.

The library was busy for a Friday morning, so Kate didn't have time to look up the numbers until she hid in her office with the Riverside phone book during her lunch hour. She learned that a Concordia man named Carter Russell had started the citizens' group in Riverside and was organizing one locally when he'd been killed on Waterbury Road, coming home from a meeting the previous Friday night. He'd been bitten by a snake on a long, deserted road, walking away from a car he'd apparently lost control of and ditched. Kate cringed at the thought of snakebites and tried to block the image from her mind.

With some trepidation, but with the encouragement of the person who now headed the Riverside group, Kate called the man's widow, who was willing to meet. The woman had her husband's files and hoped someone would take and use them to fight AMCI's plans to mine phosphate in the watershed of the Calusa River.

———⊶◉⊷———

RAY WAS AT HIS DESK, calculating how much pressure he could put on a judge to try and get that search warrant for Ledbetter's tools before the rule of diminishing returns kicked in. The phone rang, and he picked it up. "Hello."

"Hi," Kate said. "Can you come with me tonight to meet with a woman who has some papers to give me on the AMCI proposed phosphate mine?"

He didn't really want to commit to an evening spent on phosphate ranting. "Do you really need me to go?"

"No, I don't *need* you to go, but I thought you'd want to. From what I learned today, this woman's husband, Carter Russell, was really the moving force behind getting the group in Riverside going. He was some kind of expert on phosphate, and he was highly motivated to stop AMCI. And he was planning on starting a group here."

"Was?"

"He died in an accident. His car was found wrecked on the outskirts of the Calusa River watershed at night, and somehow he got snakebit, apparently by a rattlesnake, twice, and he died."

Ray winced at the thought of dying that way and wondered why the man had left his car and gone into an area where snakes would have been. It didn't seem likely he would have been foolish enough, or unlucky enough, to step on a snake on the highway.

"His widow is looking for someone to work with the Riverside people in starting a group here," Kate said.

"And you think that'd be you?"

"No, Ray, I think that would be *us*."

"If he lived here, why'd he start a group in Riverside first?"

"Because the original mining operation was slated just for there. They've been fighting AMCI for over a year now. I guess the story didn't make the local papers until the plans impacted Concordia. So Russell started there, in Riverside. Just in the last few months, the group learned—and I mean they learned this before any public announcements—that AMCI was planning to expand."

"Yes."

"Yes, what?" Kate's voice had that familiar edge to it.

"Just yes. I mean..." He didn't really know what he meant.

"She's expecting us around seven thirty. She lives in Riverview Estates."

Might as well. Maybe he'd ask Kate about the ring. She still had it, but she wasn't wearing it, at least not when he was around. "All right, I guess I'll come with you. Pick you up around seven then? Or do you want to get dinner first?"

"I'll fix us something. You come over when you can."

Ray put the phone down, rubbed his eyes, and wondered if he should bring up the ring during supper. He never seemed to know what to say to a woman or when to say it.

The only time he knew what to say was when he was drinking, somewhere in that space between the first buzz and full-faced drunk. No, that wasn't exactly true. He knew what to say while interrogating a suspect. But if Cindy Lu had taught him one thing, it was that hardnosed grilling didn't work on a woman you loved.

THE HOUSE DIDN'T LOOK like a house where company was expected. No lights shone out front, and the place was dark except for a vague glow from a nearby street lamp. After they got out of Ray's car, he held Kate's arm a moment to hold her back as he scanned the area. Satisfied that nobody was lurking in the shadows, he checked out the house itself: nice, big, well kept, a half-acre lot, and in a good neighborhood.

"You sure this is the right place? You didn't write the address down wrong?"

"This is the place." Kate's voice had a snip to it.

Still, Ray checked the address again before he knocked on the door. A woman answered. She'd obviously been crying.

Kate apologized for disturbing her, introduced herself and Ray, then offered condolences. When the woman didn't respond, Kate added that she'd called earlier.

The woman finally nodded. "Yes, of course. Please come in."

Ray and Kate stepped into the foyer, but the woman made no move to take them farther into her house.

Kate took Ray's hand as if afraid he might leave, which he had considered doing. "We're sorry to bother you at such a sad time, but Peter with the Riverside group told me you were anxious to find someone locally to take over for Mr. Russell."

"Yes, yes I am. All his work just sitting in a big box seems a waste. I should take it over, but I just... I mean I don't work or anything, so I could, you know, timewise and all. But I just can't."

Kate gave the woman a sympathetic nod. "I understand. It would just be too much right now."

"You're the librarian Peter told me about, aren't you? He called to tell me he'd talked with you. He was really pleased at getting your call. When my husband got killed—" The woman's voice broke, and she stood still, lost in her own foyer.

Kate let go of his hand and eased closer to her. "I'm so sorry. Perhaps another time. We'll come back. I'm sorry to intrude."

Ray stepped from behind Kate as she turned back toward the front door. "We're sorry for your loss, ma'am."

The woman looked up at Ray. "He was coming home from a meeting with Peter and the people in Riverside. On Waterbury Road. You know how lonesome it can be in places. Somehow, he swerved into a ditch, which wasn't like him, but he'd had so much on his mind lately. He must have tried to go for help or something. Nobody really understands it, but he fell down and got bit on the hand and on the face. Out there by himself." She paused and seemed to struggle to breathe for a moment.

"Oh, please, please," Kate said, "you don't have to—"

Ray cut her off. "This happened in what county?"

"Calusa," Mrs. Russell said. "Just barely over the county line."

A flare of interest jumped up inside him. "When?"

"Last Friday night."

"Who investigated it, ma'am?"

"A state trooper found the car in the ditch. He saw the tracks and followed them till he found... Carter."

"Do you happen to remember the officer's name, ma'am?"

"No. The officer who came and told me was tall, and he was kind, but I don't remember his name." The woman swiped at her eyes with the back of her hand.

Kate tugged at Ray's hand. "I'm very sorry. We'll leave now."

"No, wait. You came for his papers. And I need to be getting used to this. I mean, he's going to be dead a long time, isn't he?"

"Yes, ma'am," Ray said.

"Come. I've got his stuff in the den. Somebody needs to take this over for him. I just don't think I can. But he was passionate about it. Obsessed really. He blamed phosphate mining for killing both of his parents. Cancer, you know. It could have been anything that caused that cancer, but nobody could ever convince him it was something other than those mines."

Kate made comforting murmurs and followed the widow into the den. Ray waited, his mind spinning around the idea that Carter Russell's death on the same night as Alton Weaver's murder might not have been coincidental. He had nothing factual to suggest a connection, but something in the pit of his gut said it was true.

A few minutes later, Ray and Kate left. He stashed the storage box full of papers in the back seat. As Ray drove off, Kate started fussing at him for interrogating the woman.

"I just asked her—"

"You just started cross-examining her. If I hadn't stopped you—"

"You didn't stop me. All I wanted to know was where and when and the name of the trooper. I can go by the state troopers' office tomorrow morning and get a copy of the report."

"Honestly, Ray, why? Not every death is a case for you."

He didn't mention his vague suspicion there might be a connection to Weaver's murder. She would just jump on him for being paranoid, an accusation he'd heard before. "No, but maybe this guy was such a pest that the phosphate people went after him."

"Damn it. It was an accident. He lost control of his car, probably dodging an armadillo or something, and got snakebit in the dark. You know that shrubby area's full of rattlers. The phosphate companies don't murder their opponents. You've been a policeman—"

"Too long," Ray finished for her. He'd heard it before.

"Yes, too long. You need to stop thinking everything's a crime. Sometimes, things just happen. Like accidents, okay?" Kate snapped her words out as if she wanted to revive the argument.

A tinge of anger outweighed his common sense. "So you're the instant expert here. You know for a fact this was an accident, that phosphate companies don't harm people?"

"Stop it. All right? Just stop it." Kate's voice rose just shy of yelling. "Phosphate companies don't hire killers to stop environmentalists. That's what they have lawyers for."

Ray pressed his lips together and gripped the steering wheel. Kate shifted in the seat, pushing against the passenger-side door as if to get as far from him as possible. They rode in silence as he fought the urge to speed—or to retort.

———◉———

TO GET THE LAST WORD, and because he worried about Kate getting involved, Ray called her the next morning with a copy of the accident report in his hands. He got her voicemail and left a message, which gave him time to ponder the report again.

The state trooper's investigation couldn't really explain the death, though the report concluded it was accidental. Carter's car had swerved into a ditch, and the front wheel busted open from hitting a tree. But Carter was found about a quarter of a mile from the car, in the swampy outreaches of the Calusa River watershed, sprawled next to a rotting log. The trooper who spotted the car had been looking for the driver when he'd noticed footprints a few yards away that led off through a damp area. He called in a report and then followed the tracks until he lost them in the palmetto thickets. Traveling mostly on instinct, the trooper had kept going through the low scrubs and cypress muck until he'd found the body.

Ray bet that trooper wished he had turned back and let someone else find the gruesome sight. The ecchymosis, the purple and black discoloration, and the swelling from the rattler's toxin would have been a grisly sight. Ray made himself stop thinking about what the man's last moments must have been like, bitten on the hand and the face, and left to die, and hoped the man's widow was ignorant when it came to rattler bites.

Still, it just didn't add up. He couldn't figure out why the dead man would have ended up a quarter mile into the swamp. The logical thing for a stranded traveler to do was to stay with the car and wait for help. Even if it was the next day before someone came along, that would be much safer than risking a hike through that kind of shrub territory at night. Carter Russell sounded like the type of man who would know that.

There was only one explanation. Someone, or some*thing*, scared Carter off the road and into the swamp.

Yet the report stated there were no other tracks but the ones that matched the shoes of the dead man and no skid marks to indicate a second vehicle had been present. Nothing else indicated Carter had been chased or followed by anyone or anything.

A follow-up report said Carter Russell worked as a handyman. When Ray read that, he leaned back in his chair and stared at the ceiling, thinking about the man's large house in that pricey neighborhood. That seemed to be too expensive a place for a handyman to own. And the wife had told him that she didn't work.

Ray pondered that, wondering when the man had bought the house and if there was a mortgage. He called the trooper and left a message asking the man to give him a call.

Chapter Thirteen

Kate stared wearily out the library window at the evening downtown sky as sirens sounded in the distance. She was hiding in her office after her official shift to organize the information from Carter Russell's pile of random reports and studies into a presentation. That morning, she'd placed a small ad in the A section of the newspaper, announcing the formation of a citizens' group to fight AMCI's plans to mine phosphate anywhere near the Calusa River or the creeks feeding into it. The meeting would be at her house on Friday night.

She glanced at the clock and saw that it was a little after seven, a good time to call Ray back.

As soon as he answered, she asked, "Do you know that the strip mine and processing plant AMCI proposes would use thirty-seven million gallons of water a day? And this when there's a drought and such a water shortage in the area that we're not allowed to water our lawns and we're supposed to turn off the water while we brush our teeth?"

"Um... hi, Kate."

"Aquifer drawdowns of up to six feet," she said.

"I've got the trooper's report on Carter Russell's death. We need to talk about it."

"You're the cop, not me." She could hear Ray breathing on the other end of the phone and imagined he was still angry from the night before.

"Kate, I love you."

She paused, thinking for a moment it was time to make up her mind one way or the other about him. But she decided to wait. "AM-

74

CI plans to put an unlined one-thousand-acre slime pond on Cattle-guard Creek. You know that'd be bigger than all of downtown Concordia, and it'll contain eight billion—eight *billion*, Ray—gallons of toxic phosphate waste. That's seven hundred times more than the amount of oil spilled from the Exxon Valdez."

"Are you ever going to say anything about your ring?"

"This is about phosphate. Are you listening to me?"

"Yes. Are *you* listening to *me*?"

Neither of them spoke for an awkward moment.

Finally, Ray said, "I'm just worried about you, all right? That trooper's report makes Russell's death seem suspicious."

Kate bit back the urge to say *everything* seemed suspicious to him. "Come to my meeting. We can talk afterwards." She said a hurried goodbye and hung up the phone.

———◉———

FRIDAY NIGHT, TWELVE people, including Ray, sat in Kate's living room while Maggie the pug snorted from lap to lap, acting like each person had come to admire her. Kate outlined the facts about the proposed phosphate mine.

"What can we do?" a thin man in a polo shirt and dark-green pants asked.

"Frankly, I'm not sure yet, but I have a few ideas." Kate looked at the list she'd jotted down the night before. "Write letters to the editors to get more publicity. Make our opposition known to the permitting agencies. Write letters to the Central Florida Regional Planning Council—they have to issue a permit. And write the Department of Environmental Protection in Tallahassee—the DEP has to issue a permit. And get some petitions started. The first permit they need is the water-use one from Swiftmud—"

"Swiftmud?" asked an elderly lady in a bright flowered dress.

Maggie the dog wiggled in her lap and licked Blue Corn chip crumbs from the woman's dress.

"Sorry. That's the Southwest Florida Water Management District. They issue the water-use permits for this region, and AMCI has to get a permit from them. The paperwork indicates that AMCI has already filed its permit request. We need to get a copy of that. I think it's public record, and—"

"Shouldn't we hire a lawyer?" a heavyset man in a white shirt and tie asked, cutting her off.

Kate glanced at him. "Well, if any of you know any environmental lawyers, it might be worth seeing if you could talk them into volunteering. But right now, we're just gathering information, sharing ideas, and exploring options, and we don't have the budget for legal help."

"You sound like a damn bureaucrat," the heavyset man said. As he snapped at Kate, Maggie jumped down from the woman's lap, circled the man's feet, and started lapping beer from the glass on the floor by his chair.

A well-muscled man with a sunburned face leaned forward to snag a chip. An odd tuft of gray hair swirled over his broad forehead. When he sat back in his chair, he snickered and tilted his chin toward Maggie as if to show Kate he saw what the dog was doing. She'd seen him in the library, though he didn't look like a library sort. Rather, he seemed more like an aging linebacker going soft at the middle and showing his years in his jowls. But what made him really stand out was the heavy camouflage boots he wore, footwear unusual in Florida on anyone except a man who worked outdoors, hunted, or rode motorcycles. His weathered face fit being an outdoorsman, so she shrugged off the boots.

Maggie dashed over, sniffed his legs, and wiggled. The man picked her up and scratched behind her ears as the dog went into a frenzied dance on his lap. He grinned at Kate, and she smiled back at him.

When Kate looked around the room again, Ray was sitting with his arms folded tight across his chest and a scowl on his face. Kate almost wished she hadn't asked him to attend. His expression implied he wished she hadn't either.

Chapter Fourteen

Luke drove with one hand on the steering wheel, the other fiddling with the new tie Lilliana had given him as a just-because gift. "It's not going to work, you know, us trying to convince Ledbetter to agree to an interview."

"You see any other choice we have after Judge Goddard denied our request for a warrant?" Ray tapped his fingers on his thigh as if he were typing.

"Nope, none at all."

Without the warrant, all they could do was ask nicely that Ledbetter come in and talk. *Fat chance.*

Luke parked the car in front of Ledbetter's trailer and, keeping his eyes peeled for the dogs, got out, a stiffness in his lower back that made him feel his age. "This ought to be a lot of fun."

Ray crawled out of the passenger side of the car and crossed the weedy yard. Luke stretched then caught up as Ray knocked on the door.

Ledbetter cracked open the rusted door. "Get the hell off my property."

"Hey, there." Luke gave him a little wave. "We just want to talk a minute. No reason to be unfriendly."

"Unfriendly my ass." Ledbetter opened the door wider. "Get 'em, boys."

Three mutts varying in size from medium to extra-large hurtled out of the trailer, aiming straight for Luke and Ray. The black dog attacked Ray, sinking its teeth into his leg, while the brindle dog leapt for Luke's throat. The third dog, a broad-chested white one with a black ear, stood to one side, apparently not interested in joining the fray.

Though the brindle snarled and snapped its jaws while lunging repeatedly at Luke's face, it didn't manage to get a bite in. Ray was getting the worst of it as the black dog dug its teeth in deep and tried to shake his leg like it was small prey. While swatting and cursing the mutt, Ray drew his gun.

"Don't shoot it, damn it." Luke made a fist and punched the brindle dog in the face.

With a yelp, the dog dropped into a crouch. Freed of the brindle, Luke spun around and brought his foot up fast and hard under the black dog's jaw. The force of his kick lifted the dog and broke its grip on Ray's leg.

The white dog suddenly came to life and lunged at Luke. Before he could move, the dog's teeth were in his leg. Luke reeled around and swiped at the animal, but the dog hung on.

Ray hit the white dog on the top of its head with the butt of his gun. It took two hits before the dog finally let go. It curled, growling, in the sandspurs and dry grass. The other two dogs joined the white one. The black one licked the white one's head, while the brindle barked at Ray and Luke.

"Back off. Slow. Look 'em in the eyes," Luke said, glancing at the empty porch and closed door of the trailer. "Don't run."

Once they had dragged themselves back to the car, Luke got behind the wheel and called the sheriff's office. A deputy agreed to come and arrest Ledbetter for assaulting officers of the law.

"Too bad it's outside our jurisdiction. I'd love to arrest that guy," Ray said. "Leaving it to the deputy to arrest him doesn't sit right."

"High sheriff or us, don't matter. An arrest'll get his attention," Luke muttered. "Hey, bet you never pistol-whipped a dog before. Another glorious career first."

"Just don't tell Kate I hit a dog, even if it was in self-defense."

"I suspect the less said about this sorry affair, the better. But look on the bright side. Now we've got something on Ledbetter. Once the deputy Mirandizes him, maybe we can get him running his mouth so he can step on himself."

"A lead would be good, real good."

The chief had been down that morning again before they'd headed out to Ledbetter's, and the press was getting ugly about the stalled murder investigation. At least James Gilroy had stopped bugging them. He was probably too busy securing the governor's appointment as acting state attorney to replace Weaver.

Nobody really questioned them about Greenstreet's murder anymore, but that one played on Luke too. They were not getting anywhere, and each day that passed without a clue, a witness, a bit of evidence, or something, the greater the odds were that the two crimes might not be solved.

Luke started the car then winced as he pressed on the brake.

Ray asked, "You okay?"

"Yep. How about you?"

"I'm all right."

Luke cut his eyes toward his partner's bloody leg but couldn't see how bad it might be because the torn pants covered the wound. "We'll just head to that doc-in-a-box the workers' comp folks want us to use." Luke gripped the steering wheel harder with both hands and gave the car more gas.

They hadn't been at the walk-in clinic more than a few minutes before Luke blurted, "Hell, maybe it's time to get outta Dodge. We could go out east to Hardee, maybe Highlands County, and get a little orange grove. Go out and live with some nice quiet people."

"Cope with the vagaries of the weather instead of the criminal mind?" Ray snickered as he rubbed his leg.

"Vagaries, huh? You picking up Kate's vocabulary now?"

"Beats picking up yours."

"Well now, don't get all critical on me."

"I like Hardee and Highlands. Lots of open spaces. We both got our retirement vested. Nothing's stopping us." Ray leaned over his outstretched legs, lifted the torn cloth of his pants, and stared at the bloody wound. "I guess we have to get tetanus shots again, don't we? Think we should trust those rabies tags or call in animal control?"

"Hell, call in animal control to check out those dogs. Ledbetter looks like the sort who might be slack on the shots, you know? And it wasn't like we got a chance to actually read the date on those tags." Luke glanced at his own swelling puncture wounds and torn pants and wondered if the department would reimburse them for their ruined clothes. "How long you reckon we got to wait?"

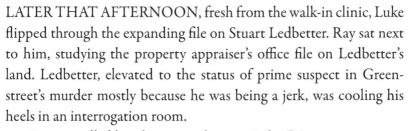

LATER THAT AFTERNOON, fresh from the walk-in clinic, Luke flipped through the expanding file on Stuart Ledbetter. Ray sat next to him, studying the property appraiser's office file on Ledbetter's land. Ledbetter, elevated to the status of prime suspect in Greenstreet's murder mostly because he was being a jerk, was cooling his heels in an interrogation room.

Dayton rolled his chair over closer to Luke. "You going to question that guy or what? Now you got him cooling off in a cell on assaulting an officer with a deadly dog charge."

Dayton kept a straight face when he said it, but Luke had tired of the jokes. He tried to tamp down the prickle of irritation and forced himself not to push Dayton's chair away or to snap at the young detective. He could almost remember what it was like to be young and green, but he didn't think he'd ever been as green as Dayton.

Almost against his better judgment, Luke asked, "You want to join us? You might learn something from Ray here."

Ray looked up from the file, narrowing his eyes at his partner.

Dayton grinned. "Heck yeah, I want to come. Why you think I been hanging around y'all all morning?"

"Don't you say a thing. You just listen," Ray said.

"Sure." Dayton reached for a file from the table. "So, now you got him arrested and read him his rights and all that, what're you going to try to weasel out of him?"

Neither Ray nor Luke answered Dayton, so the rookie lowered his head to study the notes that Luke had just finished reviewing.

A few seconds later, Dayton said, "I mean, wow, how's this guy get the money to pay cash for a hundred acres of land?" He flipped back to the front of the file. "If Ledbetter was born in 1945, he was only twenty-eight when he paid sixty grand in cash for some property in east Calusa County in 1973. I mean, he's just some low-life guy, right? No trust fund in that boy's background." Dayton looked at Luke then at Ray. "I mean, is there?"

"No, Dayton," Luke said. "That was kind of one of the things we sort of meant to ask him about."

"Well, come on," Ray said, getting to his feet. "We know as much as we're going to know about him from all this paper. Let's see what he has to say."

Luke opened the door to the interrogation room and led Ray and Dayton inside. Just to be sure, Luke ran through the Miranda rights again.

"Hell no, I don't want some dumb-ass lawyer." Ledbetter pushed his chair back as if he were going to stand but then seemed to think better of it. "I still owe on the last dickhead's bill. I had to pay him for screwing me over. And I don't mind talking about anything I want to talk about because y'all ain't got nothing on me. If you did, you wouldn't have done that chicken-shit arrest over the dogs. Now just what the hell do y'all want to know so damned bad?"

Dayton strode closer and loomed over Ledbetter. "Where'd you get the money to buy that land?"

Luke reached out and pulled Dayton back. He gave the rookie a look that said, *What part of "Don't say anything" did you not understand?* The younger officer's face reddened, and he took a seat at the end of the table.

"I don't see where that's any of y'all's business, now is it? And I ain't seen no warrant or nothing." Ledbetter smiled as if satisfied with his own brilliance.

They spent nearly two hours interrogating the man, but Ledbetter didn't give up anything they didn't already know. Tired and frustrated, Luke told Ledbetter they had a witness who'd described a man who looked like him hovering around Wyman Greenstreet's house the day he was killed. That was a bold lie on Luke's part, but the US Supreme Court had never said police couldn't lie to suspects they were interrogating. "Can't beat them but can sure trick them" was Luke's summary of the law.

Ledbetter laughed. "I don't give a flying crap how many folks said I was near Greenstreet's place. I wasn't, and I can damn well prove that, but I ain't telling you how 'less you arrest me. Then I'll tell it in court and make you look like the dumb-ass cops you are. So you fools can just piss up a green rope, you sorry-ass motherfuckers."

Ray jumped out of his chair, heading for Ledbetter. Luke stood to intervene, but Dayton, who was closer, hopped up and slid between Ray and Ledbetter.

"I need me a soda," Dayton said, so smoothly that Luke was impressed. "How about I bring one back for everybody?"

"Why don't you take a break and go with him?" Luke said, eyeing Ray. "Bring me back a Coke."

"Bring me back a Michelob." Ledbetter snickered.

Ray slammed out of the room with Dayton a few steps behind him.

Once the door closed, Luke gave Ledbetter a hard look, which netted him some more cuss words from the man. The narrow, dank room smelled of trapped, stressed male bodies.

"Pissed off permanent-like, aren't you? I know the type. My old man was just like you," Luke said, not sure why he was bothering. "Mad at everything. Nothing ever went right, and nothing was ever his fault."

Ledbetter sat there, glaring with tired red eyes.

"Know what it got him?" Luke bent over Ledbetter close enough that he could smell the sweat on the other man.

"Like you think maybe I give a shit."

"Got him ten acres of nothing but sand and palmetto shrubs and a wife and kids that went way out of their way to keep away from him."

"Got a point, or you just thinking I might care about your family life?"

"I got a point. I don't think you killed anybody because you don't have the balls for it. But you're going to sit here and be pissed off and not say a damn thing to help yourself, and then we're going to put you away."

"Yeah? We been over this. I didn't do it, so you can't put me away."

"You're a damn fool. Don't you know prisons are full of folks who didn't do it?"

Chapter Fifteen

Kate resisted the urge to turn around and walk right out of Morgan McKay's top-floor corner suite. Morgan, the local phosphate corporate officer, had called her at the library and invited her to meet with him "to discuss the situation." At first, she'd said no, but thinking she might learn something she could use, she'd agreed.

His secretary led her into his office and quietly left them alone. Kate studied the tall, broad-shouldered man. He wasn't pudgy but close to it. If he wasn't careful, he would soon have a middle-age spread to hide with his expensive suit coat. His hair had gone completely gray with a few streaks of pure white, and he had a straight nose and thin lips. He was definitely attractive, reminding her a bit of Gregory Peck.

He walked around his desk. "Kate, thank you for coming." He held her hand too long for polite convention, dropping it only when Kate rather pointedly pulled back from his grip. "Please," he said, gesturing toward a couch along the side wall. "Have a seat."

As she stepped toward the couch, Morgan stood to the side and placed his fingers lightly on her back as if to guide her. She stiffened, and as he withdrew his hand, he stroked the small of her back and across the top of her hips. The touch was so light it almost could have been her imagination, yet definite enough to make an imprint.

He sat beside her, a little too close, and smiled. "What can I get you to drink? Wine, coffee, whatever you'd like. I'll order out for champagne if you'd like some."

Kate shook her head. "I shouldn't even be here."

"Am I that reprehensible?" Morgan's voice was soft, but he grinned at her in a way that made her flush deepen.

"No, but you are not going to change my mind."

"Well, we'll see. At any rate, I appreciate your willingness to listen and to look at my plans for the AMCI mine. Let me assure you, we will protect the environment. I live here too. Did you know that?"

"No."

"Yes, just off the bay, with a channel out to the Gulf for my boat. I've had the place for years. Had to get a special permit to enlarge the dock for my boat." Morgan waved toward a photograph of a boat on his desk.

She glanced in that direction. From her seat on the couch, she couldn't see the picture clearly, but she got an impression of a wooden sailboat.

"Of course, I have to keep a condo in Bartow since I spend a great deal of time working at Antheus's headquarters there. But I consider Concordia my home, and I wouldn't be a party to anything that would degrade this area." He didn't smile, but he caught and held her gaze. "I grew up here, in this county. Did you know that?"

Surprised how sincere he seemed, she shook her head. She didn't know a thing about the man except that he was a big shot in a phosphate company she hated.

"Yes, I did." He paused and grinned. "Not, you understand, in a big house on the water. No, that was too rich for my mother, my sister, and me. I grew up out east, in the orange groves and tomato fields. During college and my early business career, I always wanted to come back home, though, and have a place on the water. AMCI gave me that chance."

Not knowing how to reply, Kate merely nodded.

"Please, let me get you something," he said.

"Just water."

He rose and buzzed his secretary to ask for two Evians. On his way back to the couch, he picked up a large album. "Here," Morgan said. "I put this together just for you." Sitting beside her, he started flipping through the book of plans, studies, charts, and artists' colored renditions, all more or less designed to show that AMCI would not harm either the air or water quality.

"I'm always curious about why people get so alarmed over phosphate mining. We're much safer now, and we reclaim the land. And it's not like we are digging out plutonium to build bombs." He shifted toward her, his shoulder touching hers, and smiled as if he were sharing a juicy secret. "After all, it's just fertilizer. Phosphate—"

"Feeds the world. Yes, I've heard your slogan."

"Not my slogan, though I wish I had come up with that one." He turned to a page with a photograph of a scenic lake surrounded by lush green trees. "This is a reclamation project, one of our best. People in and around Lakeland go there to fish. I've eaten fish caught in this lake myself."

As he continued to flip pages and make his point, Kate sipped the water and listened, feeling the warmth from his skin when he periodically tapped a finger on her hand as he made a point. Morgan's personal tour of the marketing and public relations album was a classy show, she realized, but a show nonetheless. But more than that, she didn't like the way the man made her feel, not slimy as she'd expected when she'd agreed to meet him, but frankly aroused. The man turned her on. The flush of her skin and the damp tingling made her feel guilty, as if she were already cheating on Ray. "Thank you, but I've already taken up too much of your time." She needed to leave before he saw the effect he had on her, if he hadn't already picked up on it.

"To the contrary, I've enjoyed your visit." He stood and moved in front of her. "I would be happy to show you around a mine or headquarters or a reclaimed lake." He held out his hands.

She ignored his hands and rose from the couch, a little unnerved by his stare.

"Have dinner with me tonight," Morgan said.

"No." Kate fled the office.

———◉———

KATE FLUNG THE PAPER across the kitchen table at Ray. "Will you look at that story. Under the mandatory federal drug sentencing law, a twenty-two-year-old girl gets twelve years just for telling a narc where to go buy pot. That's beyond crazy. Even the judge was upset and called it unfair. That narc should've been ashamed to even arrest her."

Ray glanced over the story. "They had evidence she was also involved in selling it. She took the DEA officer to a house where people she knew were running a large-scale operation and—"

"But she didn't *sell* the pot. She didn't have any pot on her or in her car or in her house. This guy just asked her at a party where he could score, and she told him she knew some people, and she took him to the house, and he busts her along with the rest of them."

"I know you think pot is a victimless crime and all that, but what she did was against the law. It was complicity. That's what they tried her for, and Congress has specifically—"

"Damn it. She's a kid who was trying to be nice to a guy at a party, and now she's going to lose her youth in some godforsaken prison. And you think that's okay?" Sometimes, she purely hated Ray being a cop, but mostly, it was his unflappable self-righteousness she disliked. If she wasn't careful, it would be easy to take the next step and dislike Ray too.

He watched her for a moment, as if he were thinking it over carefully. "If I answer you truthfully, you'll just get madder."

"Well, say it. Lying's never been your strong suit."

"She broke the law. Even if it was just a little contribution, she was part and parcel of the whole illegal drug market. You don't understand, I know, but cops get killed by those sorts of people."

She slapped the newspaper out of his hands.

"You remember Jerry, don't you?"

"I've heard that story before. Lots of times. Your buddy, played in the minor leagues as a pitcher till he threw his shoulder out. He joined the police and was shot in a pot bust." She was sorry she'd started the conversation. Ray couldn't help thinking the way he did. He was a cop. His friend had been killed over a pound of pot, a horrible waste.

"Jerry wasn't the only victim. His wife was too."

She knew that story, too, but she had the sense to keep her mouth shut.

"A month after the funeral, Luke and I went to see his widow. We found her crying at the kitchen table because their youngest boy had carried a sack of groceries in and dropped it, breaking the jars of peanut butter and jelly and sending glass into the bread. She couldn't afford to replace the ruined food."

"I'm sorry, Ray. Really." She paused, wondering if she should just let it be. "But that girl in the newspaper story, she wasn't part of Jerry getting killed."

They glared at each other.

"Do you think arresting her was the right thing to do?" She lowered her eyes to the paper. What she really wanted to ask was whether he would have arrested the girl.

"Yes," Ray finally said, "I think arresting her was the legal thing to do." He got up, put his coffee cup in the sink, and left the house.

Kate sat for a long time, staring at the door. He would have arrested that girl. And if he would have arrested *her*, then he would have arrested Kate too.

⎯⎯◉⎯⎯

THE NEXT DAY, A MAN in a white florist jacket delivered a dozen yellow roses to Kate at the library. The card only had Morgan's name printed on it. She put the flowers by the circulation desk and tried not to look at them.

That evening, while Kate was in her office finishing up the last of the day's paperwork, Jenny tapped on the frame of her open door.

"You're here late," Kate said, surprised.

"Yep, working the reception desk. I have a term paper due in Freshman English, and I'm trying to get some of my own research done."

While on the clock, Kate thought but shrugged it off. "What's up?"

"A real handsome man's asking for you at the circulation desk." Jenny grinned like she was sharing a secret.

"Ray?" She figured he had come to see her to make up after their fight.

"Not Ray. Even better looking, if you don't mind me saying so."

"Better looking than Ray? Ah, the impertinence of youth to make such a crass judgment," Kate said teasingly. Since getting the roses, she'd been in far too good a mood, considering how mad she and Ray had been at each other at the breakfast table.

Curious and trying to pretend she didn't hope it was Morgan, Kate fluffed her hair and smoothed her dress before strolling out front, trying to act casual. When she saw Morgan standing at the circulation desk, she stopped, feeling as flustered as a teenager.

Behind her, Jenny laughed. "I don't care if he's old. If you don't want him, I'll take him." She giggled then veered left and headed toward a woman waiting at the information desk.

Forcing herself to calm down, Kate approached and said, "Hello, Mr. McKay." She tried to put a chill in her voice. He was the enemy after all, Mr. Phosphate-Feeds-the-World.

"Call me Morgan, and please join me tonight." He leaned toward her. "I made reservations at The Sand Dollar. I hope we can drive out to the beach, watch the sunset, and enjoy a late dinner."

Kate made herself stand still, though she wanted to lick her lips and smile. She had to agree with Jennifer. Morgan was disarmingly handsome. His eyes were brown, heavily shaded by dark lashes, with lines crinkling around their outer edges. His hair appeared to be razor-cut, precisely so. He was expensively dressed with a silk tie in soft blues that brought out the silver threads in his suit jacket and his hair.

The man must be vain to be that excessively well groomed. She glanced down at his hands. No rings, but his nails gleamed. She wasn't used to men who got manicures. She wasn't used to men who got their hair cut in salons. She cut Ray's hair herself, in the backyard with scissors from the Dollar Store.

Handsome, well-to-do, successful, stylish, she added it all up quickly. Rich. Not the kind of man to lavish attention on her. It had to be some scam, something he was doing to shut her up over the phosphate. But that didn't make a lot of sense either. It wasn't as if her first protest meeting had been a big success. She couldn't be that much of a threat to a man like him.

"Why are you doing this?" she blurted.

Morgan put an elbow on the counter and leaned back, tilting his head as if to see her better. He appeared relaxed and confident, a pose that one might take for a magazine photo shoot. She wondered suddenly if he'd been a male model when he was younger.

When he just gave her a slow, lazy smile, she repeated, "Why are you doing this?"

"Because I want to walk on the beach with you, eat dinner with you, and get to know you. You intrigue me." As he spoke, his eyes never left Kate's face.

"You are not going to change my mind about AMCI."

"I don't care about that anymore."

"I'm engaged."

"Where's your ring?"

At home in a drawer, she thought but didn't say. "Look, I'm not the kind of woman that this happens to, so you can save yourself the trouble of the reservations and the walk on the beach. Men don't..." She paused. *Men don't what? Flirt with her?* Some did. Ray had. Weaver had too. But no rich, handsome man with a house on the water and a boat that required a specially permitted dock flirted with her.

"That's because most men are fools. I'm not a fool. And I want to know you." He straightened and took a small step toward her, his hands open at his sides as if he might reach to embrace her.

She took a step back and looked carefully into his eyes, straining to see some sign of deceit. "Why?"

"Because you are intelligent, you obviously have great passions about what you believe in, and your eyes are a smoky green that remind me of the Appalachian Mountains at dusk."

Ray would have spit up before saying something that sweet and corny about her eyes. But Ray wouldn't have sent roses, worn a suit, made reservations at the area's most expensive restaurant, or gotten a manicure. Kate didn't like the way she was making comparisons.

"Trust me," Morgan said. "Or if you don't trust me, meet me there. Plenty of other folks around to keep me behaving like a gentleman." He winked at her.

Kate inhaled slowly and thought about it as she held his gaze. Maybe she should go. She might learn something that would help them stop the phosphate mine. Or she might be able to persuade him to halt the expansion into her county.

Besides, she'd never eaten at The Sand Dollar. It claimed to sell only local fish, so perhaps somebody she grew up with made money off the fancy restaurant.

Or maybe she just wanted to go out with him and hear what else he might say about her eyes or her passions.

Feeling guilty but also intrigued, Kate agreed to meet Morgan at the restaurant at a quarter to eight. She went home and fed the Maggies. After walking the dog, she took a long shower and carefully chose a fitted dress both shorter and lower in the neckline than her usual dresses, in a dark green she knew highlighted her eyes. She thought about Ray's ring in her drawer, then she pulled it out of the box and put it on. Feeling even guiltier, she took it off and put it back in the box. She hurried out to her car before she could change her mind.

Chapter Sixteen

The following evening, Kate went into the microfiche room and hunted down the 1972 *Tallahassee Democrat* for another look at what Weaver might have been reading the day before he'd been killed. She needed a distraction from thinking about Morgan McKay.

The fiche was filed in the bottom drawer of a cabinet tucked into a corner behind the storage room door. As Kate bent over in the cramped space to retrieve the film, she realized how awkward it would be if someone opened the door and hit her butt. A wave of claustrophobia swept over her. After getting the film, she backed out into the open space of the room and stood there, breathing deeply for a moment before going to the reader.

Damn, there's got to be another spot where we could put that cabinet.

Scanning the paper, she carefully avoided the story about the two kids killed on the beach. There just had to be something else that interested Weaver. *This can't be about those kids on the beach.* Maybe he'd been reading something about someone involved in a current case, a criminal who had a long history and was being tried again, twenty years later. That might make sense, but she didn't know the names of any defendants in any of Weaver's cases. Ray would know, or he could find out, but she'd have to take the film to Ray, and she wasn't ready to do that. *Not yet, anyway.*

Jenny came over to the other reader with another community college student, and they gossiped about a teacher as she showed him how to thread the machine.

Turning away from the student, Jenny grinned at Kate. "Brownie points for working late for both of us, I see."

"Just a little personal research." Kate started to smile back, but she didn't really want to encourage a long chat.

"Seriously? Like you don't get enough of that during the day?" Jenny leaned over Kate's shoulder and looked at the screen. "January 1972, the *Democrat*? Damn. What is it about that that's so freaking interesting?"

Kate's initial irritation at Jenny's intrusion gave way to curiosity. "What do you mean, what's so interesting about this?"

"I've had to fetch or put up that fiche, like, I don't know, about maybe four or five times the last couple of weeks or so, and—"

"Wait. Who else asked for it?" Kate hoped her voice didn't sound as stressed as she suddenly felt.

"Well, I don't really know. But a couple, maybe three weeks ago, this guy came in during the evening, and I had to pull it for him. Then two weeks ago, I pulled a whole bunch of '72 *Democrats*, all winter ones, for the same guy. And get this. At the end of the week, I picked up the film and dumped it back in the box in the microfiche room to refile later, and it disappeared from there and ended up back out here."

"Are you sure it was this one? I mean, how can you remember the dates?"

"Hell, you should see where I have to go to get it and put it back." Jenny huffed a bit, as if exasperated. "I remembered because I had to be hunched over, hanging out in this tiny little corner, just asking for somebody to come in and swat my butt with the door. Let me show you, and you'll see why I remember crawling around—"

"No, I know what you mean. I thought of that when I pulled it out of the drawer today."

"So like I said, what's so interesting about that issue? I mean, even that cute deputy guy came in asking about it."

"A deputy? When?"

"On Monday night. He looked like Troy Donahue. Man, my mom was hot for that guy. I must've watched him and Sandra Dee in that *Summer Place* movie a hundred times with my mom, and she says—"

"Troy Donahue?" Kate's heart did a weird thrum. That sounded like Dayton. He had that kind of cute, blond-headed look to him. "You sure it was a deputy, not a police detective from the city?"

"He was cute, and I flounced around, you know, flirting, but he didn't ask me out."

"What did he ask?"

"He asked me if that dead state attorney guy had been looking at some old microfiche, and if anybody else had, and—"

"What'd you tell him?"

Jenny held up her hands. "Hey, after that fussing out you gave me for telling that woman what books her son had checked out—you remember, she thought he was researching, like—I don't know—how to build a bomb or something because he was checking out stuff on worm farms and fertilizer—"

"Yes, I remember. Now what did you tell the police officer?"

"Nothing. I remembered you told me a patron's research and what they checked out was all private and we weren't to tell anybody anything."

"Good girl. But what did you tell him specifically? That you wouldn't tell him or *couldn't* tell him or what?"

"Or what. I wasn't going to get into some big argument with a policeman, so I told him I didn't have a clue and that I mostly told people where the copy machines and bathrooms are."

"Would you recognize the man you got the fiche for those two times?"

"Maybe. I mean, he was, like, this middle-aged guy in a suit. They all kind of look alike, but I might recognize him."

"Hold on a minute. I'll be right back." Kate went to the current newspapers and pulled out some issues of the *Concordia Herald Tribune* with photos of Greenstreet, Weaver, and a random middle-aged man featured in the business section for opening a new downtown deli.

When Kate returned, Jenny was reading through the issue on the screen. "Man, I don't see anything so fascinating," she said.

"Here." Kate spread the three photographs on the table next to the machine. "Were any of these the man who asked for the film?"

Jenny leaned over and studied the grainy black-and-white photographs for several seconds. "Sure. Maybe, that is. This one." She pointed at Greenstreet's photo.

"Thank you. This is important. But please, don't say anything to anyone—I mean *anyone*—about this, all right? Not yet."

"Whatever." Jenny straightened. "So what's all this about? Does it have something to do with those kids killed on the beach?"

Kate's heartbeat ratcheted up another notch. "What do you mean?"

"Hey, don't snap at me."

"I'm sorry. Tell me what you're talking about? Please."

"That first guy, the one whose picture you just showed me, he was copying all these stories about those kids killed on the beach up in the panhandle."

"How do you know that?"

"Because like most men, he was totally useless on the copy machine. He couldn't get it to work right, and he had about a half dozen copies of the story, some too dark, some too light, and some with the corners cut off. I mean, really, how smart do you have to be to copy something?"

Kate pushed her reading glasses up into her hair to keep her bangs out of her face. She tilted her head back, shut her eyes, and tried to slow her breathing. *This is about those kids. Damn, damn, damn.*

"I had to throw them all out, the bad copies, you know. Then, like, he wanted a refund for the bad copies, but I explained—"

Kate lowered her head and looked at Jenny. "Please, don't—I mean really—do *not* tell anybody else about this. Okay?"

"Yeah, cool. If it means that much to you." Jenny shrugged and walked off.

———◉———

LATER THAT NIGHT, AFTER feeding and walking Maggie the dog and appeasing Maggie the cat with a good head-rubbing session, Kate dug out an old photo album from under a bunch of quilts in the cedar chest in the spare bedroom. She flipped right to the photo she wanted to see. Nicky and CeCe stood with Kate and her mother in the yard at her old house in Dolphin Cove Fishing Village. Kate remembered the day with terrific clarity, even though she'd only been ten years old. It was her mother's birthday, and her father had taken the photo with a new camera he'd purchased as a gift for her. A minute later, they'd all piled into his pickup and gone to the Burger Barn because "you didn't make a woman fry fish on her birthday." Kate could hear Tank saying that, making her mother laugh.

Kate tugged the photo out of the plastic sleeve and turned it over. Somebody, probably her mother, had penciled in 1963 and some of their names. But the pencil had faded out, like her mother had, and only the pale faint lines of an N and the date were legible.

Carefully handling the fading photo, she looked around for a new place to hide it. In a strange panic, she wasn't sure why she needed to hide it, but she knew Ray must not see it. He must never connect her and Nicky. She went to the bathroom and slipped the picture into the plastic makeup bag where she kept her diaphragm. Ray would never look there because her bathroom stuff made him nervous.

After she returned the makeup bag to the drawer, she stared at her reflection in the mirror, looking for the girl she'd been and thinking about Nicky, CeCe, and Tank back then. In the good old days. Before the fishing went bad and they'd fucked everything up.

Nicky.

Where is he now?

She hurried out of the bathroom and went to the den, where she grabbed the phone book. She flipped through the Calusa County pages, looking for Cecilia Delacort. It had been years since they'd spoken, though Kate often spied on her at her B and B. She wasn't sure CeCe would tell her where Nicky was, but it was worth a try. She needed to warn him, and she needed to find out what he knew.

Almost too tired to stand, she slumped into the chair beside the phone. Maggie the Cat jumped into her lap and started purring. Kate dialed the number with one hand and rested the other on Maggie's back. When CeCe answered, Kate involuntarily tensed her fingers in Maggie's fur so sharply that the cat hissed and swiped a claw at her before jumping down.

"CeCe, it's Kate."

"Kate?"

"Kitty, you know. From before. It's been a long time. Remember when I came back to Florida and called you?" They hadn't had much to say in that conversation, so she hadn't called again. "How've you been?"

CeCe didn't respond, but Kate could hear her breathing.

"I'm sorry to bother you, but I need to find Nicky."

"Why?"

"It's a long story, and I'm not sure you really want to know. But I won't hurt him. You know that, don't you?"

"I... it's been a long time, you know?"

"It's important." Kate didn't want to beg, but if CeCe made her, she would. "Please, I need to see him."

"What makes you think he's anywhere around here where you could see him?"

"Nothing. I mean, I don't know. If he's out west or something, I'd like to call him." In the following silence on the line, Kate couldn't even hear CeCe breathing anymore and wondered if she'd put the phone down. Kate wouldn't really blame her if she had.

"Listen, you can't tell Nicky I told you, okay? I'm the only one who knows. You just can't tell him."

Kate laughed with relief. "It won't be the first secret we've kept from Nicky, would it?"

"He's in Tallahassee. He goes by Keith Brothers and has a tree-trimming business. He's in the yellow pages, but I can give you a home number."

"How about an address?"

"Okay. In for a dime, in for a dollar, I guess."

Kate wrote the address down and thanked CeCe. She wished she knew how to say more to the woman who'd been her best girlfriend all those growing-up years. They'd been two fishermen's daughters in Dolphin Cove, tanned and leggy and strong and happy, a little wild because there was no reason not to be in those days. "It's been a long time. I miss you," Kate said.

"Sure. Me too. You take care."

When Kate told Ray about her plans to drive up to Tallahassee for the weekend, she gave him a vague explanation about wanting to visit a friend who'd called her and needed some company. "Girl talk, all right, Ray? Don't worry."

Chapter Seventeen

"Damn it all." Luke put down the phone and looked around his living room. He gathered up what he needed and headed out the door.

So much for his peaceful Saturday afternoon at home. He didn't know where his wife and kids were, and he had been thinking he might actually finally clean the garage. Instead, he was headed to the hospital. He thought about calling Ray but decided he might as well let his partner have his afternoon free, at least for a while.

Twenty minutes later, he pushed open the door to the room number he'd been given. At least the guy wasn't still in Intensive Care, though that was where he'd spent a couple of days. From Luke's point of view, they were wasted days in which evidence and witnesses' memories had faded away. But when the paramedics had brought the man in, he didn't have any ID on him, and it took a couple of days before he could talk and tell them who he was.

An aide had Richard Constantia sitting up in bed, his shirt off while she sponge-bathed him. She spun around and glared at Luke. "You can't come in here."

Constantia had been creamed on his bike at Hali Beach and was miraculously still alive. His face was bruised, with one eye swollen shut and a righteous cut on his chin. Road rash ran across his upper chest and right shoulder. He appeared slack-jawed, probably on some serious pain medication. A bandage circled his torso, possibly to cover more road burn.

"Police detective." Luke fished out his badge and held it up for the woman to see. "It's critical that I speak with him."

"The police have already been here, and they talked to the witnesses. This man needs to rest. Now get."

"The others were hit-and-run traffic investigators. I'm Homicide-Robbery."

"I really liked that bike," Constantia slurred.

"Sir, you need to leave," the aide said.

"Ma'am, I only need a minute." Luke stepped around the woman and moved to the other side of the bed. "Richard, how are you?"

"Fucked." Constantia rolled his good eye toward Luke. "All those years on the boats, nobody... ever tried... to kill... me."

On full alert, Luke leaned closer. "Who tried to kill you? And why?"

Constantia's one eye stared at Luke, giving his battered face an off-balanced cyclops look. "Big... black... car." His voice was so soft it was difficult to understand.

The officer who'd called Luke had told him about the big black car, so that wasn't new. One bystander even claimed to have gotten a tag number, but it hadn't led to anything. The hit-and-run investigation was currently stalled.

"Did you see—"

The aide jabbed a finger at Luke. "You are agitating the patient, and if you do not leave, I will get security to take you out."

"I didn't see... a face." Constantia inhaled as if gathering his strength. Or planning his answer. "I saw... asphalt." His head lolled as he closed his eye.

The aide picked up her sponge and gave Luke a serious hard look. "The pain meds have put him out, so you're wasting your time. Now will you leave?"

Luke leaned over Constantia, watching his breathing for a moment. "Richard?" He resisted the urge to shake the man awake.

"I'm calling security." The aide reached for the phone on the bedside table.

"Call them if you want. But it would be in their best interests not to lay a hand on me, and that goes for you too. Anyway, he's down now. So you have a nice day." He pantomimed tipping a hat. "You might want to ask for a refund on that Dale Carnegie course you took. I don't think you got that 'how to win friends and influence folks' part down too good."

Luke took one more look at Constantia splayed out in the bed. Judging from the old scars on the man's chest, the lawyer had seen some rough times. He wondered what the Florida Bar might have missed in their background check on Constantia.

⸺⸺●⸺⸺

SATURDAY AT NOON, JUST as he'd promised, Ray put Maggie the pug on a leash and headed toward the sidewalk. But his mind wasn't on the dog but on Kate. Since the night she'd held that meeting at her house, she hadn't been herself. The bickering between them only got worse, and he didn't know what to say or do to stop it.

Then last night, Kate had looked him straight in the eye and told him she was driving up to Tallahassee for the weekend. But her story was too vague and didn't ring right. There were no overt signs of nervousness about her, no shifting eyes, nothing that signaled deceit when she talked about an old girlfriend who needed some company. But Ray knew she was lying to him. He didn't know how he knew, but he had, and he couldn't figure out what he should do about it.

The dog yelped, pulling Ray out of his thoughts. The pug had no better sense than to tug so hard on the leash she practically choked herself. The only way to walk the animal without strangling her was to jog along at the speed she set. He picked up his pace.

He grinned. For a fat little dog, she had surprisingly good wind and an unnatural abundance of energy. Even if the animal seemed addlebrained, he had to admit she was a natural clown. He could see why Kate adored her.

A good five blocks from her house, the pug quit running. The dog sat down and wouldn't budge. After a few minutes of cajoling, Ray picked her up and carried her home.

He put the dog in the fence before going inside Kate's house. For the first time in their relationship, he was tempted to snoop. Better judgment winning out, he poured a glass of water and debated making a pot of coffee. Deciding against it, he sat at the kitchen table, trying not to think about the situation. If Kate was lying, it was for a good reason, not anything that would hurt him. Or that was what he told himself.

She was a good person. He'd recognized Kate's kindness the first time he saw her, which was over a year ago. That day, some teenagers had been harassing a homeless man and, fearing for the man's safety, Ray decided to take him in. As he was getting out of his car, a woman in a long, loose dress came out of a Cuban grocery store and approached the small group. She reached into her bag, pulled out a peach, and handed it to the man. She said something to him that Ray couldn't hear, and the man perched on the edge of a concrete planter on the sidewalk and started eating the peach. She sat down beside him.

The kids who had been heckling the man shut up and drifted away. When the man finished the fruit, he asked for another one, and the woman obliged. She continued to sit with him, neither of them talking. After a few minutes, she handed him her sack of groceries, touched his arm lightly, and went back into the store.

Ray followed her. Tagging along behind her, he picked up the same items he saw her putting in her small basket. Over the plantains, he asked her how she prepared hers.

"There are some recipe cards in the back. They're free," she answered and walked off abruptly.

After that, Ray started going into the Cuban grocery store regularly, making small talk with her when he found her there. After a few weeks, he asked her out. She said no. It had taken him over two months before she finally agreed to join him for coffee.

While they dated, she hadn't revealed much about herself, even when he asked. Though he avoided talking about his time in Vietnam, he did tell her his father was part of the American army that liberated France and had found his future bride among the stunned survivors of Nazi occupation. His mother remained reclusive, and his father sold shoes and was a jackleg preacher. Ray told Kate they had been good enough as parents—he and his siblings never went hungry or were abused, and all three had made decent enough lives. Ray had quit college at nineteen and was promptly drafted, but during his early years on the police force, he'd managed to finish his B.A. at night school. His sister and brother had sailed through their college years and married. Both seemed healthy and happy. Yet Ray remembered his mother hiding inside the house and his father's harsh, inflexible rules and religiosity more than he recalled having any fun growing up.

Kate listened, asked the right questions, and showed interest. But when he asked about her parents, all she shared was that her mother had been Cuban, her father had fished out of Dolphin Cove, and they were both dead. Months later, he asked again, and she'd told him quickly that she had nothing more to say about them. Ray had gotten the message.

Maybe they really didn't know each other that well, he realized as he sat at her kitchen table, listening through the open jalousie panes of the back door to the snorting noises her dog made as she scratched at the door to get in. Maybe they didn't know each other well enough to get married. *Could be that's why she's never said anything about the ring.*

He got up and started to go to her bedroom, curious to see if he could even find where she had put the ring. Before he got there, Luke came up to the back door and called for Ray to let him in.

"What are you doing here?" Ray used his foot to hold back Maggie the pug.

Luke came into the kitchen and took a chair. "I got some news I thought you'd want to know about. Real interesting."

Ray opened Kate's refrigerator and pulled out a bottle of guava juice. He handed it to Luke. "So what'd you have to tell me?"

Luke held the bottle up in front of him. "What's this?"

"Expensive. Cuban. Drink it slow."

"She got any just plain old coffee? I could use the caffeine."

"I'll make a pot of coffee. Now quit stalling and tell me what you came to tell me."

"Naw, forget the coffee. We can pick some up at the hospital." He twisted the top off the bottle of juice and sniffed it.

"The hospital?"

"That Karma guy got hit on his bike at Hali. Hit-and-run. He was in the ICU a couple of days because he didn't have any ID on him. Once he came to and gave his name, it took a while for it to get back to me."

"He's okay?"

"That's kind of relative, I guess. But he's not dead, and unless he's really unlucky, he's not going to be dead. From the accident, I mean. He's got a concussion, some bruised ribs, bad-looking road burn, and a swollen eye. But he's basically okay for a man who got hit and dragged."

"You figure this hit-and-run ties in with Weaver's and Greenstreet's deaths?" Ray didn't even know why he asked. Of course it was connected. Neither one of them believed in sheer coincidence anymore.

"Yep, it's got to. Just too damn interesting otherwise with Mr. Karma, who suddenly gets shut-mouthed on us, then him getting hit like that."

"When did it happen?"

"Thursday. After work."

"Any leads?"

"Not so it's going to help much. I picked up a copy of the hit-and-run report for you." Luke pulled out a folded sheet of paper and laid it on the table. "A guy saw it happen and claimed he got the tag number. A detective located the car with the matching tag, but it was about a hundred-year-old Datsun, and no way it met the description from the other witnesses. The tag was still on the Datsun." Luke drank some of the juice, frowned, and looked at the door, where the pug was frantically scratching and howling to get in. "High-strung little thing, isn't she?"

Ray opened the door, and Maggie dashed into the kitchen. She skidded on the terrazzo floor and slid into her water and food dishes, spilling water and knocking chunks of food onto the floor. Then she scurried over to Luke, tracking the water and food with her. Maggie started jumping up and down in front of him and snorting.

Luke laughed. "What do you reckon is wrong with this dog?"

"Brain damaged if you ask me," Ray said. He opened the closet and got out a mop. "But don't you ever say anything about her to Kate."

"Be like telling a momma her baby is ugly."

Ray started cleaning up the mess. "Could be somebody stole the tag and put it back on, if it was a planned hit."

"Naw, our guys looked into that. They said the tag was pretty well rusted on. They just figure the witness got it wrong."

"What kind of car did the witnesses say it was?"

"Well, not surprising, there's some disagreement on what make and model. But the general consensus was that it was big and black."

"A big black car? Well, that certainly narrows it down."

"Yep, don't it though?" Luke picked Maggie up and looked her straight in the eyes. "Calm the hell down," he said in a low, soft voice.

Maggie wiggled, snorted, and spit on him in her excitement.

Luke put the dog down then bent over and picked up some of the kibble. "Saturday or not, you get done here, we got to run over to the hospital and talk it over with Mr. Karma again."

"Again?"

"Yep, I stopped by on my way here. Didn't get much. He's doped up. But I figure by the time we get over there, he might be coming off the meds some."

"How long's he going to be in the hospital?" Ray put the mop away.

"I don't know. But now that the hospital knows who he is and that he's got a regular job and insurance and all, I reckon they'll keep him a bit longer."

Ray didn't like any of this, not one bit. Constantia could have been their third murdered lawyer. If he and Luke didn't figure this mess out soon, somebody else could die.

Chapter Eighteen

After pulling over at a roadside park in Old Town, Kate parked in the shade and flexed her stiff fingers before getting out of her car. Standing by a railing on the high bank, she stared down at the Suwannee River and ate a sandwich she'd brought from home, washing it down with lukewarm coffee she'd picked up in a drive-through north of Tampa. She raised her face toward the late-morning sun, which was already hot on her skin, as she swallowed the last of the meager meal.

She walked down the crooked stone steps that led from the railing to the narrow beach below. At the base of the steps, a wooden sign noted the high-water marks of the big floods of 1984 and 1972 and, at the top, the biggest flood of all—1948. She slipped off her sandals and walked barefoot in the damp grit beside the waters of the Suwannee.

When the beach ended in a dense stand of live oaks heavy with Spanish moss, she stood a long time, breathing in the dank, humus smell of the river and watching the patterns in the water made by the wind and the currents. From downstream, the grind of an outboard motor filtered up to her. The river itself brushed against the banks with an almost imperceptible sound of blood pumping through an artery.

Under the shade of the live oaks, she watched the tea-colored waters and remembered being there with her father. In those days, when they traveled US 19 and US 98 between Dolphin Cove and the fishing village in Apalachicola, they often saw wild boar along the highway and once spotted a black bear at a roadside picnic table. They'd seen moccasins or rattlers, too, but her father always told her to let them be, that the snakes had just as much right to be there as anyone or anything else.

The last time Kate remembered being at the Suwannee park with her father, it was just the two of them. Her mother had died the same year the mortgage company forced them out of their house.

That day, they were on their way to Apalachicola because her father had lost his boat to the bank the week before and was moving to get work on his cousin Jimmy's shrimp trawler out of Apalachicola. "Like a damn hired hand, cousin or not," he said. He'd made a joke about "square grouper" over the phone the night he made the arrangements with Jimmy, and Kitty pretended she didn't know that meant a bale of marijuana.

Tank blamed himself for losing the boat and the house, but Kate knew it wasn't his fault. She'd seen the others failing, too, and knew those men worked hard day and night, struggling even more when everything turned against them. Yet no matter how rigorously Tank had worked, the further behind he got. Bank crap he didn't understand on the mortgage—and worse, on the boat—plus new government regulations that cost him a ton to refit the netting and rigging on his boat, and a market dump of cheap fish from China had just about done him and all the other fishermen in. What had been a way of life for generations faded out as the big corporate fishing fleets took over and, with the apparent help of banks and regulations, pushed the family fisherman out.

That last day together on the Suwannee, they'd watched the river for a long time because neither of them had wanted to continue to Apalachicola. They drank warm soda and ate cheese sandwiches then got into her father's pickup and went on, whether they wanted to or not.

Her father had stayed in Apalachicola, but within three months, Kate had packed her few belongings, caught a Greyhound, and gone back to Dolphin Cove, where she lived with CeCe, Nicky, and their folks. She slept on a rollaway cot in the corner of CeCe's room and worked after school and weekends at the fish-packing house and in the tomato fields to help pay for her room and board. Apalachicola had been too far away from CeCe and Nicky. Her father didn't try to stop her from leaving even though she was only fourteen. When he could, he sent money, and he called her once a week. Four years later, when he asked her and Nicky to come up, they moved in with him. By then, Jimmy had turned things on the trawler over to a local thug named Bobby. Tank might still pilot near the coast, but Kate eavesdropped enough to know Bobby was the one running the show.

Still troubled about Tank and Bobby, Kate walked back to her car, wiped off her feet, and got back behind the wheel.

Halfway between Fanning Springs and Perry, with its stink of paper mill, she spotted the ruin of an old roadside tourist trap. She remembered when the high cage out front, visible from the road, held a lone camel. For a good sixty or more miles on either side of the exhibit, crudely made roadside signs advertised exotic animals. For a fee, travelers could walk behind the plywood and tin and see an assortment of poorly kept animals in small cages.

Over the earlier years, when her family went to Apalachicola to visit their cousins and sometimes to work the scallops, Kate had watched the camel in the cage out front and wanted to see the other animals. Her mom had always refused.

On one trip when she was eight, Kate had pestered her dad for miles to stop. Her mom, slumped against the door, didn't say anything. Her dad stopped. They paid their money, and the three of them, her mom leaning against her dad and sucking her Coke through a bent straw, started through the zoo. The animals had vacant looks and smelly, rough coats, and Tank turned Kate away before they were through the exhibit. In the pickup, Kate cried and begged her dad to go back and free the animals.

"*Mi princesa, es mucha tarde.*" Her mom pulled Kate into her lap and stroked her hair.

"They been in cages so long they don't know how to take care of themselves," Tank said.

Kate rubbed her face against the rough cotton of her mother's dress and smelled her Ivory soap scent. She'd eventually quieted, repeating under her breath what her mother said. *It was too late.*

As she drove past the old zoo, Kate rejoiced to see that the place had fallen into a mess of rubble and scrap tin. She still hoped those animals had somehow escaped.

In the early afternoon, Kate pulled off Apalachee Parkway in Tallahassee into a parking lot and pulled out her map. It had been a long time since she'd been in the city, and she'd forgotten what little she'd known about getting around its streets. She consulted a piece of paper from her pocket, repeated the address out loud, and studied the map until she found the street.

Northwest of town, off Meridian Road, it looked easy enough to find. Kate pulled back into the traffic.

Twenty years. She shook her head. It had been two decades since she and Nicky had left Dolphin Cove for Apalachicola to visit her dad, flush with plans to save some money, get married, and attend Florida State University. She remembered him as a young man, not much more than a teenager, with long white-blond hair, fine and straight, hanging past his shoulders, and strong, tanned arms and legs. His blue eyes, even at twenty, had squint lines around them, and his forehead was creased from the relentless sun, wind, and salt spray of the Gulf of Mexico. He was a fisherman who was the son of a fisherman, like she was the daughter of a fisherman.

Thirty minutes of traffic later, she pulled into the driveway of a small house in a heavily shaded lot. It seemed like a slightly newer version of her own home, the kind of house single people bought in neighborhoods of people just starting out, or finishing up, with their lives, the kind real estate agents like to describe as a "good starter home."

Kate got out of the car and walked up to the front door. She wiped her hands on her jean shorts several times before ringing the doorbell.

A man with short, thinning gray-blond hair answered. Dressed in jeans and a T-shirt, he looked at her pleasantly enough but with some puzzlement on his tan, lined face.

"Nicky?" Kate said, her voice more tentative than she'd have preferred.

The man squinted at her. "Jesus. Kitty?"

"Nobody calls me Kitty anymore."

"Nobody calls me Nicky." He stuck his head out the door, checked out her car, then looked up and down the street. "Anybody follow you?"

"No."

He swept his hand in a gesture to invite her in. She followed him into the house and glanced around the living room, noticing it was neat, if a bit shabby. They stood facing each other for a long, tense moment.

"Damn. I mean, I don't know what to say. You look great. Really." He reached out to her and pulled her into a bear hug. "It's been a long time."

At first, she stiffened and tried to pull out of his grasp, but when he wouldn't let her go, she relaxed and hugged him back. He kissed her cheek then moved to her mouth. When he finally released her, she started crying.

"Don't cry. Sit down. Tell me..." He stuttered to a stop, looking at her, the frown lines on his face deep.

Tell you what? Why, after twenty years, your old girlfriend shows up at your door?

"Please sit down." He collapsed on the old couch and patted the seat beside him. "Kitty. Good God, Kitty."

She sank onto a chair across from the sofa. "I told you. Nobody calls me that anymore. I'm Kate. And you're Keith now, aren't you?"

"Keith. Well, you know." He grinned, but the grin disappeared almost as quickly as it had appeared. "How'd you find me?" He leaned forward. "I mean, I changed my name. I moved away. Hell, I went out west for several years."

"I'm a reference librarian now. It took me a long time to get to college, but I did, and I learned a lot. I know how to look things up, even name changes. Anyway, you came back to pretty much the same area you left. Apalachicola's only a couple of hours away."

"It was that easy?"

He looked so worried that Kate wanted to confess, but she had promised CeCe she wouldn't tell. "Don't worry. Anybody who'd wanted to find you would have done so a long time ago."

"I guess so, but you know, you can't be too careful."

"I know. I took my mother's maiden name. Katherine Maria Garcia." She had gone to the courthouse in Athens, Georgia, paid twenty-five dollars, and filled out a form. She had prepared an elaborate lie, but nobody asked why she wanted to change her name. The new name caused some delays with her high school transcripts when she finally applied at the University of Georgia, but otherwise, dropping Tank's last name hadn't been a problem.

"I like that. It's pretty. Suits you."

"I need to know where Bobby is. *Who* he is." She stood and stepped toward him. Straightening her back, she tilted her head only slightly to look down at him. Ray had taught her about the power positions to take during interrogations, so she figured she might as well try it.

"No you don't." He jumped up. "I mean, leave it be, okay?"

"Just tell me what you know about Bobby." She glared at him.

"Nothing. Which is all you need to know about him. That, and he's a dangerous son-a-bitch."

"I guess I know that much. Come on. You spent time with him. You have to know something more."

"Aw, come on yourself. You know how it was. You didn't ask for last names. You didn't even look too closely at anybody's face. We all had beards and long hair and wore baseball hats and big old sunglasses during the day. I doubt I ever saw his eyes in the daylight. I never wanted to."

"You must know his real name or where he was from. Something. After all, you worked for him."

"Let me just check my W-2."

"Look, don't get mad. I wouldn't be here after all this time if it wasn't important. I'll tell you why—"

Nicky jerked away as if she'd suddenly exhaled fire on him. "Oh God, no. Don't tell me. I don't want to know."

For a moment neither spoke. She glanced around the room, taking note of a couple of framed school photos, then cut her eyes back to Nicky. The lines in his face made him seem older, and all that beautiful long white-blond hair was just a short, dull fringe now. He'd aged. A lot. Maybe she had too.

Nicky suddenly strode toward a door leading deeper into the house. "I could sure use a beer," he said over his shoulder. "You?"

"Yes."

For half an hour, they made nervous chitchat. Nicky told her that he was divorced and had a little girl. He owned a small landscaping business and said he was doing well enough.

While he talked, Kate kept thinking about Bobby. Her father had said Bobby was a local boy from Apalachicola, and in ways she hadn't figured out yet, he was the key to those murders back in Concordia. If she were going to find any hint of who Bobby was and where he was now and how he fit into the whole mess of things, Apalachicola was the place to start.

Nicky started a story about his little girl and something she did in school, but Kate couldn't listen anymore. She broke in and asked him to go with her to Apalachicola.

He sat still for a moment and seemed to struggle to smile but didn't pull it off. "They've reinvented themselves," Nicky said. "What used to just be a small fishing village is this hot vacation spot. Still famous for Apalachicola Bay scallops and oysters." He paused, glancing at a framed photo of his little girl. When he looked back at Kate, his eyes narrowed into grim slits. "Why do you want to go there? It's just a tourist place."

"I don't care if it's the new Disney. We have to go there. Now."

Nicky finally nodded, though he obviously wasn't happy about it.

After they settled into her car, Kate took US 98 and was surprised at the changes. A new white concrete bridge crossed the bay at the mouth of the Ochlockonee River, where the sewage from South Georgia flowed down and made its way to the Gulf of Mexico. Boat repair shops and out-of-business fish houses were still sprinkled along the highway, and Pigott's Cash and Carry was right where it'd always been. But young houses rose up on their flood-insurance-regulated stilts, their newness in sharp contrast to the low cypress-wood houses with sloped tin roofs and the camper trailers where whole families lived with privies out back. In the spots closest to the Gulf, the highway was patched with new asphalt replacing the sections swept away by hurricanes and erosion.

After two hours, with Nicky sitting morose and silent, Kate parked on the main drag of Apalachicola. They crawled out of her car, stretched the long drive out of their backs, and looked around the central street of the village with the restored Gibson Inn centered among gift stores with "shoppe" in their names.

"Gone touristy but in a good way," Nicky said. "Didn't I tell you?"

"Very picturesque, I guess, if you didn't try to make a go of fishing here." She looked down the street toward the marina with its long docks crowded with boats. It was a bit early for the fishermen to be coming in, but somebody would be there. She started rolling up her shorts, curling the denim until she was showing plenty of thigh, while Nicky, leaning against the side of her car, watched.

Her Cuban ancestors had left her with skin that tanned even when she just walked to the mailbox in the mornings. With her after-work jogs around her neighborhood and the weekend runs at the beach, her legs were muscular and dark. She pulled up the tail of her T-shirt, a green one with Selby Gardens and a picture of a red hibiscus on it, and tied it in a side knot, exposing her flat stomach. She intended to use her body to pull information from men famous for their suspicious and taciturn ways around strangers. Showing some skin might encourage somebody to slip up and talk. *Who knows?*

"Go on over to the library and see if they have any yearbooks from the late sixties, will you? I'll meet you there." She didn't want Nicky with her as she prowled the docks.

He stopped staring at her legs and pushed off the side of her car. "If you're going to the docks, I ought to go with you."

"No. Just go to the library. Look for pictures that might have Bobby in them, something that might give us his new name."

"Look, just because he fished out of here didn't mean he was really *from* here."

"Tank said he was a local boy. You remember that, don't you?" She glared at him.

After a moment, he turned away and headed toward the library. She stared down at the marina. *Let it be. Get back in the car, warn Nicky, and go home.* That would be easier and probably just as helpful. But she sighed and started walking. Somebody was killing people who knew about Bald Point. That put Nicky at risk and maybe her. It was time she finally understood what had happened, time that she faced it once and for all.

The place to start was in Apalachicola.

With Bobby.

Chapter Nineteen

Kate looked down the sidewalk. A few straggling tourists wandered among the pale glow of the streetlights. Nicky slouched beside her.

The kid working at the library had just kicked them out. Past closing time, he told them, and maybe they didn't have anything better to do, but he did, and they had to get.

"Nothing. Nobody at the docks remembers anybody like Bobby or a boat called *The Jackpot*." She wiped her hands on her cutoffs, which she had rolled back to their normal length. The aged dust from the stacks of high school yearbooks had turned her fingers grimy, and rubbing them on her shorts didn't help much. None of the photographs had looked like how Nicky said he remembered Bobby.

"Is there anything else about the way he looked that you haven't told me?" She tried to keep the frustration out of her voice. "You know, a tattoo, a mole, a scar?"

"He had a scar on his right side, in the front below his ribs. And his nose had been busted somewhere along the way and was kind of crooked."

Kate remembered the scar once Nicky mentioned it. She'd seen it that night at the farmhouse when Bobby had ripped off his bloody shirt. But she didn't even pretend to remember what his face looked like or the crooked nose. Earlier in the library, she'd just marked the page of any yearbook with a Robert or Bobby with dark hair and made Nicky look at it.

"Hungry?" Nicky asked. "I could use a drink. That's for sure."

Kate nodded, for once willing to let Nicky change the subject.

He gestured across the street. "We could get us a room at the Gibson. It's been fixed up real nice since what it was when we fished around here. All Victorian and stuff. We get us a room, then eat in their restaurant, and—"

"No."

"Come on. It's getting late. You're tired. You got to be with all that driving. Let's get us a room so we can catch up good with each other."

"No!" She spoke so loud that a woman in a flowered straw hat turned to stare as she walked past.

He waited until the woman was out of hearing range. "Don't you remember what it was like between us?"

"No." Kate turned away from him and started walking toward where she'd left the car. "No, I don't." When she reached the vehicle, she hopped in behind the wheel.

He climbed in after her. "Look, we gotta eat."

"I saw a place coming in, looked like a hangout for the locals, not the tourists. We'll stop there."

It was just an old fried-shrimp-and-beer type of dive, like a hundred others along the Gulf coast. The gray cypress structure sloped down toward the beach, constructed on shifting sand but grandfathered in to be exempt from modern beachfront zoning and only a few years away from falling into the elements.

When they walked into the diner, the fishermen and their women stopped talking to look them over. A jukebox played in the corner. By the time the server brought them their red plastic basket of fried shrimp, french fries, and hushpuppies, nobody was staring at them anymore. They split a pitcher of beer. Nicky tried to talk, but Kate just ate.

When she finished, she excused herself. The narrow hallway leading to the bathrooms was lined with photos of fishermen, boats, and the aftermaths of hurricanes. She was too tired to give them more than a glance.

When she came out of the bathroom, Nicky was standing rigid in the hallway near the men's room.

"You look like you've seen a ghost," Kate said as she stopped beside him and looked at the cheaply framed picture that seemed to have caught his attention.

"Damn right, yours and mine." He pointed at the image.

Under a greasy piece of glass, the photo was framed in rusty metal. A shrimp trawler dominated the scene, but off to one side, two men stood on a wooden pier. One had long dark hair, a drooping mustache, and a full beard. He wore aviator sunglasses, a white T-shirt, and jeans. He stood with his legs wide apart, his pelvis jutted out in an aggressive and vulgar way. Beside him, a bulky man in a denim shirt with the sleeves cut off had his bare muscular arms crossed over his chest. The gray cardboard mat around the edges covered the men's feet and the corners of the photo.

Nicky pointed at the man in the sunglasses. "That's Bobby." He moved his finger to the other man's face. "And that man on his left, that's his pit bull, Rock."

Kate wiped the cover glass clean with her T-shirt hem and squinted, trying for a sharper focus on the faces. She didn't recognize either man. After checking to make sure no one was watching, she took the picture down and slid it under her arm, letting her purse dangle over it. "Let's go."

Chapter Twenty

Too tired to talk, Kate drove in silence. Every now and then, she'd finger the photograph on the seat beside her. She glanced at the dashboard and wondered if turning on the radio would help keep them awake. As she reached for the dial, the sign for the turnoff to State Road 370 appeared on the right. Kate braked and turned off onto the narrower road.

Nicky, who had been staring off into the blackness outside his window, turned and put his hand on her thigh. "Don't do this. All right? Don't. Please."

Kate ignored him and kept driving.

"Please. You don't want to—"

"Yes, I do."

She steered down the lonely stretch of road that wasn't much more than a paved ridge through the salt marshes. The eerie shadows of the Spartina grasses appeared like thousands of sharp silver ropes in the beams of the headlights.

Once on the gator-shaped peninsula itself, Kate headed past the driveways and lights of beachfront houses on stilts, most of them with a for sale or for rent sign stuck in the front. The last time she'd been there, the road had cut through uninhabited darkness with nothing but the silhouettes of pines and dunes to break the pattern of the black sky against the black land.

Kate slowed and veered off 370 onto a road they'd nicknamed Sand Ditch Road some twenty years ago. The asphalt eventually gave way to sand and oyster shells. *Thank God that this end is still undeveloped. Something in this state ought to be left the way it was.*

When she got to the end of the road, on the eastern tip of Alligator Point, she stopped the car but left the high beams on. "Get out."

Nicky didn't respond for several seconds. "You're long out of it. So am I. Let it be, all right?"

"Get out. Now. We're going to talk about what happened that night." She slid out of the car, stretched, then walked several feet away to stand with her back to Nicky. Looking out at the Gulf of Mexico, dark waves on dark water with only a hint of whitecaps visible, she wrapped her arms around her body and shivered despite the warmth of the summer night.

He lumbered up beside her. "You know, I used to really like it here."

She jammed her hands into the stiff pockets of her cutoffs. *I used to love this beach too.* "What happened? Last time I saw you, in that farmhouse, you were curled up like some baby on a mattress, so scared you couldn't talk. You couldn't even hold water down. All you told me was to get out and go to that park in Georgia and wait for you. But you never came."

"Bobby and Rock kept me like a prisoner. When I broke loose, I lit out for the park, but I couldn't get to it right off. When I did, I camped there for a couple of months, hoping you'd show. But I figured you were safe."

"Safe?" She spun around to glare at him. "Safe? Yeah, right. Bobby was all hyped up and crazy when he came in that night, the way the rest of y'all looked before you shoved me into the bedroom and collapsed. And you telling me not to go back to Tank's. So after I left the farmhouse, as soon as I got to a phone, I called CeCe, and she told me Rock was already there looking for me. How safe do you think I felt after that?"

"You were right not to go back to Tank's. CeCe told me Rock didn't get you there, so I figured you were all right."

The night breeze whipped her hair around her face, and the salt spray stung her eyes. "All right? My van—*mine*—was in that sinkhole with bodies in it. I waited nine years, *nine whole years*, before I came back to Florida. That's how 'all right' I felt."

"I did the best I could."

"Fine. You did what you had to do."

Nicky gulped in a deep breath, the sound oddly loud over the waves. He held it for a moment then exhaled in a puff of warm air that licked Kate's face. He put his hand out as if to touch her but dropped it to his side after just grazing her fingers.

Kate collapsed into the sand, the crushed shells scraping her knees. "My God, Nicky. I wasn't even there when my father died. Nobody knew how to find me."

He knelt and wrapped his arms around her. Pulling her toward him, he said, "CeCe was with him. You knew that. She took care of him. He wasn't alone."

She rested her head against his chest and listened to him breathe.

"It wasn't supposed to go down like it did." He lifted her head just enough to look into her eyes then kissed her forehead. "You know that."

Part II
The Panhandle, 1972

Chapter Twenty-One

Nicky leaned over the starboard side of the shrimp trawler he'd spent the last three days on and studied the freighter perched on the horizon. No more than a hundred seventy feet, its white wheelhouse gleamed in the Caribbean sun. Rusty but with patches of red and green paint still showing, it looked ancient.

Bobby jutted his head out for a better look. "Got to be the mother ship."

"Hardly looks like it'd stay in the water," Nicky said.

Polky snorted. "Don't kid yourself. It just looks like shit. I bet that freighter's got a better engine and equipment in it than the fucking Coast Guard. They just made it look like it's on its last leg so nobody pays it any attention."

"You the expert now?" Bobby asked gruffly. "Punk-ass redneck."

"And you're like, what? The Captain Kirk of the high seas?" Polky took a step toward Bobby.

Nicky's heart hit an extra thump. Wishing he'd never agreed to this, he put a hand out to stop Polky.

Bobby snorted and turned, dismissing Polky and focusing on Nicky. "Glad we don't have to wait. Came up here this one time, and another fishing boat was up against the mother ship like it was... what do you call those fish that suck on sharks?"

"Suckers." Polky laughed.

"Remoras," Nicky said, beginning to wonder if Polky had been drinking, even though it was against orders.

Bobby nodded. "Remoras, yep. Tank said you were smart and going to go to college with your money." He glanced at Polky, who was still laughing. "Anyway, that time, we had to wait our turn. We were conspicuous as hell sitting in the water like that." Bobby turned back to watching the mother ship as their trawler drew closer to it.

"Well, stay cool, okay. Won't be long till we rock and roll." Bobby picked up his M-16, a serious weapon he called Babydoll, and nudged Nicky with the barrel.

While Nicky was no expert on guns, he understood why Bobby favored his M-16. The rifle held more ammo than most and looked badass enough to put the fear of God in just about anybody.

Bobby prodded Nicky again with the rifle, and Nicky slapped it away.

"Stop poking me with that damn thing." Nicky picked up his own rifle, an M-1 he'd bought off a Vietnam vet.

Bobby gave him one more jab. "Fucking new guy. Now stop being a pussy."

Polky fiddled with his bolt-action rifle, rocking back and forth on his heels, getting in the way, and making Nicky's gut roil. Bobby's right-hand man, a big guy called Rock, was in the wheelhouse, easing the trawler through the water. A man named Dave stood nearby. But even with those two, and Bobby and Polky on deck, Nicky felt strangely alone.

"How you going to do this?" Nicky asked, wishing he'd asked Tank more questions before agreeing to the trip. "I mean, get the pot over onto the trawler?"

Bobby snickered. "Any way we can. Sometimes the mother ship'll put down a floating platform. Tricky as shit and not for the clumsy. Sometimes they use cargo nets. Worse comes to worst, the men just toss the bales over. Good thing the water's calm." He glanced at Nicky. "Go tell Rock to get out here. And tell him to bring the cash. You get in the wheelhouse and take the helm. Watch the radar. You see another blip, you let us know right away. Stay cool."

Nicky hurried into the wheelhouse, glad to be off the deck. "Rock, Bobby says get your butt out there. Bring the money." Nicky flattened himself against the opening as Rock grabbed a duffel bag and pushed his linebacker bulk past him. Dave switched spots so he was in the doorway of the wheelhouse.

Nicky could see why Bobby would want Rock out there on the deck. The man was older than the rest of them by a good ten to fifteen years, but he looked to be the best fighter among them. He'd said he was out of Jacksonville, but late one night, Nicky had heard Rock talking on the phone in a kind of fast language that sounded like a family of Louisiana Cajuns he'd fished with once.

Nobody really cared where any of them were from or if their names were fake. Each man could handle the trawler, though the inlanders, Dave and Polky, weren't completely trustworthy yet at the helm. They all knew how to shoot and had duffel bags full of guns and ammunition. Still, Nicky figured that if the dark men on the freighter chose to do so, they could kill them. As well armed as Bobby's crew was, the five of them might slow it down, but they couldn't stop a slaughter.

Nicky balanced his rifle on top of the compass housing, near the throttle and within easy reach if he needed to grab it and run out on deck. His hands were sticky with salt mist and his own sweat when he took the wheel. He checked the instruments and thought for a moment how he loved this boat, *The Jackpot*. A seventy-five-footer with a 350 horsepower diesel and a large trawl from each of its riggings, it could drag the Gulf for three hours or more in depths of thirty to three hundred fathoms and carry some twenty-three hundred cubic feet of shrimp in its fish hold. But they weren't trawling for shrimp.

The low guttural hum of men speaking in heavily accented voices carried over the sound of the boat and the ocean.

Nicky cocked his head to listen but couldn't make out any words. "What do you see?" he asked Dave.

"Here, I'll watch the radar and the wheel. You go look." Dave skirted past Nicky.

Nicky hesitated. Dave was new to boats, and Bobby said one of the best men should be at the wheel during the transfer. But it was Nicky's first time, and he wanted to see what was going on.

Muttering, "Yeah, man," Nicky picked up his rifle and moved into the passage, where he could hear better.

The voices belonged to two dark men huddled around Bobby. Rock and Polky stood on either side of Bobby, creating a tense semicircle. The barrel of Rock's shotgun rested on his shoulder while his right hand gripped the trigger guard. Polky held his bolt-action with the barrel pointed at the deck. They were ready, but Nicky kept his own guard as Bobby traded his rifle with Rock for the money then followed the two dark men back toward the bigger vessel. Nicky wouldn't have gone on that ship alone and unarmed for all the dope money in Florida.

After Bobby was out of sight, Rock watched the other boat, humming softly. Polky paced, while Nicky breathed slowly, waiting for something to happen.

A few minutes later, the men on the mother ship started pulling burlap-covered bales out of the hold with a pulley. Half a dozen or so of the ship's crew started transferring the marijuana to the trawler. The men were dark and squat looking, and most were shirtless in the tropical heat. They grunted with the effort of lifting the bales, each of which weighed around sixty pounds.

Transferring the thirty-eight bales took just over two hours, and by the time they finished, Nicky's shoulders were spasming in pain from standing still and holding his weapon ready. He took the wheel again and eased the trawler back out into the open Gulf waters. Going home ought to be easy, as long as no Coast Guard cutter thought the trawler looked suspicious and wanted to board. He could smell the pungent odor of the weed, but Bobby wouldn't let any of them touch it until they had it back on dry land.

"I'm not sailing through the Caribbean with a ton of pot and doped-up fishermen," he said when Polky started in again on sampling the goods. "The reason most dope runners get in trouble is they get fucked up on their own stuff and mess up."

Polky muttered a disgruntled, "Yeah, man," and turned away.

Near dawn, Rock took the helm so Nicky could get a cup of coffee. The liquid steamed his face as he tried to sip it. Too hot. Too strong. Nicky blew on it and tried again but burned his lips. He couldn't seem to get enough coffee or water or anything into his mouth to wet his tongue.

Bobby slunk up beside him and laughed. "See? What'd I tell you? Easy or what, man?"

Nicky nodded. The dry inside of his mouth had a rotten taste to it, and his shoulders still hurt from the tension. *Easy, my ass.*

Nicky knew that since Tank Pettus had moved to Apalachicola, he'd been hauling bales of marijuana. The man even joked about his square grouper. Years ago, Tank had fallen in with his cousin, Jimmy Chukenears, a wheeler-and-dealer sort who outgrew just fishing. Though Jimmy had grown up in Dolphin Cove like the rest of them, he'd left his family and moved to Apalachicola a few years before Tank had. He'd chased the oysters and scallops at first then went after something far more lucrative. Soon Jimmy had the financing and the connections in Colombia to make the deals. Tank praised smuggling as an easy way to make the money they couldn't make from fishing anymore. While Tank had the years on him that the hired crew with the big guns didn't, he was one of the best pilots around for getting back into the hidden inlets along the Big Bend coast.

The first couple of years, Tank had been Jimmy's main man on the trawler. But then Jimmy cut back to just the Colombian end, with a well-armed and observant Bobby in tow, and left the Gulf haul to Tank, who as captain knew the little coves, the shallows, and the hidden spots like his own handprint. When Tank took to coughing too much, Bobby had eased into his place on the trawler.

As far as Nicky could tell, Bobby was Jimmy's main man, but they kept Tank involved because of his knowledge. Understanding the shorelines like Tank did, sometimes all he did was run a little john-boat out to the trawler when it came back in loaded with marijuana, climb on board, and pilot the trawler the last few miles through some out-of-the-way channel. Other times, Tank met them on the beach with a rented truck and smaller boats to relay the pot from the trawler to the shore.

While Bobby was closed-mouthed about his connections, Tank, with a couple of beers and in the relative safety of his own porch in his four-room rented cypress house, had spilled what he knew to Nicky the week before. Like he was seeking a convert, Nicky had thought as he listened to Tank while Kitty puttered around in the kitchen, frying some mullet from the day's meager catch.

"It's grown up in the Guajira peninsula of Colombia," Tank had said. "Look it up on an atlas, will you? I'd like to go there myself some time. Jimmy, so he says anyways, been there a few times." He coughed then wiped his mouth with a handkerchief. He sat quiet a moment before he got the breath to continue.

Nicky spotted some rust-colored stains on the handkerchief. The coughing spell wasn't too bad that time, and Tank hadn't needed the syrup for it, yet he'd winced with pain. Jimmy kept Tank going with codeine cough syrup and paregoric, but from the way Tank shifted around trying to find a way to sit that was comfortable, Nicky feared the medicines weren't going to be enough for much longer.

"They got a whole organization there," Tank continued, "with airstrips for four-engine planes they sometimes use and all kinds of storing and loading places for their freighters. They use this route they call the Windward Passage, runs between Haiti and Cuba, and sometimes they—"

"Supper's ready," Kitty said, sticking her head out the back door. "Why don't we eat out here? House is pretty hot tonight."

Nicky wiped sweat from his face and wondered again if he hadn't made a big mistake throwing in with Tank. Still, the hard truth was that Nicky could make more money in one or two runs than he could make in an entire year from fishing. So the money was a hook, but not letting Tank down was part of the decision.

But the biggest reason he went was simple. Nicky wanted to give Kitty a better life than that of a fisherman's wife.

Chapter Twenty-Two

As near as Nicky could figure, the first time Bobby had seen Kitty was at Jimmy's fish house on the outskirts of Apalachicola. He and Bobby were sitting in Bobby's pickup, waiting for some folks to leave so they could talk in private with Jimmy. Kitty was working part-time during the scallop season. Jimmy'd brought in a truckload, and though he kept telling her not to, Kitty hoisted a heavy sack over her shoulder and carried it to the scales. She weighed sack after sack while Nicky admired her long tan legs and the way the muscles in her arms bunched and hardened as she lifted each bag onto the scales. Even though it was September and a cool breeze broke the bright sun, it was hot. Kitty wore a T-shirt and cutoffs and looked all of sixteen with her long hair pulled back into a thick rope of a braid down her back.

Everything was cool until Nicky glanced over and saw how Bobby was looking at Kitty. Nicky's stomach flopped over and twisted.

"That's Tank's daughter," Nicky said sternly. "And my girl."

"Got it." Bobby nodded. But he didn't stop looking at Kitty.

A minute later, Jimmy waved them over. They got out of the truck and went toward the side of the fish house. They stood in the shade with Jimmy while he spoke in a low voice. Kitty was busy with a couple of tourists wanting to buy some scallops and didn't seem to notice them.

Nicky hardly listened to Jimmy. He kept swinging his head back and forth between Kitty at the scales and Bobby, standing beside him and staring at her. If Bobby had been a dog, he would have had a string of drool hanging from his mouth.

When Kitty finished weighing the scallops, she quoted the tourists a price so quickly Nicky hadn't had time to do the math in his head. He was good at numbers, good at math, but Kitty always beat him to the final figures.

She wrote the price and her initials on a scrap of paper and handed it to the buyers. "So there won't be any misunderstanding," she said without a hint of a smile. "Pay that man over there." She pointed at Jimmy. Then she nodded at Nicky while ignoring Bobby, who was still half hidden in the shadows.

Nicky could see the white ridges of several small scars from shucking oysters as well as some new cuts and rough redness about her knuckles from working the scallops. She was too smart to stay there, smelling of fish and trying to make a go of it against nature, the tides, and government regulations.

Nicky had to get her into college and give her a chance in life.

And he had to get her away from Bobby.

———◉———

"HOW'D IT GO, BOYS?" Tank asked as Nicky and Bobby scrambled up the porch steps.

Nicky glanced around, looking for Kitty. He didn't want her to hear their business, and he didn't want Bobby to see her again.

"If you're looking for Kitty, she ain't here," Tank said. "She had some things she needed to go do. Not sure when she'll be back." He sat on a rusty lawn chair perched kitty-corner on the porch. The table in front of him held a plate with an uneaten sandwich and an empty beer bottle. His tan had a gray undertone, and the whites of his eyes had a yellow cast. His pupils were small pinpoints of darkness. "Now, how'd it go?"

"Fine, Tank. Everything's cool. Your boy here's slick." Bobby grinned.

"Well, sit down. No reason to stand there when it's a hundred in the shade. Who'd've thought it'd still be this hot this late in the season?"

"No, sir. Just dropping your boy here off. Come up to say hey to you. See how you're doing."

"Gettin' lazy is how I'm doing. Got my daughter to run, fetch, and cook for me, and now I got my son-in-law here to do my work. What more could a man ask for?"

Nicky thought a man might ask for a decent set of lungs and an air conditioner. He didn't care what Tank said, if he had to drive all the way to Tallahassee to get one, he was going to buy the man a decent window unit.

"Y'all be cool." Bobby backed down the steps and waved.

As soon as he was out of sight, Nicky collapsed on the chair across from Tank. "I don't want Kitty getting around him. Or any of the shit we bring in. If we're going to keep doing this, we do it out of Jimmy's place or Dave's. We're not—"

"Knock that shit off. You're not my son-in-law yet, no matter what I told Bobby. Even if you were, you're not telling me what to do. Besides, I'm not letting Kitty in on any of this. You're going to give me what money you got, and I'm sending her to Tallahassee with it. Get her away from this shit." He paused, breathing heavily. "We just got to convince her to go."

Nicky nodded. Getting Kitty to leave Tank would not be easy. "How you going to get her to go?" He didn't figure Tank would just out and out order her away, but he might.

"She and me talked about it. Course, she thinks you're working the bay with Bobby. She don't know what you're really up to."

"She thinks I'm getting this kind of money off fishing?"

"No, she'd know better. But I told her most of the money's mine. I told her I been saving up for her, for her college fund. She didn't want to leave me till I stop with the coughing, but I just about got her convinced to go on to Tallahassee. She'll get a place, find a job, maybe start college. But you're going to have to give her a push too."

"Sure, I'll do that." Nicky was already forming the argument in his mind.

"And when you get enough money so's you and her can both get to college, you quit with Bobby." He rested a few seconds. "Bobby is... I pulled him out of a bar fight a few years back." He inhaled loudly, picked at the sandwich, then eyed Nicky. "Bobby killed the man, so I couldn't take him to the hospital. Bobby was cut bad, but I nursed him better than his own mother could've, then I put him to work with Jimmy and me. That was a while back. Now I've made him promise to stay away from Kitty and to take care of you, and he agreed. But a shark can't help being a shark, so you keep that in mind. You understand what I'm saying?"

Nicky nodded. He had wondered why Bobby seemed so close to Tank. That story would explain it.

"And I don't care if I can't crawl to the pot to throw up in it. Once you get enough money for college for you two to go and to get married, you go. You leave me, and you get yourself to Tallahassee. Bobby might have all those nice-boy manners, and he's smart, real smart, but like I said, that man's a shark. I want you done with him soon as you can be." Tank started coughing so bad that he had to take some codeine.

By the time Kitty got home, Tank was dozing on the porch. As soon as Kitty came inside, Nicky took off. He returned a few hours later with a window unit and put it in Tank's bedroom.

If the old man was going to die on them, at least he could do it in the cool of the bedroom, not splayed out on the porch, open to whoever walked down the sidewalk.

Chapter Twenty-Three

Nicky never thought he'd be so glad to be back on land as he was when he hunkered down in a cramped rental cabin on the bay. They were back from the run, safe from the Colombians and the Coast Guard. Nicky rotated his head, trying to loosen his neck muscles. His back hurt, and he was glad to be done with the offloading.

Polky sat down on the worn couch and began cleaning a couple of buds, picking out the seeds with his fingernails. "Third time's the charm, reckon?" Polky grinned at him.

"Reckon so," Nicky said then eased around him, not wanting to listen to him anymore.

There hadn't been any problems on the first two trips, but transferring the bales from the mother ship still scared him. However, Nicky would be damned before he let anyone see that fear.

In the living room, Bobby reported to Jimmy in a low mumble. Nicky didn't even try to make out the words. Rock and Dave leaned against the wall on either side of the only exit, sweeping the yard with their steely gazes. Four bales of pot were propped against the wall in the kitchen, and a buyer was expected within the half hour. The rest of the pot had been divided between two vans, and they'd already argued about how to get it to New Orleans.

Earlier, after the pot had been loaded onto *The Jackpot*, they acted like just another shrimp trawler out in the Gulf of Mexico and ran the boat up into the Big Bend area of the Florida gulf coast. A big trawler averaging seven to eight knots couldn't possibly outrun a Coast Guard cutter if one took after them, but they moved slowly around the places a trawler out for shrimp would be and counted on looking normal and having luck.

After cutting back through the Gulf, they had eased the trawler into an inlet near Carrabelle as far as they'd dared. Dave, Polky, and Nicky took the dinghy to an isolated beach, where Tank met them with a rented ten-wheeler loaded with a couple of small aluminum boats. The men relayed the bales of pot in the dinghy and aluminum boats while Rock stood guard with his shotgun. When they finished, Rock helped them load the bales into the truck while Tank stood guard with Rock's shotgun. As Nicky had strained to push the last of the bales into the truck, he'd wondered who had rented it and under what name.

Back in the relative safety of the rental cabin, Nicky tried to relax the kinks out of his back. Jimmy and Bobby came in from the kitchen, and Jimmy started going through a stack of papers. Polky picked the sticky buds off the stems, rolling them between his fingers till they fell in small bits into the lid of a shoe box. Rock and Dave kept their guard by the door.

When Polky had a handful of clean pot, still gummy with the resin that made it potent, he spread some in a thin, narrow line on a cigarette paper. He twisted the paper tightly then licked it along the seam to seal the joint. After lighting it and taking a hit, he passed it to Nicky.

Nicky inhaled deeply, feeling the smoke burn the back of his throat. Coughing a bit, Nicky drew down again, pulling the smoke deep into his lungs and holding it there. He passed the joint to Bobby, who shook his head and handed it to Jimmy.

"No way, man. I'm no fool. I'm a pure-D businessman," Jimmy said and passed it back to Polky. Nobody offered it to Dave or Rock, as they were on guard.

Jimmy shook his head, a grin on his sunburned face. "You boys pass out and see God if you want. Bobby and me are planning the next trip. Going to bring in a bigger load this time. You get straight, we'll talk again. Might bring y'all in for a share of it this time."

Bobby and Jimmy walked back into the efficiency's cramped kitchen. Nicky took another hit when Polky passed him the joint.

"Might, my ass," Polky said. "I'm gonna get me a share this time, whether Bobby means me to or not."

"What d'you mean?" As Nicky spoke, smoke billowed out of his mouth. He inhaled again, ignoring the etiquette against holding on to a lit joint too long, then passed it.

"Nicky, you're so sweet sometimes, it scares the shit out of me. You think Jimmy and Bobby are gonna miss a bale? A couple of bales even? When they go off like the—what'd the shit Jimmy call themselves?—pure-D businessmen? When they go off to count money, leaving you, me, Rock, and Dave to load the stuff on the trucks, you think they notice if I kick a bale or two out in the sea oats, come back and get it later?" Polky stopped talking and inhaled. Tears from the smoke collected in the corners of his eyes. He started coughing, and smoke heaved out from his lungs. When he settled down, he said, "Man. Well shit, you don't get off good 'less you cough some." He toked on the joint again then passed it to Nicky.

Nicky was already stoned, but he took another hit. He forgot what he was going to say, or maybe he'd already said it: *Hell yeah, Bobby will notice if you hide a bale or two of prime Colombian pot in the sea oats.*

NICKY STOOD BESIDE Tank's house and watched Kitty hanging up laundry in the backyard. She turned around and stared back, squinting in the sunlight.

Tank called out, "Hey, you, you get up here, right now."

Nicky turned and went up on the porch. Tank gave him a hard look, and Nicky glared right back. *What right did that man have to order him around like he was hired help?*

Nicky stopped glaring, ashamed of being mad at a sick old man, and gave him a sheepish grin. "What's up?"

"Sit your butt down." Tank kicked a chair toward Nicky without rising from his own. The older man's coffee cup reeked of whiskey. "You got to help me get Kitty out of here. She's saying she won't leave me."

Nicky started to say he didn't blame her, but he kept his mouth shut.

"I made Bobby promise again to stay away from Kitty after I caught him studying on her earlier today. With him sitting in his pickup, she didn't see him. But I mean it, you keep your eyes on him." Tank's voice sounded gravelly, almost like he was growling.

"He promised you?" Nicky hadn't forgotten the time he'd seen Bobby giving Kitty a good once-over at the fish house and smiling like he liked what he saw.

"Sure, he promised. Called me his main man and patted my damn leg like I was his pet dog. And I got Jimmy to tell him if he so much as looked at Kitty, Jimmy'd bust his head in two. But you watch his ass, and you watch out for Kitty."

"I promise. I will watch out for Kitty, and I will do what I can to get her out of here. And I won't let Bobby get near her."

"All right then. Now, you ready to talk business?"

"Yeah, shoot."

Tank leaned forward. "Jimmy and me are making plans for a much bigger haul this time. Up to ten tons."

Nicky shook his head. *That's too big a load.*

"I see you shaking your head, but we can do it. Same way, just more so."

"Why? Things are going all right the way they are."

"I need to get a big bankroll for you and Kitty, get you two out of here, in college, and away from all this shit. You can't be fishing for a living unless you want to starve, and I won't have the two of you running drugs no more." Tank paused long enough to draw in a deep breath, his face turning red.

"You okay?" Nicky studied Tank, suddenly wondering if he should call Kitty.

"The damn banks and the damn government regs have killed fishing for the likes of us. And those giant commercial fleets are taking more than their share and selling it cheap. Hell, I couldn't even take care of my own family. My wife... sick and no insurance, and Kitty—damn it all—dressing her from the church thrift shop, and her having to pick tomatoes and work in the fish house. I won't have you two living like that." Tank seemed to have exhausted himself with that speech. He leaned back in his chair, his cheeks puffing with the effort of his breathing.

"Let me get Kitty." Nicky didn't want Tank to die on him, and Kitty always seemed to know how to calm him down.

Tank coughed and reached for the coffee cup by his chair. His hands shook, and he spilled more of it than he drank. "Wait a minute." Tank steadied his hand and gulped more whiskey. "We got to talk about this next haul."

"Maybe later."

"Now. This is for Kitty." Tank put the cup down and folded his hands in his lap as if to hide their shaking. "Bobby put me in charge of the shore crew. This'll be more than just the regular guys can handle. Jimmy'll make the connection with Colombia and the financing." He paused again to breathe. "You and Bobby run the trawler, but I'll be getting extra trucks and more men this time to haul it off the trawler. Get some men I know and trust with a gun to stand guard."

"You up to doing this?" Nicky hated to ask, but he would also hate to see Tank kill himself taking on more than he could handle.

"Have to be, don't I?" Tank stared hard at him. "You can't run the shore crew on a deal this big. You don't know the locals yet like I do."

Nicky nodded, not taking his eyes off of Tank. A grey-yellow tinge made the older man's face look shadowed, even in the full light. He was sicker, no doubt about it.

"After this next big haul, we quit. Both of us. Jimmy and Bobby can keep it up if they want, but you and me... son, we're done after this run."

Chapter Twenty-Four

Kitty sat on a folding chair in Tank's bedroom and listened to him ramble. Between the paregoric, the cough medicine, and the whiskey, he was comfortable enough. By sucking down the codeine syrup, he could talk without too much coughing. Even with the drugs and whiskey in him, he still made sense.

"You go on. I mean now. You go on to Tallahassee." Tank waved a finger at her. "Go on now. Quit arguing with me."

Kitty nodded, even though she knew there wasn't enough light in the bedroom for him to see her. She didn't want to leave him, but he had ordered her to go and had become agitated when she'd refused. The only way she could quiet him was to promise to leave, though she planned to come back on weekends. She would definitely return toward the end to be with him. But she understood the only way she could offer her father some peace of mind was to leave. And she knew it was because of the drug running business.

They both pretended she didn't know Tank started running dope soon after he had moved to Apalachicola. But Nicky had to know that she understood what was going on, especially after the night following his third run when he had told her to dress up because they were going to New Orleans. Tank had been over in Sopchoppy, tending to what he'd told her was some fishing business, and would be gone a couple of days. If he'd been home, Kitty wouldn't have gone with Nicky, and even with that, she'd had to think about it awhile.

Right before they left, two men drove up in a van with electrical supply signs on the sides, and they talked with Nicky. Kitty had her own paneled van, a gift from Tank when she was in high school. It still had Lloyd's Plumbing signs on it. Without asking her, Nicky had the men load some boxes into the back of her vehicle. As the men readied to leave, one of them handed Nicky a small gun, which he slipped under the driver's seat of the van.

Kitty watched from the kitchen window, unsure of what she should do. When Nicky came into the kitchen and asked if she was ready to go, she nodded and grabbed her backpack.

Nicky drove her van through the night, traveling the backroads toward the Big Easy, with a couple of quilts thrown over a stack of stereo component boxes. The fetid smell of Mobile Bay drifted in through the windows but didn't wash away the pungent odor of the marijuana inside the boxes. From time to time, in the glare of lights in the towns in south Alabama and Mississippi, Kitty caught sight of the other electrical supply van just ahead of them on the road. She figured that made her a mule after a fashion, though once in the city, she waited in a motel room until Nicky finished with the business.

They spent the next couple of nights in the French Quarter, doing touristy things, until Kitty said it was time to go. As they crossed back over the Pontchartrain Bridge, she told him that she wasn't doing that again.

That was the closest they'd come to talking about what Nicky and Tank were up to. After that, they just pretended she didn't know anything, the same way she pretended with Tank.

There they all were, stuck in the mess they'd made. Kitty sat in her father's bedroom, listening to the rasp of his breathing as he finally calmed and went to sleep. She didn't know what to do.

Nicky came into the room and stood beside her. "Why don't you come on to bed now? He's asleep."

"Why don't you leave me alone?" she snapped. Hurrying past Nicky, she went outside to the porch, where she breathed in the damp night air ripe with the smell of the bay and fish. She was only eighteen, yet she felt as though she'd already ruined her life.

LEANING AGAINST THE door facing, Kitty listened to Nicky's call with CeCe.

"Stay with Tank," he said. "Help out, and we'll pay you." He paused, then his face turned red. "Okay, okay. I know he's family, and family doesn't ask for pay. Just room and board and gas money then. Kitty's going to be in Tallahassee during the week, so Tank—*we* really need you."

Nicky twisted the cord on the phone around his fingers. "She'll just be in Tallahassee during the week, you know, to get a job and find an apartment. So me and her can go on to college after..." He turned away from Kitty. Over the long-distance line, CeCe must have filled in the blanks. Nicky couldn't say "after Tank dies."

Kitty moved up next to Nicky and rested her head on his shoulder. She started to take the receiver away and speak to CeCe herself, but a wave of exhaustion washed over her. She couldn't make herself reach for the phone. But standing so close, she could hear CeCe's talking.

"Damn Kitty. How's she just take off and leave her father for somebody else to take care of? That's her daddy." CeCe's voice had that sharp grating sound like her mother's when she would fuss at them.

"She needs to get a job," Nicky said, "and the only good jobs around here are in Tallahassee. She's been working some in Jimmy's fish house, but you know that's not steady and the pay is crap. I'm fishing regular with a guy named Bobby, but we still need the money."

After a long pause, CeCe said, "Bullshit. Tell me what's really going on. What the hell is Kitty hiding from?"

"We just need you. That's all. *Tank* needs you."

"Tank's too proud to be letting me nurse him."

"I got that covered. You're going to call him and tell him you got all kinds of problems after breaking up with this guy and you need to get away and you need Tank to let you stay with him a while. Make it like he's helping you."

"Okay," CeCe said so softly that Kitty had to push up closer to Nicky to hear. "That would be a good way to do it."

"It's settled then." Nicky sounded relieved.

"But I'm going to let Kitty know what I think of her running off and leaving me to take care of her father."

Nicky said a quick goodbye and hung up the phone. He pulled Kitty into his arms. As she pressed her face against his chest, she knew her friendship with CeCe was over. She also figured it wouldn't take long before CeCe understood what was going on.

But what CeCe might do about it, Kitty didn't know.

Chapter Twenty-Five

Nicky shivered in the dampness of the January night. *What a crock of shit.*

Bobby slammed down his cup, and it shattered against the hull of the trawler, splashing hot coffee across Polky's feet.

"Man, watch out." Polky scrambled out of the way of the coffee, but not out of reach of Bobby, who drew back his fist and smashed Polky's left cheek.

The punch knocked Polky off balance, and he dropped to the deck, landing in the spilled coffee. Bobby drew back his right leg as if to kick him while he was down.

Dave jumped between the two of them. Rock sprinted over, his twelve-gauge already pointing at Dave. Polky pushed himself halfway up and wiped his face on his sleeve.

"How the hell do you get lost and run out of diesel when you're hauling ten tons of pot?" Bobby screamed.

Nicky didn't blame Bobby one damn bit. For a moment, his own foot itched to kick the stupid fool. Marijuana boats liked to carry a maximum amount of marijuana and a minimum amount of fuel, but running out of diesel was both a big risk and a big embarrassment.

"It's your fucking boat, big shot!" Polky shouted back. "You ought to at least know how much diesel to—"

Bobby drew back his leg for a kick. Polky spun out of reach and jumped up, fists at the ready.

Dave held up his hands. "Cool it, all right. Both of you. Just be cool. Nicky and me can run the dinghy in, and one of us can get a boat and get more diesel. We're not far out from Carrabelle. All right?"

Polky kept his fists up until Bobby nodded slightly and lowered his hands. Rock's grip on the twelve-gauge loosened a bit, but he kept his eyes on Polky. Taking a step backward, Polky rubbed his face. He smelled of coffee and whiskey and, even in the chilly night air, a sour sweat. The night before, drinking against Bobby's strict orders, he'd let them run badly off course, delaying them and wasting precious diesel for the heavily loaded trawler.

"Let me get my hat, and I'll go with him," Nicky said. He was eager to get off the trawler. Ever since they'd loaded the marijuana from the cargo ship, Bobby and Polky had been sniping at each other. And now, not far from their drop site on Bald Point, they'd run out of diesel.

"Then go and get it." Bobby pointed at Polky. "And take this worthless piece of shit with you."

"And leave you and Rock with the pot? No way, man," Polky said.

"What do you think we're going to do with it out here?" Bobby stood with his legs wide apart, and his right hand balled into a fist. "Thanks to you and your navigational skills."

"Polky, get out of here. Go with Dave, and I'll stay here with Bobby." Nicky was afraid that if he left Polky on board, Bobby would kill him, especially since Polky didn't have any better sense than to keep egging the man on.

Dave grabbed Polky's arm. "Come on. Let's go."

NEAR DAWN AND HOURS behind schedule, Nicky looked at his watch in the dim light when they finally eased the trawler as close to shore at Bald Point as they could without running it aground. They were coming in from the Gulf, but on the other side, the Ochlockonee Bay filled in a hole between the shorelines of the point and the mainland.

Earlier, Polky and Dave had gone for diesel twice. They came back with Polky in the dinghy, low in the dark water and smelling of diesel. Dave ran a fifteen-foot Terry bass boat with a fifty-five-gallon diesel drum each trip. Nobody asked Dave where the boat had come from that late at night.

Nicky studied the horizon. "Reckon we got time before it gets light? Takes a while to unload all this shit." Still a good two hours before dawn, the sky had a thick cloud cover, and a light, cold rain peppered the choppy bay waters. "We could wait till tomorrow night."

Bobby shook his head. "Tank's supposed to have the guys and the trucks there. Let's do it tonight. Start it anyway. Weather'll keep people off the Bald. It'll be dark a bit yet."

Cradling his M-16 and standing beside Rock, Bobby winked at Nicky. "You be cool. Keep your eyes open."

Nicky, Dave, and Polky took the dinghy to Bald Point, where they expected to meet Tank. When they pulled up on the beach, they looked around. In the beams of their flashlights, only the dunes, the sea oats, and the yaupon holly on the dark beach were visible. No one was there. No Tank, no trucks, no guys to lift and tote the bales.

"Shit." Polky waved his arms. "What'd we do here, land on the wrong beach?"

Nicky held up his finger for Polky to be quiet, and he listened. He heard nothing but the sounds of rain, waves, and wind. "Polky, stay put. Dave, go that way up the beach, and I'll go down this way. Let's see where they're at."

Polky pointed his flashlight in Nicky's face. "Hey, man, who died and put you in charge?"

"If I were you, boy, I'd keep a low profile," Dave said and started walking up the beach, the beam of his light bouncing off the sea oats and sand a few feet in front of him.

"Hey, what I do?" Polky asked.

A half hour later, Nicky, Polky, and Dave came back together on the beach.

"This one's snakebit for sure," Nicky said. "Tank was here, but he must've given up and pulled the men off."

Using his flashlight, Nicky pointed out the tracks the various vehicles had made in the sand as they'd turned around and left. A red Ford pickup with mud covering the tag was parked near a dirt trail they called Sand Ditch Road. When he checked, the key was dangling from the ignition. Nicky figured Tank must have left it for him, which was good thinking. He understood why Bobby kept Tank in the game even though he was sick.

"We better take that truck and go check on Tank," Nicky said, eyeing first Dave then Polky. "He's staying in Carrabelle with the men he rounded up to help."

"We need to see what happened here and then set up for tonight." Dave headed off toward the truck.

"I could go, and you two could get back to the boat," Polky said.

Dave didn't even slow down as he advanced on the truck.

"Naw, not a good idea," Nicky said, hurrying after Dave.

"You think I'm too much a screwup to find the old man, don't you?" Polky ran ahead, stopped in front of them, and puffed out his chest like he wanted to fight.

Dave gave Polky a hard look Nicky hadn't seen him use before. Nicky stepped between the two men. Fighting among themselves wasn't going to help.

Dave moved around Nicky and grabbed the front of Polky's wet shirt. "You're a fuckup, sure. Mess up again, boy, and I'll save Bobby the trouble. You get it?"

Dave let go of Polky's shirt and opened the driver's door. Before he got in, he spun back to Polky. "You ride in the back. I don't want you pushing up close to me."

Nicky climbed in the passenger side while Polky vaulted over the tailgate and slumped down in the bed of the truck.

When Dave stopped at a stop sign in Carrabelle, Polky hopped out of the pickup and took off running. Dave grunted. Nicky thought they ought to chase him down, but he decided not to mention it. Dave eased forward through the intersection and headed to the old, nearly abandoned motel where Tank and his men were supposed to be holing up.

Nicky sat still, his lips pressed tightly together so he wouldn't say what he was thinking. *Polky's going to fuck us over.*

Chapter Twenty-Six

Nicky pulled into the sandy parking lot of the old motel where Tank had told him he'd be staying, and his heart seemed to ricochet into his gut. *What the hell?* Scruffy men in T-shirts and jeans were hanging out in rusted patio chairs, drinking coffee, and shouting stuff back and forth. Several of the doors were wide open, and inside one room, a shotgun leaned against the wall. The parking lot was crowded with pickups, moving vans, trucks with boats on trailers, and even a ten-wheeler. His own blue pickup was parked near the office. He guessed Tank had driven it from Apalachicola. Nicky climbed out of the truck and headed for the group of men.

Dave scrambled out of the driver's side and slammed the door. Catching up with Nicky on the busted concrete that passed for a sidewalk, he said, "Scenic, isn't it?"

"Hell, why don't y'all just put in a phone call to the DEA and tell them you're here," Nicky muttered.

"Nobody cares, okay? This far back off the road, if it wasn't for the drug runners, this place would have shut down after the last hurricane."

When Nicky and Dave got closer, the men stopped talking and watched them with their wary eyes.

"Where's Tank?" Nicky asked when he reached them.

One man glanced over Nicky's shoulder, nodded at Dave, and pointed to his right. "Room at the end." He picked up a revolver and set it in his lap.

Nicky jogged down the sidewalk, Dave on his heels. When he reached the end of the building, he opened the last door, somehow not surprised it wasn't locked, and stared into the dark room.

Tank lay in one of the beds, passed out or sleeping or maybe even dead. A couple of other guys slept bunched up in chairs, and one man was stretched out on the floor, snoring.

Nicky edged closer to Tank and stood over him, watching with relief as the old man's chest rose and fell. He gently shook Tank's shoulder.

Dave skirted Nicky and tapped Tank's thin arm. "Wake up."

Tank's eyes fluttered open. "What the hell happened to you?" His voice sounded surprisingly strong for a man as sick as he was.

"We had to refuel," Dave said. "We got to the beach around dawn, but you were gone." He gave Tank a look that told him not to push the matter.

A man wandered in from outside, scratching his arm and sucking on a cigarette. He dipped his chin at Dave and Nicky and said, "Good morning," around the cigarette.

"This is Lloyd, out of Sopchoppy." Tank struggled into a sitting position on the bed but didn't stand. "I had him up on top of the ten-wheeler last night, listening for y'all and looking for any lights."

"Damn cold on top of that truck." Lloyd glared at Nicky, squinting like he might recognize him from somewhere. "Raining, case you didn't know."

"Waited four hours past what Bobby said." Tank started coughing and reached for a glass of amber-colored liquid on the nightstand. He gulped until the glass was empty. But when he put it down, he started coughing again.

"See," Lloyd said, "we figured out something was wrong. We didn't much like the idea of being there with a bunch of men with hunting rifles, all them boats and moving vans, and a ten-wheeler when the sun come up."

"I pulled everybody off," Tank said, wheezing between his words. He reached over to his jacket, which hung on a chair by the bed, and pulled a bottle of codeine cough syrup out of a pocket. No one spoke while he guzzled about half the bottle.

"We can do it again tonight," Dave said in a matter-of-fact tone as if it wasn't some big screwup, as if Tank wasn't dying in front of them.

Lloyd grunted and kept scratching. The other men in the room started stirring, and the one on the floor sat up, grabbed his gun, and glared at all of them.

Polky was right to haul ass. But Nicky couldn't leave Tank, who was still coughing. Nicky wondered if the older man could stay awake with all that codeine in his system.

———◉———

PILOTING A SKIFF IN the early-morning light, Nicky spotted *The Jackpot* in the open waters of the Gulf of Mexico, just west of the mouth of Ochlockonee Bay. He pulled alongside the trawler. Tank tried to stand but slipped. Nicky and Dave helped him up and onto the trawler, where Bobby and Rock stood, both of them armed and frowning.

"Polky skipped," Dave told the two waiting men.

Bobby cut his eyes at Rock with a message in the look, but Nicky wasn't sure what that message might be. He didn't really care, though he figured Polky was a dead man unless he was long gone.

"It's just a matter of doing it all over," Nicky said. "This time without Polky to screw it up." He couldn't make himself look Bobby in the eyes, so he glanced over at Tank.

"I can promise you—" Tank coughed. "My men and all them trucks will be there at midnight." He coughed again so hard Nicky grabbed him by his arm and held on in case he fell. "On Bald Point. Just like before. I'll go back... get everybody arranged." Tank wiped his mouth with the back of his hand, but he didn't pull out of Nicky's grip.

"You could've stayed back at the motel," Bobby said.

"My screwup, getting scared and pulling everybody off." Tank leaned hard on Nicky. "I wanted to be the one to come tell you we'll be there tonight." He coughed again and sprayed blood on the deck, apparently too tired from the long night to get his handkerchief out in time to catch it.

"Why don't I send Nicky back with you to keep you company," Bobby said.

Tank nodded. He shook loose of Nicky and reached into his back pocket to pull out the bottle of cough syrup. "Yeah, I could use me some company," he said then drank the codeine in strangled gulps.

"Let me grab some stuff." Nicky wanted his rifle if he was going back among that strange army Tank had collected at the motel.

Bobby followed Nicky, and once they were out of Tank's hearing, he grabbed Nicky's arm to stop him. "First damn thing you do, you get Tank into a hot shower then to bed. When he wakes up, if he doesn't look any better, you take him to a doctor."

"He won't go. Me and Kitty tried our best, but after that last time, he won't—"

"Don't ask. You understand me?" Bobby poked him in the chest. "Just do it."

"Yeah, all right."

"Next thing you do, you round up the men Tank hired, and you take a good, long look at them. If Tank's able, get him to stand with you. Any of them don't seem cool, you cut them loose right then. But pay them." Bobby let go of Nicky's arm, reached into his pocket, and pulled out a thick billfold with a rubber band holding it together. "Nothing in this but money that can't be traced. I'm trusting you." He thrust the wallet into Nicky's hand.

Nicky nodded and tucked it into his jeans pocket.

"You cut anybody loose, you pay them a couple hundred from that billfold. Send them away happy so they don't try anything. Plenty of hundreds in there, but don't be wasting it." Bobby glanced over his shoulder. "I just hope Tank can make it through this." He cut his eyes back to Nicky as the morning sun broke through the mist. "And you." He glared at Nicky, something almost feral in his eyes.

"What?" Nicky asked to break the tension.

"Get a van," Bobby said. "Not a pickup and not one of those hippie things, but like a working man's van. I'm going to give you a share of the pot. You load up from Bald Point, and when we're done there, you go on. I got this squirrelly feeling. Maybe you better take off from there, not go back to the Crawfordville house where we planned to meet. You take the van and the pot and get. Take Tank, and you find him some help. I don't care what he says. You get that man to a doctor or hospital. If you can't handle that, call Jimmy."

"I can get Kitty's van. It's still got the Lloyd's Plumbing sign on the side. We can—"

"No." Bobby poked him again. "Don't put her in this. I promised Tank not to get her involved. You rent something if you have to, but don't use your real name. You got the cash now. That doesn't work, you steal something. But don't use Kitty's van."

"Okay, sure." Nicky nodded, feeling the pressure of Bobby's grip and wanting to be long done with him and the whole deal.

As Nicky started to walk away, Bobby said in a low voice, "One more thing. You're in charge of the offloading now. Get Tank to tell you what he's got lined up, but don't you let that old man go out on the beach tonight."

With Rock's help, Nicky half-carried, half-dragged Tank to the skiff and got him loaded. Tank never said a word, but the loud rasp of his breathing sounded as if he were shouting.

When they reached the shore, Nicky tied up the skiff at the marina and drove back to the motel in his pickup with Tank dozing beside him. He sat in the parking lot of the motel for a few minutes. He had to decide if he was going to follow Bobby's orders or take Tank, get Kitty, and run for it.

Chapter Twenty-Seven

Nicky leaned over and made sure he could reach his rifle when he saw Lloyd hurrying toward him.

Lloyd opened the passenger-side door. "I can help you get him in."

Nicky nodded. They managed to carry Tank into the room he'd been sleeping in earlier. Once the older man was settled, Lloyd left, and Nicky, grateful the other guys were gone and Tank had drifted back to sleep, perched on a chair beside the bed.

If he were going to run, he should have just taken Tank straight to Kitty in Tallahassee. But it was too late, so he needed to find a van. Carrabelle didn't have any kind of moving van rental place, and Nicky was too nervous to fool with that anyway. He didn't have a clue how to steal one unless some fool left the keys in it, which would be luck he couldn't count on. He didn't seem to have any other option. He had to get Kitty's van, no matter what he'd promised Bobby.

He called Kitty and told her he needed to borrow her van. "I don't have time to drive over to Tallahassee and get it, so you got to bring it here to that old motel back of Carrabelle."

When she didn't answer, he wondered if she had hung up. But then he realized he could hear the low hum of the connection.

"Listen to me, please." Nicky heard the begging tone in his voice and hated it. "This is important. After you drop off the van, you can take my truck and get back to Tallahassee. You pack, gather up all the money, and be ready to go first thing the next morning. Tank and me will come get you in the van."

After a few more seconds, she said, "I told you I wasn't going to do this again."

"This is different. This is real important. I'll tell you more when you get here. Just come here. Please."

He listened to her breathe as he watched Tank's chest rise and fall. *Hell, this is never going to work.* He looked at the alarm clock on the nightstand and wondered where Polky was. He didn't know how to tell if the men Tank had pulled together to unload the pot were okay. "Damn it, me and your dad need you."

Tank moaned and rolled over in the bed. He coughed loud enough that Kitty must have heard.

"Where's CeCe?" she asked.

"Back in Apalachicola at the house, waiting for somebody to bring Tank back. We told her we'd just be gone one night."

Tank coughed again, ending with a low moan.

"All right. I'll be there," she said.

Two hours later, Kitty knocked on the door. Nicky opened it, and she went straight to the bed to check on her father.

"I'm not leaving him like this," she said, looking at Nicky as if he were to blame for Tank's condition. "Anyway, I'm already packed, and I've got the money. We can make a bed in the van for Tank and leave for Dolphin Cove now."

"No." He spoke with as much authority as he could, returning her hard look. "I've got... something I have to finish. For Tank."

"Fine. I'll wait here with Tank until you get back."

Realizing that was the best he could hope for, he laid half of the money Bobby had given him on the nightstand and told her if he didn't get back by ten the next morning to take Tank back to Dolphin Cove in his pickup.

"And just leave you here?" she asked.

"I'll catch up with you there."

"What about CeCe?"

"She'll be just fine. We'll call her later." Nicky didn't want to send Kitty back to Apalachicola to get CeCe, not with how mad she was at both of them. CeCe could find her own way back to Dolphin Cove, or she could just stay put. Nicky didn't care. He had Tank and ten tons of pot to worry about. He would make everything up to Kitty later, he promised himself as Tank started coughing again.

"Lock the door behind me." He stepped out, waited until he heard the click of the dead bolt, then walked back to the truck to meet with Lloyd. They had a lot to organize.

———◦◉◦———

THE NIGHT WAS COLD and lit by an eerie-looking three-quarter moon when Nicky brought the skiff alongside the trawler, which sat low in the dark waters inside the Ochlockonee Bay.

Nicky had hauled the skiff from Carrabelle on a trailer using Lloyd's pickup while Lloyd followed in Kitty's van. Lloyd had chuckled at driving the van with Lloyd's Plumbing still painted on the side.

Nicky tried to recall everything Tank had sputtered out at him by way of advice, but he couldn't remember any of it. As best he could tell, Lloyd was the leader of the assortment of men Tank had pulled together. Most of them had the raw-boned, sunburned look of fishermen. A couple of black kids Lloyd said were college students and a handful of Cubans who didn't seem to speak English rounded out the crew. Nicky hadn't let any of them go because he saw right off that there were hardly enough men or small boats as it was to get the ten tons of marijuana off the trawler and onto the trucks on the beach before daybreak.

He guided the skiff closer to *The Jackpot*. As he approached starboard, the light off the trawler lit a bright circle in the dark, and Nicky could see the boat's name painted on the side. He threw out a line, and Rock caught it. A minute later, Nicky scrambled over the stern and boarded the bigger boat.

Bobby stood on deck with his right hand cupping the trigger guard on his M-16. Rock's cut-down twelve-gauge pump hung over his shoulder in a rope sling. Neither of them bothered to say hello. Rock tied off the mooring line and reclaimed his twelve-gauge off Bobby's shoulder.

"It's ready," Nicky said. "Dave and me can load up this skiff. Rock can come over on the dinghy if you want him to, and we can start the relay."

"Rock stays with me," Bobby said. "Hear anything from Polky?"

"Naw."

"Where's Tank?"

"Back at the motel, sleeping." Nicky looked at the gun in Bobby's arms. He thought about the .38 Bobby kept in a holster on his belt and the little .22 strapped in his boot. "Here," he said, handing him the billfold. "I didn't cut any of them loose, but I left some of the money with Tank. Just in case."

"All right. We'll count it out later. Get going," Bobby said, moving back to the shadow of the wheelhouse.

Bobby paced, his M-16 at the ready. The way things were going, Nicky figured Bobby would as soon shoot him as anybody else, so he eased around carefully. The boats with Tank's men started to come into view, and as if they had triggered it, a soft but steady rain began to fall.

A rubber raft arrived first, and a couple of bulky men, one in a John Deere hat and the other in a Braves hat, climbed onto the trawler. At Rock's direction, the pair started dragging bales of marijuana from the fish hole onto the deck. A small aluminum johnboat pulled alongside, and a guy in a blue jacket tossed his line to Dave, who looped it loosely around a cleat. Dave bent over to grab a bale, but before he could pick one up, Braves Hat hurled a bale at the johnboat.

"Hey, don't throw the pot down so hard!" Dave yelled. "You want to sink the damn boat?"

Braves Hat, who looked twenty and stupid, grunted and went back for another bale. John Deere went to the rail and flung a bale as hard as Braves Hat had. The little johnboat rocked hard.

"Cripes, man, don't throw any more like that!" Blue Jacket shouted.

Bobby raised his rifle and pointed it at John Deere, who had picked up another bale. "Put it down."

John Deere stared at Bobby then tossed the bale over without looking. The heavy block hit the bow of the johnboat, causing it to dip enough that some water rushed in. Blue Jacket and the three bales slipped into the cold bay.

"Fucking shit." Bobby's finger tensed on the trigger.

Nicky jumped back, his heart banging hard.

Dave pushed Braves Hat and John Deere Hat toward the ladder. "Get back on the beach and lay down some plywood. Make us a platform so we can pull these little boats up easier. Now get your asses moving."

After a glance at Bobby, the two men scooted down the ladder and got back on their raft. From one of the small skiffs, Lloyd fished Blue Jacket out of the water. Wet and shivering, the man crawled into Lloyd's boat and cursed. Lloyd called out that he'd take the wet man back to shore and start a fire to dry him off and warm him up.

"No fucking fire!" Bobby shouted. "Put him in a truck and turn the heater on."

Nicky stepped toward the ladder. "I better get in a boat and start carrying the stuff to shore."

"I'm going in too," Bobby said. "Otherwise, we'll never get the stuff off the boat. Rock, stay here for now, and don't take any shit from anybody."

"What about the bales in the water?" Nicky asked.

"Leave them," Bobby said. "We only got about four hundred more to worry about."

They started a relay between the trawler and the smaller boats, with everybody but Rock bending their back to it. Even the two raft men got the hang of it when they rejoined the offloading, though Nicky made sure Lloyd kept a tight rein on them. Rock stood still in the glow of light from the wheelhouse, an arsenal within easy reach of his large, quick hands, his eyes darting about.

Bobby loaded pot, and Nicky ran a small boat to the beach. They switched off occasionally to give the one loading a rest.

Lloyd kept the men moving fast for the first couple of hours, but it was a cold night, and the steady, light rain continued. The pace began to slow even though they were running out of time. Bobby worked like a madman, yelling and pointing to push the men along.

After another hour, Nicky was shivering with fatigue and cold on the beach. He didn't know how much longer he could keep up the work. He wasn't the only one worn out. Most of Lloyd's men were huddled a few yards away, and the bunching together made Nicky nervous. He stopped dragging a bale toward a truck and watched Bobby and Dave pull up on the shore, one right after the other, in small johnboats.

"Get over here!" Bobby shouted at Nicky.

Teeth chattering, Nicky jogged over to Bobby and Dave.

Bobby pointed at Dave. "You go over there with Lloyd's men. See what's happening. Nicky and me are going to walk down the beach a bit and make sure nobody else is out here." Bobby picked up his M-16.

Nicky wished he had a better gun and a thicker jacket. He wished he were in the van with Kitty and Tank, heading back to Dolphin Cove. But he trudged along beside Bobby in the loose sand, moving away from the men and heading toward Sand Ditch Road on the other side of the dunes.

As soon as they were out of earshot of the others, Bobby slowed his pace. "I don't have any choice here but to have everybody meet back at the farmhouse outside Crawfordville, just like we planned. But there's no reason why you can't take your pot—I mean right now—load up the van and go on. Soon as you have it loaded, you go. Dave, Rock, and me can handle it from here. That Lloyd fellow seems like a stand-up guy. Tank must've known him pretty good."

Nicky was hours away from being done with the job if he didn't go, but he had to ask. "Why?"

"Why what?"

"Why are you letting me go now?"

"Man, don't look a gift horse in the mouth. Take the shit and go. Get Tank and Kitty and get out of here." Bobby glanced back at the beach. "You weren't ever one of us. You know what I mean? I want you and Kitty and Tank out of this before the shit hits the fan because I feel it coming. I owe the old man that much. I can't save him, but maybe I can save you and the girl."

Before Nicky could ask another question, Bobby jerked his head toward the dirt road at the sound of a truck with a bad muffler. "What the fuck now?"

Nicky flinched, not sure which scared him more, Bobby or the approaching truck.

"Got a gun?" Bobby asked without taking his eyes from the lights of the approaching truck.

"No."

"Here." Bobby handed him the .38. "Keep it handy. Now, be cool." Bobby bent over, pulled a .22 from his boot, and shoved it into the holster on his belt. He raised his rifle and held it across his chest. "Babydoll here," he said, patting the M-16, "will make most folks take note."

When the pickup got closer, they saw that four people were crowded into the front seat, three men with a girl sitting on the lap of the man by the passenger door. Nicky could smell the marijuana smoke drifting out of the open windows. The driver pulled up beside them and stopped.

"Got a little gang bang planned, you guys need to take it down the road some," Bobby said.

Nicky didn't like the way this felt, and he wondered—not for the first time that night—where Polky was.

"This ain't no private beach," the driver said, turning off the engine but leaving the headlights on. His whiskey breath wafted out as he spoke.

Bobby muttered, "Shit. Stoned and drunk both. Great, just fucking great. Stupid, too, mouthing off in front of a damn M-16."

Nicky didn't think for one second the guy would believe him, but he wanted to try and head off what he thought might be coming. "Tonight it's private. We're the cops, got a stakeout. This place is off-limits. Now get."

"Cops, my ass." The driver opened his door and hopped out. As soon as he was standing on the ground, he swung a rifle up and pointed it at Bobby.

Bobby jerked his weapon around and fired into the man's face at point-blank range. The girl screamed as bits and pieces of skull, skin, mucus, and brain sprayed back into the cab of the truck. She pushed open the passenger door, jumped out, and started running.

Bobby swung his rifle toward the two men still in the pickup. "Don't even think about moving."

The girl, still screaming, tripped and fell. When she stood, she shut up and, without looking back, took off running again. Bobby kept the rifle on the men, but with his left hand, he pulled the .22 out of his belt. Before Nicky could say anything, he raised the pistol and fired three rounds at the girl. When she collapsed like a rag doll, Bobby put the .22 back in its holster and held the M-16 with both hands, one finger on the trigger.

Nicky looked at the man crumpled in the sand near his feet and vomited right on top of the bloody stump of a head.

"Well, you're a handy man to have around. Get your damn gun up," Bobby said to him. He wiggled the M-16 at the two men in the pickup. "Get out. Real slow."

Nicky raised the gun and pointed it at Bobby for a split second. Then he turned it toward the pickup as the two men climbed out. One of the men was older and dressed in a plaid flannel shirt, but the other was just a kid with pimples and wearing a jean jacket over a Pink Floyd T-shirt.

The sound of feet pounding the sand carried over the rush of the tides. Bobby held his rifle on the two men but twisted slightly toward the noise. "Don't take your eyes off of them," he told Nicky. "And don't you ever point a gun at me again."

Lloyd and Dave ran over. When Dave saw the body, he stopped and stared.

Lloyd hurried over to the girl and knelt beside her. "She's still alive."

"Yeah, a .22's not a real serious gun, is it?" Bobby said.

"We should try to do something for her," Lloyd said.

"Like what? Call an ambulance?" Bobby glanced at Lloyd, his eyes narrow slits in his dark face. "You see any phone booths, you let me know."

"Let her be and get over here a minute," Dave said.

Nicky stood still, trying not to throw up again while avoiding looking at the dead body. The gun shook in his hand, but he kept it trained on the newcomers.

Slowly Lloyd turned away from her and walked back to Bobby. "I didn't bargain for this."

"None of us did. This shithead jumped me." Bobby pointed his foot at the weapon under the body. "Get his rifle, Dave."

"I done told you. We didn't bargain on no killing." Lloyd glared at Bobby in the reflected glow from the headlights. "I'm taking my men, and we're getting."

Keeping his revolver pointed at the ground near Lloyd's feet, Dave stooped and picked up the dead man's rifle with his left hand. He shook the weapon a little, dislodging a clump of gore from the stock.

Bobby skirted around the dead man and moved closer to the two men from the pickup. "Let me fucking think here a minute."

Dave eased nearer too. "Damn it all!"

"Quiet," Bobby said. "Don't be yelling."

Nicky figured the girl's screaming and the gunfire had alerted anyone in hearing range, so Dave's shouting hardly mattered. He felt like screaming himself.

Dave was breathing hard, almost gasping, with his eyes wide and his lips parted. He cut his eyes from man to man as if looking for someone or something then lifted his gun and pointed it toward the two men from the truck. Watching Dave's stricken face, Nicky stepped back, ready to run if Dave started shooting.

"Be cool," Bobby whispered.

Dave stood still for a few seconds as his breathing became normal. He lowered his rifle and turned to Lloyd. "You okay with just taking the pot you got loaded already and going to the farmhouse? We'll meet you there and pay you off, and you guys get."

Bobby jerked around and glared at Dave. "When did you take over?"

The older of the two pickup men lunged toward Nicky. Startled, Nicky jumped back and pulled the trigger. The bullet went wild. The man continued his leap and tackled Nicky around the ankles. Nicky brought the gun down hard on the side of the man's head, knocking him loose. As the guy rolled away, Nicky kicked him in the side.

Dave poked the nose of the dead man's rifle against the older man's face. "Get back over there with your friend."

When the .38 slipped from Nicky's sweaty hand, Lloyd snatched it up and held it loosely at his side. "I want the money now, here."

"Yeah, right, like I'm carrying it with me," Bobby snapped. "You want the cash, you got to come back to the farmhouse."

Nicky gulped air and tried to stand steady. Lloyd looked furious, but Nicky was too terrified to be mad. Still, if he were Lloyd, he'd skip meeting at the farmhouse and just take the trucks full of pot and be in New Orleans before the whores in the Red Light district woke up.

"I ask you again," Dave said, his voice now calm. "You cool with leaving, taking your men and the trucks back to the farmhouse? We'll be right behind and pay you off. You don't even have to unload the vans at the farm. Just take the pot out of your own trucks so you can leave clean."

Lloyd stared at Bobby. The scavenged .38 still dangled at Lloyd's side, pointed at the ground. Nicky had a stitch in his side as if he had been running hard, and his mouth tasted bitter from the vomit.

"Nope," Lloyd said. "I ain't cool with that, but what choice I got? We'll leave right now. But I'll take that girl and drop her off first house we come to in Carrabelle, get them to call in help for her. Then we'll go to the farmhouse. You give us the money, and we all forget this beach."

Bobby looked over at Nicky. "See if there's any rope in that truck, something to tie these two up with. I'm getting tired of holding this gun on them."

Dave moved to stand beside Bobby. "I got them." He pointed the rifle at the man who'd tried to jump Nicky.

Glad to have something to do that took him away from the bloody mess on the beach, Nicky started rummaging in the truck. A minute later, he came out with some electrical wire and fishing line.

"That'll work for now," Lloyd said and snatched the wire from Nicky. He and Bobby tied up the two men while Nicky stood, shivering again, and watched.

Dave never took his rifle off the men, even after they were tied up.

"Yeah. That's what we'll do," Bobby said as if he had carefully considered it. "You're part of it now, Lloyd, like it or not. That'll keep your mouth shut, won't it? You might want to think about how much you're going to like Raiford before you go dropping off that girl at some house up the road. That prison's full of men who'll love helpful folks like you."

Lloyd didn't say anything but went back to the girl. He bent as if to pick her up then straightened. "Don't matter now. You put enough .22s in a person's back, I reckon it'll do the job."

"She's dead?" Bobby asked.

Lloyd just shook his head and started walking back to his men and the trucks.

"Dave, you go with him," Bobby said.

Lloyd stopped walking as if waiting for something else to happen. He still held the pistol in his hand.

"No," Dave said. "Send Nicky back with him to bring the van up. We got to get these bodies dumped somewhere, and we can't be driving along in this pickup with two dead bodies rolling around in the truck bed and those two tied up. And get some line off one of the boats. I don't trust that electrical wire on those two."

Bobby scowled. Nicky figure Bobby didn't like Dave acting like he was in charge, but Dave was making good sense.

"Here." Dave held the dead man's rifle out to Nicky. "Take this with you."

Nicky took it but shuddered as he wrapped his hand around the stock.

"Now don't you worry none," Lloyd said. "We're not going to hurt Tank's boy. He don't need the rifle." He started heading back to his own men.

Nicky hesitated, not sure if he was supposed to follow Lloyd or not. Dave had been staring hard at the tied-up guys, but he stopped, went over to the girl's body, and turned her over. Not wanting to see any more, Nicky started walking away, staying a few steps behind Lloyd and dragging more than carrying the dead man's rifle. A few steps down the beach, while he was still in the glow of the truck's headlights, he dropped the rifle in the sand.

Behind him, Bobby said, "Reckon it was too messy for the boy."

Nicky spun around and lurched toward Bobby. He was tired of being called "boy," and he was tired of Bobby being the badass and Dave calming down so easily in the face of a dead girl and a blown-up head.

"Cool down, Nicky," Dave said. "We got bigger problems." He reached into the truck and dimmed the headlights. Motioning to Bobby, he walked a few feet away into the dark mist. "Come over here, will you? You too, Nicky. Hang back a while with us before you go get that van and check on Lloyd's men."

"What?" Bobby whispered when they were all together.

"That boy, the one still got the pimples on his face, that's Polky's kid brother. The girl, I'm not sure." Dave looked back over his shoulder toward where her body lay in the sand. "They might've been passing her back and forth between them, or she might've been one of them's girlfriend, but she's been hanging with them since they left Polk County."

Nicky clenched his hands into fists. *Damn Polky. He must have put them up to this.*

Inhaling deeply as if to calm himself, Bobby asked, "How do you know this?"

"I brought them out of Polk County with me. We met in a bar in Bartow. The girl and the kid are underage, but it was that kind of bar. We all wanted to get out of Polk County before we ended up working in the phosphate mines or drowned in one of the damn pits they leave behind."

"But Jimmy said—"

"Sure, Jimmy said what you wanted him to say. What'd you expect?"

Bobby let the shotgun drop by his right leg. He rubbed his eyes with the back of his sleeve. "We can't be leaving that kind of loose end."

"Tell me."

"There's a big sinkhole over near Perry. I know the trail, and I think the van can get back there. I've dumped shit in it before. We take the bodies there and weigh them down with something."

Dave sniffed then rubbed his nose against his sleeve. "Could work. The gulls'll get any of the mess left from the guy you blasted. Weather like this, nobody's coming to the beach this morning. Anybody sees blood in a day or two won't think human."

"Right." Bobby spit, pointing away from Dave but at Nicky's feet. "So what do we do with the other two?"

Nicky glanced out at the Gulf, figuring it wasn't going to be that long until dawn. Whatever they were going to do, they needed to be doing it. Rain or not, daylight wasn't the time to be moving bodies.

"Tell them we're going to let them go then plug them at the sinkhole and shove them in." Dave caught Nicky's eyes when he spoke as if to warn him not to object.

Bobby nodded. "Only way."

"Can't leave loose ends like that, especially when they know me." Dave shook his head. "I remember the only thing that girl ever said directly to me. That night at the bar, I asked her if she needed to go home and pack or anything. She grabbed up her purse and said, no, she had her driver's license, ten bucks, and drugs if we needed them."

"Well, traveling light didn't help her much in the long run, did it?" Bobby snickered.

At the sound of Bobby's half laughter, Nicky started to lunge forward, but Dave grabbed his arm and got between them, moving so smoothly that Bobby didn't seem to notice. The three of them walked back to the two men, Dave between Nicky and Bobby.

When they got to the truck, Bobby squatted in front of the two bound men. "I don't think you guys are upstanding members of the community. So it's just your word against ours as to what happened here. Besides, I'll just bet you came out here to steal some dope. That makes you part of the dope running, so under the law, you're just as guilty as anybody who pulled the trigger. That's called a felony murder rap."

"Where's Polky?" the younger one asked. "He's my brother, and he'll—"

"Shut up," the other man said. "Jus' shut the fuck up."

"Naw, kid, you talk all you want to. What're you saying?" Bobby asked.

"Polky's my brother, man. He'll vouch for me. He's supposed to be down there now, unloading."

"Yeah, well, he isn't," Bobby said.

"Aw, man. I knew I shouldn't've given him those 'ludes."

Bobby's jaw twitched. "Reckon not."

"Don't matter, does it?" Polky's brother sounded desperate. "He told us to come up and help out. Said y'all was shorthanded. Elmo there, he just got freaked, you know, when you said you was cops."

"What about the girl?" Bobby asked, rocking back on his heels.

"Aw, she don't mean nothing. Just some tail, that's all. Kind of a shame, though. She had real nice tits."

Nicky kicked the kid in the gut, and when he flopped over on his side, Nicky kicked him again in the kidney. "You must have some serious inbreeding in your family."

Bobby smirked. "Don't let my morally righteous friend here bother you. We'll just load you up in the van, take you out deep in the woods, give you some money, and a bale or two of pot. By the time you walk out, we'll be gone, and you'll have the dope and the money. Work for you?"

The kid groaned, writhing in the sand. The other man said nothing.

"Go on then, Nicky. Check on Lloyd and bring back your van."

Nicky turned and headed back toward where Kitty's van waited with Lloyd and the others. He kept his eyes out for the rifle he'd dropped but didn't see it.

Might be just as well.

Chapter Twenty-Eight

Lloyd's men were gathered in a knot and mumbling so loudly Nicky could hear them as he approached. Two of the trucks had their headlights on, and the brightness hurt Nicky's eyes.

"I heard shots, and I just started running down the road to get away," a young man in a frayed corduroy jacket said. "I was fixing to leave, let me tell you, man, 'cause I figured if somebody was shot, I wasn't going to stay around. And then I got about halfway down the road, and I thought, I'm just freaking out, and if I leave, that would probably be the worst thing I could do."

The man he was talking to nodded. "Yeah, I was on the trawler and heard them shots. Four of them, I counted. I thought I'd jump in the water and swim to shore and hightail it out a there, but that water's cold. But let me tell you, I left that bale of pot on the deck, jumped in my little johnboat, and got back here."

In one of the rented trucks, Blue Jacket sat in the cab, sucking on a fifth of whiskey. Lloyd opened the door, reached in, and took the bottle. After Lloyd took a couple of long gulps and coughed, he wiped off the mouth of the bottle with the hem of his jacket and passed it to Nicky. Nicky took a sip and tried not to puke again.

"Go on, you earned a better shot than that," Lloyd said.

Nicky nodded and took a bigger swig. He promised himself that if he got out of this alive, he was never going to smoke another joint in his life.

"Let me have another nip. Then you finish it if you want." Lloyd took the bottle, slurped some more down, swallowing loudly, then handed it back to Nicky.

Nicky guzzled the remaining whiskey too fast, and dizziness hit him hard for a moment. Then he followed Lloyd as he maneuvered through the men, who parted but stared hard as if waiting for some direction or explanation. Or maybe just their money. When they got to Kitty's van, a low, steady grumble rose from the gathered men.

Lloyd shoved Nicky toward the driver's-side door. "You watch your back real careful like. And don't say shit to nobody."

Nicky crawled into Kitty's van and headed back to Sand Ditch Road. With nothing but his parking lights on, Nicky pulled up near the dead man's pickup. He climbed out of the van and slunk over to Dave and Bobby.

"It's all set," Bobby said.

"What's happening back there?" Dave asked.

"They got everybody on the beach, ready to head out. Lloyd's got it under control." Nicky shook himself like a wet dog, wishing he had more whiskey.

Bobby nodded, his head a silhouette against the horizon. "You and Nicky gag those guys and throw them in the van."

After they forced the bound men into the back of the van, Bobby eyed Nicky before turning to Dave. "You better go back there and see that they go to the farmhouse and don't get any wild ideas."

"Sure," Dave said, holding the dead man's rifle up to the van's parking lights. "A puny little thing. What'd that guy think he'd do with this?"

Bobby glanced at his M-16 then handed it to Dave. "Take Baby-doll. She'll put the fear in them."

"What about you?" Dave asked. "That just leaves you with that little pistol."

"Give me your gun. Between that and my .22, I think I can handle Nicky, don't you?"

Dave made a guttural sound and handed over the Colt. He held the M-16 tightly in his right hand as he walked toward Lloyd and his men.

Bobby pointed at the dead man and the dead girl a few feet away. "You load those bodies into the van. Cover them up. Leave those guys right there in the van. They aren't going anywhere. I'm going to take the skiff and check in real quick with Rock on the trawler. I'll get me a shotgun and a couple of .38s for us."

Nicky nodded.

"Here." Bobby handed Nicky the .22 pistol. "You need to, don't shoot wild this time. And turn the damn lights out once you load the bodies." He ran off toward the skiff.

Bobby had barely disappeared when Nicky vomited out all the whiskey Lloyd had given him. Dizzy, he cut off the lights like Bobby had ordered, but he couldn't make himself go near the dead bodies. Glad for the darkness, he sank down in the sand, the cold dampness seeping through his pants. The beach tilted and spun. He hadn't slept in over forty-eight hours, and he hadn't eaten enough to count. Drinking that whiskey and drinking it fast had been a mistake. He closed his eyes, hoping the dizziness would pass.

Nicky jerked awake. The night was darker with clouds covering the setting moon. He couldn't believe he'd slept—or passed out, he wasn't sure which. He could barely see Bobby towering over him, but he heard the man's hard breathing. Rock poked Nicky's leg with his boot but didn't say a word.

"Hurry the hell up. And stop being so useless," Bobby said. "I'll drive the van. Rock, you take the pickup, and Nicky will ride with me. It's a bit of a drive, so stay close. We're going out to a sinkhole. We'll dump the bodies and be done with it all."

Nicky didn't move.

"You hear me?" Bobby snapped. "Get up. Now. We've got to hurry."

Nicky brought the back of his hand up to his forehead. "Yeah. I hear you."

"Come on, then," Bobby said. "Get in the van. We'll dump the pickup in the sinkhole, too, so there won't be any tracing it."

Neither Bobby nor Rock turned on their headlights until they hit the paved road. Bobby didn't speak, and his breathing remained harsh and loud in the cab of the pickup.

As Bobby drove, Nicky tried to stay awake. Bobby didn't speak or play the radio. Nicky rolled the window down and stuck his head out in the whoosh of air, breathing deeply.

Nicky told himself that when Bobby stopped to pee or stretch or take a break, he would run. *Get away from Bobby, just run out into the woods on the side of the road and disappear like Polky had. Then I'll go back for Kitty and Tank.* But Bobby didn't stop.

An hour later, Nicky's head hurt as if his brain had swollen too big to fit inside his skull. He wanted to be almost anywhere else than where he was going.

A pink glow had appeared on the horizon by the time Bobby turned onto an unmarked dirt road just east of the Econfina River. The narrow dirt road soon became little more than a break in the trees.

After a slow, bumpy haul, and a time or two when the wheels ground and spun, they pulled into a clearing. Bobby stopped the van and turned off the engine. From the open window, the sounds of birds, frogs, and insects drifted in with the sticky air.

"Don't you quit on me," Bobby said. "Now get out. Rock and me need your help."

They stepped out of the van, and Bobby came around to Nicky's side. As Bobby slid open the back panel door, Rock pulled up on the other side of the vehicle.

Ignoring the two bound men, Bobby stuck his head in and looked toward the back. "Where're the damn bodies?" He spun around and grabbed the front of Nicky's shirt, his one hand bunching up the fabric and the other raised like a fist.

Nicky shuddered and licked his lips. Some kind of dried crud had collected in the corners of his mouth. His lips tasted salty, and he was so thirsty he feared he'd faint if he didn't get some water. Rock walked around the rear of the van and came up behind Bobby.

"I said, where are the damn bodies?" Bobby shook Nicky a little by his shirt.

Nicky jerked away so hard his shirt tore, leaving a strip of cloth in Bobby's hand. Bobby flung the material down, pulled back his right fist, and punched Nicky in the nose. Nicky stumbled and fell, the world spinning. He rolled over on all fours like a dog and vomited. Nothing but bile came up, and he dry heaved for several seconds while blood from his nose ran down into his open mouth. He finally sat back on his haunches. Bobby pulled the .38 from his belt holster and pointed it at the young kid in the van.

Nicky cried, "Don't! For God's sake, don't."

Rock stepped between Nicky and Bobby, his rifle pointed at Nicky's head.

Bobby fired. The kid jerked then slumped to the side, a crimson stain erupting on his chest. He gurgled, twitched a bit, then fell still.

The older man inside the van tried to roll toward the rear. Bobby shot him before he'd moved more than a foot. The man spasmed then stopped moving.

Bobby walked over to Nicky, bent, and put the hot barrel of the .38 against Nicky's cheek. It felt like a caress against his cold face.

"You left those bodies on the beach, didn't you?" Bobby sounded oddly calm.

Nicky nodded.

"Well shit, boy. By the time we get back there, it'll be bright out, and I'm not trying to move bodies in the full light of day."

Bobby eased up out of his crouch and pointed the gun at Nicky's head. "You fucked up bad. You know that?"

Nicky tried to say a prayer, but his mouth wouldn't work. Somewhere in the distance, a dog barked. Nicky rolled his head to the side and looked up. The sun was breaking behind the trees, and streaks of gold and red filled the sky. He figured it would be his last sunrise. He wished he were on a beach on the Gulf of Mexico, hot in the bright blaze of a midday sun, not shivering deep in the pine forests of northern Florida.

"Room for one more body in the sinkhole." Rock toed Nicky with the point of his boot. "But I say we keep this'n. He'll be a good boy, we let him grow up some."

Bobby kept the gun on Nicky, but he eyed Rock and finally nodded. "Get up, damn you. Rock and me can use you yet."

Nicky rolled over on his side and climbed to his feet. He breathed with his dry mouth wide open.

Bobby waved at the van with his gun. "We'll have to shut that van and shove it all in the sinkhole. Hate to push the van in, too, but all that blood'll be hard to clean. We'll drive the pickup out but ditch it soon as we can."

Nicky wiped off his face with his sleeve and nodded. They rolled Kitty's van into the sinkhole, then they crowded into the pickup with Rock at the wheel and Nicky crushed in the middle. His head ached, and his gut churned like he was in the throes of a bad hangover.

Just past nine thirty, they pulled up at the farmhouse. Nicky looked up, surprised that he was actually there and not lying dead somewhere along the side of the road. He spotted his own blue pickup parked in the scattered collection of trucks and men outside the house.

How'd that get here? He eyed his truck hard, wondering if he was hallucinating. He had left it outside the motel for Kitty with strict orders that no one was to move it. Only Kitty had the key.

Bobby opened his door and stepped out of the pickup. "Get out," he snapped.

Nicky scooted across the seat and climbed out to stand beside Bobby. Rock came around the front of the truck and joined them.

Bobby pulled off his bloody shirt as he walked toward the front door. He handed it to Rock. "Burn it. And get rid of Babydoll. I won't have anybody tracking it back to me if this goes south." Once they were inside the house, he slipped off his dirty pants. "Nicky, strip down so we can burn those clothes."

Nicky pulled off his shirt, crusted as it was, but he kept his pants on. Bobby was down to his jockeys when Kitty and Polky walked in from the kitchen. As soon as Nicky saw Kitty, a wave of nausea zipped through him so fiercely that he fell back against the wall and bent over, grabbing his stomach. He'd gotten her killed too.

Bobby barely glanced at Kitty before he lunged at Polky. After Bobby's first punch, Polky got in a weak right cross to Bobby's jaw before Bobby hit him so hard that blood flew and splattered on Kitty's shirt. She screamed and jumped back toward Nicky. As Bobby continued pummeling Polky, she turned away.

Bobby finished with Polky's head and went for his kidneys. When Polky collapsed, Bobby picked him up by his belt and collar and flung him against the wall. Polky slid down to the floor and lay still.

Bobby spun toward Kitty and Nicky, his eyes crazy with his anger. He had blood on his torso, and a large jagged scar cut across his right side, the tissue raised and puckered.

For a moment, Nicky really saw Bobby's face, and his features registered maybe for the first time. The man's eyes were practically black. His nose was hooked and looked as if it had been broken, and his lips were strangely full, like Mick Jagger's.

"Nicky?"

Kitty's voice cracked through Nicky's paralysis. He grabbed Kitty and pushed her out the door. "Run," he sputtered.

But instead of running, she stood there. "What the hell is going—"

"Go. Damn it, run." He shoved her, wanting to make her sprint away, but instead, she stumbled and fell. Neither of them had time to say another word before Bobby and Rock came out after them.

"Get back inside," Bobby said, looming over Kitty.

Rock raised his shotgun a little. Nicky yanked Kitty to her feet and towed her back into the house by her hand. When he turned around, he saw Dave coming through the doorway with Lloyd behind him.

Bobby eyed Dave. "Watch them, will you?" He turned to Lloyd. "Don't you get any ideas, not you or your men. You and Rock come in the kitchen."

Nicky tugged at Kitty's arm, thinking they might make a dash for it. But Dave stepped between them and the door.

"Get in that bedroom." Dave pointed with the rifle toward an open door to their right. "Some of my stuff's in there, so put some clean clothes on. And for God's sake, keep quiet."

Nicky pulled Kitty into the bedroom and shut the door. His mouth seemed cemented shut with dried blood and vomit, and his tongue couldn't even lick his lips anymore. She went to the sink in the half bath connected to the bedroom, rinsed out a glass crusted with toothpaste, and filled it with tap water.

She carried it back to him and thrust it at him. "Here, drink this."

Nicky took a gulp but gagged at the taste of sulfur. He swallowed the bile that rose in his throat and tried again. That time, he drank it and held out the glass for more.

After his second glass, he collapsed on the bed and curled up into a fetal position. A ragged pile of clothes was spread across the end of the bed as if someone had dumped a suitcase. He grabbed a flannel shirt and pulled it over him like a blanket then closed his eyes.

Outside the bedroom door, the guttural noises of men talking rose and fell like the sound of dogs barking in the distance. After a few minutes, Kitty started washing off his face with a thin washcloth she must have gotten from the bathroom.

"Listen to me," she said. "I don't know what's happening here, but I came to get you so we can take Tank home to Dolphin Cove. I drove him to the house in Apalachicola last night in your pickup, and CeCe's with him now, waiting on me to get you and the van. He's bad off, and I can't get him to go to a doctor or hospital, but he did agree to go home. We need you. And we need the van so we can put a mattress in it for Tank."

He couldn't think of what to say. He lowered his eyes, unable even to look at her.

"Polky was hanging around Tank's house when I got there, asking for you. He was upset because his brother's missing. I got him to tell me where y'all were supposed to meet. He was all doped up, but he was able to tell me where to turn while I drove."

He nodded.

She straightened and stared down at him, the wet washcloth clenched in her hand. "Any reason you can't put on that shirt and we just walk out of here?"

"Bobby'll kill us if we don't play this right. The man's crazy."

"Oh God, Nicky. What have you gotten into?"

Hearing the fear in Kitty's voice, Nicky sat up and moved to the edge of the bed. He stuffed his arms into the sleeves of the flannel shirt, glad for its cover, though it hung huge on his frame.

He looked around the room, thinking Kitty might have a better chance of getting out if she went now and went alone. "You go." The window on the far wall was wide enough. They were lucky it was on the opposite side of the house from the kitchen where Bobby and

Rock had disappeared with Lloyd. "You got the keys to my truck? On you, I mean?"

She patted the pocket of her jeans and nodded.

"You got your stuff and the money with you in the pickup?"

"I got the money hid good in the pickup, but my clothes are back at the house."

"Forget your stuff then. Crawl out that window and get in the truck and go. Anybody tries to stop you, you just keep going. If you have to, just run into the woods, but you keep going. You understand me? Don't go back to Tank's. Bobby'll know to find you there. Don't even go to your apartment in Tallahassee. I don't think he knows where it's at, but don't take the chance."

"I have to go get Tank, Nicky. He's—"

"No. Don't you see? Bobby'd know just where to find you if you go back there now. If you run, he's got to figure you know too much and come after you. But if you stay, he might just kill us all to clean house. So you got to go, and you have to do it right now. And you can't go any place where he knows to find you."

"I can't leave Tank." She flung the washcloth at him. "Damn you for getting us into this."

"*Tank* got us into this. Now shut up and go out that window."

"I can get Daddy and be gone inside an hour."

He cocked his head, studying her. She hadn't called Tank "Daddy" since she'd been fourteen and moved in with Nicky and CeCe. "You can't take that chance."

He spun around and checked the window to make sure it wasn't painted shut. He unlatched it and got the pane up a foot or so before he turned back to her. "Bobby can be there at Tank's and shoot you both inside an hour. He could even call and have somebody waiting for you. He's already killed four people, so doing more won't matter 'cause they can't electrocute you but once."

She moaned, a small, scared sound from the back of her throat.

He went over and put an arm around her. "He won't go after Tank unless you or me are there. Tank doesn't know anything about what happened on the beach. He didn't see anything."

"*I* didn't see anything either."

"Yeah, you did. You saw him come in all bloody. You know about the pot, and Bobby probably thinks I'm spilling my guts to you right now. That makes you more dangerous. He'll figure you didn't have anything to do with it, but you know all about it and can talk to the cops. Me, I can't say anything else or I'll go to jail too. See? You can't take the chance, not with Bobby the way he is right now. You understand?"

After a moment, she nodded. "What about you?"

"Like I said, I'm part of it. You know about the felony murder rap? It doesn't matter who pulls the trigger. Everybody is just as guilty. Bobby knows that'll keep me quiet. Let him calm down, and sooner or later, he'll let me go. Now, you get. Go up to that park just over the Florida line in Georgia. You know the one we stayed at once? I'll find you there. Just promise me you won't go back just yet for Tank. Let CeCe take care of him. We'll get them both later, have CeCe meet us someplace safe. But now you've got to stay away from where Bobby can find you unless you want him to kill you, Tank, and CeCe too. Promise?"

Kitty inhaled, straightened, and eased over to the open window. "Okay."

Nicky reached out to hug her but faltered, suddenly dizzy and weak as if he might slip away from himself. She carefully knocked out the screen.

When she was halfway out the window, she looked back and asked, "Where's my van?"

Nicky stared as if he didn't understand the question. Then he collapsed back on the bed. She *was* part of it. If he didn't get her killed, he'd get her arrested.

"Oh God, Kitty. It was full of blood, so Bobby had us push it in a sinkhole outside of Perry." He paused, wondering whether it was better to tell her the rest or not.

"What?" she practically shouted.

"Quiet." He cocked his head toward the bedroom door and listened for the sound of footsteps. Hearing nothing, he looked at Kitty and whispered, "There's dead people in it."

"Damn you, Nicky. Damn you to hell and back." She didn't shout, but her tone was harsh.

"Kitty, I—"

"Fuck you!"

"For God's sake, Kitty, keep quiet."

"That makes me part of it, doesn't it?"

"Anybody picks you up, you act dumb. Tell them the van was stolen. That don't work, make a deal, even if you have to spill your guts. And don't worry about me or Tank."

"Spill my guts? Isn't that just what Bobby's going to be worried about? With me, I mean. They find that van, they come for me, and I rat out Bobby or go to jail. Great choices, huh?"

"They won't find that van—"

"You want to bet my life on it?"

"No. You got to go. *Now.* And don't be going near Tank."

"Damn you to hell, Nicky." Without looking back at him, she crawled the rest of the way out the window.

He got up and eased the windowpane down then motioned for her to go. His pickup was out on the far edge of the driveway, and a few men he didn't know were milling around between her and the truck. She walked around the men, and a few glanced at her, but nobody tried to stop her. Exhaling in relief, Nicky figured they just wanted their money and to get out. They must have seen her come in and probably thought she was all right to come and go.

Planning to distract Dave or Bobby from looking out in the yard, Nicky latched the window, crossed the room, and opened the bedroom door. He heard Bobby's voice coming from the kitchen. Then he spotted Dave coming out of the far corner and heading for the front door with the dead man's rifle in his hands.

"Please," Nicky whispered. "Let her go."

Dave turned around, raised the rifle, and aimed it at Nicky's head. They stood that way long enough for sweat to begin to pool under Nicky's arms and roll down his face.

"Shit," Dave said. He lowered the rifle. "You keep your ass right here. Don't even think about leaving."

Dave turned away from the front. A few steps later, he pushed open the kitchen door and disappeared into the room, dragging the rifle by his side.

Nicky wanted to cheer when the sound of his truck starting reached him. He stood still until he heard Kitty pulling away from the house.

Chapter Twenty-Nine

Nicky stood befuddled outside the bedroom door, thinking he needed to do something and fast. He didn't see Polky or Lloyd, and the few men still in the house were hurrying out the front door. His best bet was probably to go after them and beg a ride. But just as he stepped toward the door, Bobby stormed out of the kitchen and charged him like an enraged bull. Dave and Lloyd were right behind him.

"Motherfucker, son of a bitch!" Bobby yelled so loud spit flew onto Nicky. "You leave those bodies on the beach, and now you let your girlfriend just walk out of here."

Before Nicky could move or say anything, Bobby hit him in the jaw hard enough to snap back his head. The next punch knocked him to the floor. Bobby snatched up a rifle from a nearby table and pointed it at Nicky's head.

"Whoa, now," Dave said. "You want another body to get rid of? One associated with us?"

Lloyd stepped close to Bobby. "That's Tank's boy. You ain't killing Tank's boy."

"He's not Tank's son," Bobby said, but after a moment, he lowered the gun.

Nicky rolled over and got to his knees. Before he could gain his feet, Bobby smashed the stock of the rifle across his head. Nicky collapsed, slamming against the hard floor. Then the world went dark.

When Nicky woke up, he was lying in the back of what he figured was one of the moving vans. The vehicle was traveling fast, and an overpowering smell of pot seemed almost to smother him in the crowded darkness of the cargo compartment. His head pounded, his jaw and eye pulsed with pain, and he was parched.

He ran his hands over his body, searching for wounds, but other than the hurt from Bobby's beating, he didn't feel any new injuries. He patted his pants pocket, relieved when he felt the familiar pad of his wallet. He pulled it out and checked to make sure his money and driver's license were still in it.

Stumbling in the dark, he made his way to the back doors. When he tried to open them, they wouldn't give. But the locks apparently were designed to lock people out not in, so he jumped on the handle with his full weight. He fell over a bale of pot as he bounced off the catch, but the handle cracked and gave way.

He opened one side just enough to look out. The van was somewhere on a back road in the countryside. He thought of jumping out, but the idea of hitting the pavement at that speed seemed suicidal.

He hunkered down, resting against a bale. The only thing he could do was wait until the van stopped and hope he could get away. He meant to stay awake and alert, but as he wondered who was driving, he drifted off to sleep.

A clanking sound woke him. The van wasn't moving. With unsteady hands, Nicky eased one back door open a crack and looked out into the night. They were stopped at a railroad crossing.

Nicky pushed the doors open and jumped down. His feet hit the pavement hard enough to hurt his knees, but he ignored the pain and ran toward some buildings to his right. He sprinted between two of them and turned left once through the alley. He kept going until he couldn't breathe anymore, then he dropped to his knees, heaving in the grassy field behind a warehouse.

Once he caught his breath, he got up and started walking. When he'd gone a couple of miles, he spotted an all-night gas station with a water fountain and a bathroom. After guzzling water until he felt sick, he headed to the bathroom. His face in the mirror scared him—swollen cheeks, purple bruises, two black eyes, and blood around his mouth and splattered on the collar of Dave's too-large shirt. He used the bathroom, washed his face, and stepped back inside the station. The nervous clerk kept a tight grip on a baseball bat as Nicky picked up a Coke and a Moon Pie and took them to the counter.

"Got a bus station around here?" Nicky asked as he paid for the items.

"Truck stop 'bout five miles out of town. Bet's Place." The clerk eyed Nicky and twisted the bat in his hands. "Take the road out front, head right."

As rough as he looked, he didn't figure he could hitch a ride. He hoped he had enough money to get a bus ticket back to Tallahassee. He didn't know where he was, but he couldn't be that far from the farmhouse in Crawfordville. Five miles. He could walk that.

It turned out he was farther west than he'd realized, all the way to the outskirts of New Orleans. He had to wait a couple of hours for the next bus going east, and then it took ten hours to make it back to Tallahassee.

Once there, he walked to Kitty's efficiency apartment. He'd only been there the day he helped her move in, and he didn't have a key, so he planned to break in. But when he got there, he found the front door slightly open with splintered wood around the jamb.

He hoped Kitty had listened to him and hadn't come back. He tiptoed into the one-room apartment in case whoever had broken in was still there, but the place was empty. After gulping the last of the milk in her refrigerator and stuffing a few slices of bread into his mouth, he took a shower. Once clean, he took the time to spread some peanut butter on the rest of the bread before eating it. By the time he finished, dawn was breaking, so he sat on Kitty's lumpy bed, picked up the phone, and dialed Tank's number.

"Hello." CeCe's voice sounded strained, maybe scared.

"It's me," Nicky said. "Are you all right? Do you know where Kitty is?"

"They don't have Kitty, but they're looking for her and you both. I told her to run. Don't come here. They—"

After a rattling noise, Rock's voice came over the phone. "Where are you?"

Nicky hung up. He pulled his shoes on and left the apartment.

After walking a mile or so, he stopped at a discount store to buy a decent shirt, a Coke, and some aspirin. He threw Dave's shirt in the trash, put on the new one, headed to the highway, and stuck out his thumb as he walked. Several hours later, an old man in an ancient Dodge picked him up then dropped him off a few miles from his destination. When he got to the park, it was almost night, and he didn't see any sign of Kitty. He slept on the hard, damp ground.

The next morning, a hippie couple in a VW van had a fire going and invited him to join them for eggs and coffee. The man's beard reached the middle of his chest, and the girl had red hair to her waist. They told him they worked day labor at a place called Hopkins, a farm and produce distributor.

"Nothing much in the fields except some cabbage and winter collards," the guy said, "but we still have enough work most days to keep us busy for a few hours."

Nicky rode with them to Hopkins and got work clearing a field to plant peanuts come spring. That night, the couple gave him a thick blanket, a toothbrush, some soap, and supper. He slept beside their van.

A week later, with the Hopkins money, he purchased a cheap sleeping bag, a change of clothes, and some toiletries. Weeks passed. He stayed in the campground, working when he could, bathing in an icy creek, and looking for Kitty in the park. His beard grew in, thick and nearly white against his tanned face.

He tried to call CeCe again a few times from a pay phone near the library, but there was never any answer, and about a month later, the number was disconnected. Nicky was too afraid to go to Apalachicola and see what he could find.

On days he didn't work, he hitched into town and went to the library to read newspapers. At Hopkins, they had a TV that played all day long in the office, and he hung out there on his lunch breaks, watching the news while he ate his meager meals, more hungry for news than food.

Law enforcement had found the bodies on the beach, but they had no suspects. Some sports fishermen phoned in an anonymous tip to the Marine Patrol, saying that they'd seen bales of marijuana floating just west of Egmont Key, near Tampa. When the Marine Patrol went to investigate, they found *The Jackpot* scuttled seventeen miles off Egmont Key. Inside its hull, they confiscated almost eleven bales of marijuana and the decayed body of an unidentified man inside the fish hole.

The DEA traced *The Jackpot* to Jimmy Chukenears, Tank's cousin, and arrested him. As soon as he read that, Nicky called Jimmy's wife, who gave him an earful.

"Jimmy's still in jail," she said. "His lawyer submitted a notarized document that showed *The Jackpot* was leased to Bobby Dozier. So I expect the feds to let him go since they can't show he was directly involved with the pot or the dead body on the trawler." She chuckled in a harsh way. "Jimmy already filed an insurance claim for *The Jackpot.*"

After that, she advised Nicky to leave the area and not bother her again. A few days later, he read a story that said Bobby was wanted for questioning.

As Nicky followed the news accounts over the following weeks, he never saw anything about an arrest of Bobby, and he suspected the DEA had lost interest in the whole soggy mess. One television clip showed the man in charge standing at the marina in Apalachicola and looking out at the fleets of fishing boats. The microphone picked up words he probably didn't mean for the television crew to get.

"Nothing but a bunch of ambitious Florida crackers gone to pot." He laughed, then he explained to the pretty reporter that the dead man was a drug-running fisherman who wouldn't be bothering them anymore and *The Jackpot* would never haul pot again. "We're chasing ghosts," he added.

According to the local papers, the homicide investigators in Franklin County worked a long time, trying to find out who killed those two kids on the beach. They identified the boy as Elmo Johnson, a local twenty-year-old who still ran with the tough teenagers from the high school. The girl was from Polk County, but they didn't give her name because she was a minor.

None of the reports connected the bodies of the teenage girl and the local hood on the beach to the scuttled boat off Egmont Key. They found bales of pot floating off Bald Point where the bodies were found, but so many bales of pot were floating in the bays and inlets of coastal Florida that a whole new set of myths had been created. There was no way the law could link the Alligator Point bales with the Egmont Key bales.

In the spring, when the hippie couple decided to go to Colorado, Nicky rode west with them. If Kitty had ever come to the park, she was long gone and not coming back.

Chapter Thirty

CeCe ground up all of the Dilaudid and Valium pills and mixed the powder with the last of the codeine cough syrup. She held Tank's head up and poured the mixture slowly into his mouth, praying he could swallow and keep it down. Next, she poured in a jigger glass of whiskey.

"Damn them all," she said, putting Tank's head back down on his damp pillow. The doctor had told her the controlled substance laws wouldn't allow him to give her anything stronger or any more of the pills than he had prescribed. Anything more potent would require a hospital, and Tank didn't have any insurance, and he'd given all his money to Kitty. The hospital wouldn't take him because dying wasn't considered an emergency. If he'd had a heart attack, the hospital would have had to admit him, insurance or not, until he was stabilized, but dying of end-stage lung cancer wasn't within the applicable guidelines. Or that's what the bitch at the ER desk had said when she turned them away. So CeCe found a sympathetic doctor who wrote a couple of helpful prescriptions, but even those were playing out.

Tank thrashed a bit, moaning, then he finally began to grow still. CeCe hoped he would die soon. If he didn't, when he woke up, he'd wake up crying out in pain, and she wouldn't have anything but whiskey to give him. Eventually, she would have to think of some lie for the pharmacist or the doctor. Or she'd have to smother him.

She went out to the backyard, bent over, and vomited. When she stood up again, she wiped her mouth with the back of her sleeve and turned to go back into the house. She stopped when she saw a shadow of a man in the side yard, barely out of reach of the back porch's naked yellow light bulb.

CeCe stood still as the man walked toward her. For all she cared, whoever it was could kill her, as long as he also killed Tank. When he got closer, she recognized Dave.

"I thought you'd gone like all the rest of them," she said.

"I did, but I came back to see about you. And Tank."

"Tank's about done for."

"So are you from the looks of things."

"I'm all right. I'm not the one who's dying."

Dave nodded. "Let me help you."

CeCe led him into the house and into Tank's bedroom. The window unit had the room cold, but Tank was sweating. Dave gagged from the smell.

"That's Tank," CeCe said. "I keep him clean, but I can't... I can't fix the odor."

Dave walked over and peered down at Tank.

"I gave him all the rest of the medicine." CeCe stepped up beside Dave. "I hope he dies, because if he doesn't, I'm going to have to smother him if he wakes up. I won't let a man suffer like that anymore."

"Give me an hour, maybe two," Dave said and left.

When he came back, he had heroin and a needle. He got a serving spoon out of the drawer in the kitchen, and CeCe followed him to Tank's room. Dave tapped out the heroin into the spoon and held a cigarette lighter under the bowl of the spoon to melt the drug. He dipped the syringe in and drew up the plunger.

"Tie off his arm above the vein," he said.

She rolled a handkerchief into a rope and tied off Tank's reedy arm. Dave found a vein and injected Tank.

She touched Tank's sunken cheek. "Is that enough to kill him?"

"No, but it'll keep him comfortable."

She nodded and collapsed into a chair drawn close to Tank's bed.

"Why don't you go on to bed? I'll sit up with him. In the morning, we'll ask him if he wants us to give him enough to kill him."

"He can't talk anymore."

"Go to bed, then. We'll see how he is in the morning."

CeCe stood up. As she turned to leave, she rested her hand on Dave's shoulder. "Last thing he said to me was if he could, he'd get up out of that bed and he'd track Bobby down and shoot him. Me, I'd shoot Jimmy, too, for getting everybody into this."

"Don't you be too hard on Jimmy. He's the one who got the stuff here." Dave nodded toward the heroin. "And he says to tell you that Tank's his cousin and he'll do anything he can if you'll just tell him what. Money or if he can hire a nurse or whatever."

"Well, isn't he the great one? Where's he been before now?"

"He just got out of jail yesterday. He doesn't want to come around here till he knows the feds aren't stalking him anymore. He doesn't want to pull you or Tank or anybody else into this mess."

"Good time to think of that."

"Get some rest."

CeCe lay down on the couch and stared at the ceiling in the dark living room. She waited, already tensed for Tank's waking scream.

FOUR WEEKS AFTER BOBBY disappeared, Tank died in his bedroom while CeCe wiped his face with a cool, damp washcloth. She prayed that God would forgive Tank, would forgive them all and have mercy. Dave pulled the blanket over the old man's face and began to pack up the drug paraphernalia.

The night after she had Tank buried in Apalachicola, she opened the door of the rented house in the darkness of predawn to Jimmy.

"Nobody followed me, but I got to be quick." He pressed an envelope thick with money into her hands. "You done what you could for Tank, and I thank you. Now go someplace real nice. Forget all this."

"Where are Nicky and Kitty?" CeCe asked, tightening her grip on the envelope.

"I don't know, but Bobby didn't hurt them. Everybody just ran and scattered into hiding."

CeCe nodded and shut the door. She'd always wanted to see California, and with all that money, she might as well go.

The next morning, Dave approached CeCe as she loaded her suitcase into her car to leave. She looked up at him and shook her head. He stopped and gave her a questioning look. She shook her head again then got into her car and left Apalachicola.

Part III
Luke and Kate
Tallahassee and Concordia, summer 1992

Chapter Thirty-One

Kate woke up disoriented. She reached out to slap her alarm clock, but it wasn't there. Startled, she looked around and saw Barbie pictures on the wall and a white flowered pasteboard bookcase with stuffed bears, plastic horses, seashells, and Golden Books on the shelves. She remembered that she was in Nicky's daughter's room.

Nicky had said his divorce was amicable, with both of them determined not to mess up the little girl. Kate was glad she'd arrived on a weekend the girl was with her mother. If things had been different, she might have wanted to meet the child, but it wasn't the right time.

She sat up on the single bed with its pink-and-green unicorn sheets. The sun shone brightly through the window. Well, she hadn't been planning on making the early-morning church service anyway. It'd been well after midnight when she and Nicky had gotten back to his house from the beach at Bald Point. She was surprised she had slept at all.

She dressed quickly and walked down the hallway, listening for Nicky. In the kitchen, she found an old-fashioned percolator and started a pot of coffee. Once it was brewing, she went to Nicky's room. His bedroom door stood open, and his bed was empty. She ran her hand over the crumpled, twisted sheets. He'd apparently tossed and turned. She could still feel the warmth of him on the material. For a moment, she wanted to crawl into his bed and go back to sleep with the smell of him on the pillow under her face.

She went over to his bathroom door, wondering what they would say to each other. She heard the shower running, and imagining the hot water cascading over Nicky's body, she pressed her forehead against the door so hard her nose flattened, and she had to open her mouth to breathe.

Their first time had been in the warm salty bath of the bay outside Dolphin Cove when she was just thirteen. They'd been skinny-dipping, and she left the water and was shaking herself dry in the hot sunshine. Nicky wouldn't come out, and though she teased him, he remained waist-high in the bay. So she swam back in after him and found him erect and embarrassed. Driven by curiosity and instinct, she'd simply crawled up on him, straddled him with her strong legs holding tight to his body, and he'd slipped inside her.

That night, they met on the beach and sprayed each other down with mosquito repellant as they tumbled out of their clothes. After that, there was no stopping them, and nobody tried.

Her mother knew right away and went to the drugstore to buy them some condoms. If Tank knew, and Kate realized he must have, he kept it to himself.

Though her mother was just a gray outline of herself by then, she made Nicky sit down with Kitty, and she taught them about protection. She made them promise: no baby until they were both done with school and holding down jobs. With his face so red he looked as though he might cry from embarrassment, Nicky agreed. He had kept his word, even after Kitty's mother had died.

Now, even with the years and the dead people battering against her like flotsam against the side of a skiff in the bay, she still remembered how it had been between Nicky and her. She had lied to Nicky at Apalachicola when he'd tried to get her to stay in the Gibson Inn with him. Listening to the shower and envisioning Nicky on the other side of the door, she couldn't deny what she felt. But however much she wanted to go to him, she didn't. She couldn't risk what it might do to her and to him if she opened that door. And she wouldn't betray Ray.

She went back to the kitchen and poured a cup of coffee. Her hands shook as she sipped from the mug.

Half an hour later, Kate tried to eat the breakfast Nicky had cooked, but she couldn't swallow more than a bite or two. The night before, she'd told him what was happening in Concordia and how, thanks to the microfiche, she'd linked Weaver and Greenstreet with the two dead people on the beach from twenty years ago.

Nicky had said it didn't have to be Bobby. It could be any of them—Dave, Polky, or Rock. Even Jimmy. And she had agreed, but Kate still thought it was Bobby. He was the killer in the group.

Nicky shoved his uneaten toast aside. "What do I do? Do I stay here and wait to get arrested or shot down? Or run? Again."

"I don't know." She was flat out of answers and wondering what she should do herself.

"I mean, there's my little girl to think about. I don't want to leave her, but I'd never steal her from her mother. Her mom... she's a good mom, you know?"

Kate nodded.

"And then I got to figure I'm being selfish to want to stay around her. She's just a little girl. What happens to her if I get shot or arrested? What if she's with me and somebody shoots us both?"

Kate stood up and went behind Nicky's chair. She wrapped her arms around his neck and rested her head lightly against the top of his. "I don't know," she whispered.

"I got to figure, bad as it'd be for me to just disappear on her, it would be ten times worse for her if I got arrested. Or killed. You know?"

Kate stood behind him a minute or two more, feeling the warmth coming off him. Then she backed away and walked toward the bedroom, where her overnight bag was sitting on his little girl's dresser.

Nicky followed her into the bedroom. "Come with me," he said. "I mean, if I decide to run again, you should come. You could be in danger too. We can start over, make a new life. Have kids of our own. We're not too old, and I'd be a good father. I won't screw up this time. I promise."

Kate put the T-shirt she'd slept in into the bag and zipped it. "It's a long drive. I've got to go."

"Please. Come with me."

But she said no and left. Kate didn't have the energy to explain it to him, but she doubted she could ever forgive him or herself. She should have been with Tank when he was dying. She could live another fifty years and never forgive either herself or Nicky for running out on her father. It didn't matter that she still loved Nicky because she couldn't look into the face of a man that she blamed for so much, not day after day.

And besides, this time there was no drug money to finance a run from the law.

Chapter Thirty-Two

Ray was finishing a bag of potato chips when Greenstreet's secretary came into the detectives' office. She looked a lot better than the distraught woman he remembered from their first meeting.

A few feet away, Luke was harassing Dayton about taking Miriam dancing then turning in a reimbursement receipt for dinner and drinks. Ray had been listening to it long enough, and he hadn't even enjoyed the potato chips.

Though it was already two in the afternoon, Ray still had about ten more hours of paperwork. The chief had been after the detectives again that morning about the Weaver case, and the local troopers were giving him a hard time about interfering in their investigation of Carter Russell. The Karma guy who got creamed in that hit-and-run still wouldn't tell them whatever it was he knew. And since Kate had come back from Tallahassee, she'd hardly talked to him. She denied anything was wrong, but even LB had asked what was bugging Kate after he called her on Monday night with a school question. All in all, it'd been a crappy couple of days.

So now what? He wiped the potato chip grease off his fingers and stood to greet the woman as she approached his desk.

"Remember me?" she asked.

"Yes. You're Wyman Greenstreet's secretary. Annette Thompson, isn't it?"

"Yes. Good memory for names."

"Please sit. May I bring you something to drink? Coffee?"

"No, thank you."

Luke came over, stuck out his hand, and grinned at her. "Ms. Thompson, you're looking right fine this afternoon. I hope things are going better for you."

"Yes. Thank you," Annette said, still not taking the chair Ray had offered. "Look, this won't take long. In fact, it's probably not even important at all. It was just... when you talked to me before, you asked me if Wyman was working on anything to do with any old cases."

"Yes, a very precise question," Luke said, grinning.

"Do you have something?" Ray asked.

"Maybe. It's a phone memo. It was in the pocket of one of his suits. I was supposed to drop these suits off at the cleaners, but I forgot, with him getting killed and all. But this morning, I asked Harry—you know, Wyman's partner—about the suits, and we decided to get them cleaned and give them to Goodwill. Anyway, I found this in one of his pockets."

She handed Ray a pink phone memo that had been folded up into a little square. On the front, a note in big, loopy handwriting said, "Call James, urgent. Says you've got the number." On the back was a note in tiny print: "End of January 1972." The memo was not dated.

"Who wrote this?" Ray asked, pointing at the tiny print on the back.

"That's Wyman's writing."

"And on the front?"

"I wrote that."

"Who is James?"

"I don't know. I don't remember writing it. I mean, I write so many of these callback memos. But I did look at our client list. We have three clients with the first name James and two with the last name James. Harry doesn't know if we can give you their full names because of client–attorney privilege and all that. We didn't even know if you'd need them."

"Yes, we'd like that information." Ray wondered if the note could really be a lead or was just more work for them. "And as soon as possible."

"Sure, I'll talk to Harry about it." She paused, glancing back and forth between Ray and Luke. "One more thing. I can't imagine how it's relevant, but a few weeks ago, Wyman put an ad in the newspaper, saying he was available to do environmental work."

Ray raised one eyebrow. "Environmental work? Like what?"

"Getting permits to cut down mangroves, that kind of thing. I mean, I guess that's what he meant. He was just trying to boost business."

"Did he know anything about environmental law?" Luke asked.

Her lips twitched, and she almost smiled. "Between you and me, not much. But he took a CLE course on it from the Florida Bar. I don't think he got any new environmental clients, but you'd asked me about what kind of work he did, so I thought I'd mention it."

"Okay," Ray said. "We appreciate this. Thank you for coming in."

"Did you walk here by chance?" Luke asked. "It being a nice day and your office being close by."

She nodded, looking unsure for some reason.

"Then why don't Dayton and Ray drive you back? They can talk to Harry while they're there."

She hesitated, as if she didn't quite trust them, then she nodded again. "Sure."

Ray and Luke excused themselves and started walking over to where Dayton was scowling at a bunch of papers on his desk. Before they got within Dayton's hearing range, Ray whispered, "Why Dayton?"

"Hey, she's a good-looking woman. About the right age for Dayton, don't you think? And no ring on her finger. They'd look cute together, all that blond hair."

"When did you become Dayton's matchmaker?"

"Since he started hanging out with my eighteen-year-old married daughter with enough problems of her own, thank you."

"Yeah?" Ray looked over at Dayton. *Lilliana and Dayton?* He'd never figured Lilliana would stay with that idiot she'd married. *So Dayton, huh?* Maybe not such a bad match, though the look on Luke's face kept him from saying so.

Dayton looked up as they approached his desk. "Something up?"

"Yep. Why don't you go with Ray and that pretty lady over there and talk to her boss about getting some info on Wyman Greenstreet's client list," Luke said. "I'll hold down the fort here."

With a grin, Dayton slid back his chair and stood. "Glad to." With that, Dayton headed toward Annette, Ray walking beside him.

As Ray held the door for Annette, his mind went back to the case. *James. As in, maybe, James Gilroy.* The ambitious assistant state attorney. The man whose political career just got a huge boost from the governor's office appointing him state attorney. Courtesy of a dead man. It didn't seem like a smart man like James would kill his boss just for a promotion. Still, Ray aimed to question Greenstreet's partner about any possible connection between Greenstreet and James Gilroy.

———◉———

A HALF HOUR LATER, Ray stomped back into the detective squad's square beige room.

Luke looked up from his desk. "I don't know who's chasing the bigger wild goose, you or me. Where's Dayton?"

"Parking the car. Dayton's doing okay, you know. He was helpful over at Greenstreet's office."

"Leastways, he's having more fun with his goose. Dancing with Ms. Miriam like he's going to befriend her to the point she lets down her guard and tells him something we don't know." Luke leaned forward in his desk chair and rubbed his back.

"Maybe it all has something to do with something that happened in 1972." Ray was going to have to bug Kate again about what Weaver had looked at on microfiche no matter how much he dreaded asking.

"Beats me. So what'd you find out at Greenstreet's?"

"No connection between Greenstreet and Gilroy." Ray paused to see if Luke would react.

"I figured that would occur to you too. But I don't see it. James Gilroy has bound-for-glory written all over his Brooks Brothers suit. He'll be our first African-American governor one of these years. You wait and see. No need for him to mess things up now just to hurry. He's too deliberate for that. You know what I mean?"

That was more or less what Ray figured too. Even so, he meant to nose around some more. He might ask James Gilroy where he was in 1972 and where he was the night Alton Weaver was shot in his office, the office James currently occupied.

"So what else did this man Harry tell you?" Luke sounded impatient.

"Upshot, Harry's not going to officially give us the list of clients named James. But he gave us some case numbers, which are all public record, and told me to check them out at the circuit court. He said we could find out that way, without him breaking client confidentiality."

"Pretty decent."

Ray nodded. "He wants to catch the guy who killed his partner, but he doesn't want to get in trouble by telling us directly. That's how I read it." He stepped toward the coffee machine, hoping the pot was reasonably fresh. "Dayton's going to call that woman he's friendly with in the clerk's office and get her to pull the court files and make copies of the pertinent pages."

"I guess the three of us can divvy up the James names and give them each a call."

"All three of us?" Ray poured a cup and sipped the coffee.

"You think Dayton can handle that, don't you?"

"You're slacking up on him some, aren't you?"

"Well, I guess he's all right, but he's no rocket scientist."

Ray laughed. "Like we were at his age?"

———————◈———————

THE NEXT MORNING, RAY tried to keep the irritation out of his voice as he answered James Gilroy's endless questions while they prepped for the upcoming trial for the murder of a pretty, young real estate agent during an open house. He kept repeating the same questions as if Ray couldn't remember what he'd said from two minutes ago.

After the fourth repetition, Ray broke down and asked, "Is this really necessary? I've got work to do. You remember? Finding Weaver's murderer." He sounded angrier than he'd meant to.

They were in Gilroy's office, which used to be Alton Weaver's. Gilroy had put up some different artwork, but he was apparently just as tidy as Weaver had been. Yet the place had taken on a cold and clinical quality. There were no photos of a wife or kids or anything personal.

Gilroy took off his wire-frame glasses and studied Ray. The light from the desk lamp reflected off Gilroy's dark skin and cast shadows that made his handsome face appear distorted. Seconds seemed to pass as Ray glared back, fighting the need to blink. He wasn't going to let the man beat him at the silence game.

Finally, Gilroy said, "Tell me again exactly what the defendant said to you that night. *Exactly*."

"He wasn't the defendant then, just some guy we'd picked up on an anonymous tip."

"What did he say? And what were the circumstances?"

Ray stifled the urge to sigh. "Like I already said, we picked him up. My partner and I read him his Miranda rights, just as a precaution. Then Helms asked him why he'd done it, and he said, surprising us both, and I am quoting, 'Bitch blew me off too many times.' And then he said, 'Don't matter what I say. You don't have a case. You'll never convict me.' So we took him to jail."

"And that's it? All of it?"

"Yes, for the fourteenth time, that's all of it. The man shut up after that. Helms asked him a few more questions, but the guy didn't respond. He never invoked his right to silence. He just totally ignored everything we asked him, so we took it as tantamount to him invoking. We damn sure didn't want to screw up anything that might follow, so we quit questioning him."

"We have a weak circumstantial case. I know you understand that." Gilroy's tone softened, becoming almost friendly. "The defendant denies saying anything like that to you or your partner. You have to convince the jury that the man confessed to killing the realtor, or we could lose the case."

For a moment, Ray wondered if Gilroy was suggesting that he doctor his testimony and put words in the defendant's mouth. But Ray was far too loyal to cop work and too ethical to lie. Besides, he had been deposed too many times to change his testimony now without getting ripped on cross. Still, he had to wonder about Gilroy. The trial started next week, and Gilroy was stepping into Alton Weaver's role as the lead prosecutor. The man had to be nervous. Maybe even scared.

"Too bad your partner's dead now." Gilroy's tone was detached. "Having the two of you testifying would strengthen our position considerably."

"Helms probably wasn't happy about that heart attack either. I'm sorry we didn't have four Supreme Court justices watching as witnesses, but we didn't." Ray shifted in his chair, suddenly seized with the idea he should just stand up and leave before his temper got away from him.

"One more thing." Gilroy leaned closer to Ray. "Cindy Lu."

Damn it. Will that ever go away? But Ray kept his mouth shut.

"The defense attorney will try to make you out a bad cop. You know that, right?"

"This isn't my first rodeo, and I'd sure appreciate it if you'd knock off the condescending bullshit. I was catching crooks long before you hung out your shingle and became an instant genius." He didn't bother to keep the snideness out of his tone. Even before Internal Affairs investigated him for allegedly tipping Cindy off, defense attorneys had tried to make Ray out to be a fool, a liar, a drunk, and worse. And now this guy was acting like Ray had never been inside a courtroom before.

"I've filed a motion *in limine* to keep any mention of that IA investigation out of the cross, but the judge hasn't ruled on it. So we need to go over it."

Ray's frustration boiled over to outright resentment. He stood up. "No, we don't."

"Sit down."

"Where were you in 1972?"

"What?" Gilroy looked genuinely puzzled at the abrupt change in topic. "What's that got to do with anything?"

"I'm curious. Were you in law school by then?"

Gilroy frowned and leaned back in his chair. "No. I was a freshman, still in Tallahassee. At FSU."

"In Tallahassee," Ray repeated. "Where were you the night Alton Weaver was shot?"

For a second, Gilroy's expression remained puzzled, then a look of rage flashed across his face. "How dare you?" He jumped up, strode around his desk, and advanced on Ray.

Ray stood his ground, calculating if the man could actually hurt him if he punched first. In a fair fight, Ray figured he might be outmatched. Gilroy was younger and obviously fit. But Ray had been a cop way too long to fight fair. His hands formed fists at his sides almost without him thinking about it.

With his face inches from Ray's, Gilroy said, "Alton was my mentor. My *friend*. That man was almost like a brother to me. I miss him. Do you understand that?" He stepped back, a slight tremble in his chin. "I mourn him." The raw grief on James Gilroy's face was obvious.

Ray believed the man missed Alton. But remembering how quickly Gilroy had arrived at the scene, Roy still wanted an answer to his question. "So where were you that night?"

"You go to hell. Get out of here."

Ray stood, waiting.

Finally, Gilroy answered, "I was home. My wife was with me. Call her if you insist."

"Fair enough," Ray said and left. He'd call for sure. *Yeah, like his wife wouldn't lie for him.*

Chapter Thirty-Three

Exhausted from her sleepless night, Kate took a long walk around Riverside Park then grabbed a Cuban sandwich on her way back to the library. Back at her desk, she had only taken one bite when the phone rang.

Thinking that she was glad it was Friday, she sighed as she picked up the receiver. "Hello."

"Kate, good afternoon," Morgan said. "I have been thinking about you. How are you?"

"Fine," she lied, holding the phone tightly.

"Please join me this evening for supper. You pick the restaurant—or we can eat here at my place."

She was just too tired for that. And she knew continuing with Morgan was a bad idea. "No, I have some work here at the library I must catch up on. A... project." She hoped she sounded sincere.

"All right then. But it's perfect sailing weather. Let me take you out this weekend."

"It's a long work project." Surely he'd get the hint and stop asking her out. "I'll be busy all weekend."

"Ah, then all the more reason you should let me feed you this evening."

"Really, no. I can't."

For what seemed a long moment, Morgan said nothing. "All right. Let's try Saturday night." His voice was low and husky, a seductive tone she'd heard him use before with her. "I won't take no for an answer, at least not right now. You call me tomorrow and let me know."

They said their goodbyes, and she hung up. *I need to stop this. Now.*

Whatever this thing with Morgan might be, it wasn't fair to Ray, but since coming back from Tallahassee, she couldn't bear to be around Ray. She felt that at any minute, he would see through her and know she was linked to the murders. Also, she feared he might somehow sense that she had almost been unfaithful. That Nicky was the first man she'd loved didn't matter because she had thought about betraying Ray. So she pushed him away, but she couldn't rest, couldn't sleep, and couldn't stand to be alone. Yet when Ray called an hour later and invited himself over for supper, she told him that she was exhausted and needed to get some rest.

That night, she slept badly again, waking often from nightmarish dreams that just escaped her memory. Finally, she went out on the porch and dozed in a chair, with Maggie the cat curled in her lap. She was still on the porch Saturday morning, staring at the giant live oak and listening to the squirrels' chatter, when her phone rang.

She went into the kitchen to answer it. "Hello."

"Good morning," Ray said. "I'm just checking on you. I missed seeing you last night. Did you finally get some sleep?"

She leaned against the counter, trying to think of something to say.

"Are you all right?" Ray asked.

"I'm fine."

"Shall I come over? I have work to do, but I can spare a little while."

"No. I have some things I have to do."

"Tonight then. I'll bring the wine, and we can—"

"No." Kate spun excuses through her mind but couldn't come up with anything that wouldn't sound like the lie it was. She settled for telling him she had a project she needed to work on. That was true after a fashion, if one considered Morgan a project.

"What's going on with you? Ever since you came back from your trip, you've been... distant. Did something happen to you in Tallahassee? Why did you go?" The concern in his voice was gone, and he sounded more like a cop in an interrogation.

Kate thought of Morgan and his invitation for dinner. She thought of how Morgan never asked her what was wrong or cross-examined her. Instead, he offered distraction, comfort, wine, and delicious food. "I'm sorry, but I have to go now." Without giving Ray a chance to argue, she hung up the phone. She waited a couple of minutes to see if he would call back. When he didn't, she called Morgan and told him she'd love to join him for dinner later.

AFTER DINNER AND A long stroll on the bay, Kate went to Morgan's house with him. When he pulled her into an embrace, she let him and opened her lips.

Morgan's tongue moved against hers as his hands stroked her breasts through the thin cotton of her blouse. Even through their clothes, she could feel the heat coming off him as he rubbed his erection against her skirt.

His touch aroused her, and it would have been so easy to give in. But she thought of Ray and pushed out of the embrace. Morgan wore a sensual smile as if he expected her to pull off her shirt, or maybe his shirt.

She tucked her blouse back into her rumpled skirt. "I've got to go."

"I'm sorry," he said, stepping closer to her. "I had hoped you would stay."

"Yes. I'm sorry too." She took a few steps toward the door, relieved he didn't follow. At the door, she turned around and caught him studying her. "We can't be lovers." She said it as flat and definitively as she knew how. "Never."

For a moment, they just stared at each other. She wondered if she should explain about Ray and if she was even still in a relationship with Ray. She didn't really know.

Morgan moved toward her but paused before getting too close. "Never say never." His expression was calm, and he didn't smile or wink as he continued to stare at her.

She broke the eye contact and hurried out the door.

She drove herself home and sat on her porch with Maggie the pug snoring at her feet until the sun came up. She brewed a pot of coffee and wondered if she should call CeCe. In the early dawn, she noticed that Ray had left some wine and plantains in her kitchen.

RAY THOUGHT KATE'S excuse was so weak it was like she wasn't even trying. For a year, they'd always spent Saturday nights together unless he had to work. After he slammed down the phone, he went for a run, worked out with his weights, then headed into the office for a long day of pointless phone calls and paperwork.

That evening, he decided to drop by her house anyway and stopped by the Cuban deli on the way. Her car wasn't in the carport, and no lights shown from within the house. He rang the bell just in case. Inside, Maggie began barking, and the other Maggie scratched on the door to get out.

When he was sure nobody was home, Ray used his key. The cat slipped out when he opened the door. When he reached down awkwardly to catch her with his free left hand, she clawed him and broke free.

"Damn it!" He knew he couldn't get the cat back inside until she was good and ready.

As he walked through the dark living room to get to the kitchen light, Maggie barked at him like he was a burglar. In a way, he guessed he was.

A collection of dirty dishes sat in the sink, and what looked like at least two days of newspapers lay on the floor by the table. *Not like Kate at all.* After putting the wine and the plantains on the counter, he walked about the rest of the house, checking each room. He saw nothing out of the ordinary except that her bed was not made.

Cursing himself for the impulse, he went into Kate's bathroom and opened the drawer where she kept her diaphragm. He pulled out the flowered cosmetic bag and unzipped it. The plastic pink container was in the bag, just as he'd hoped.

As he returned the bag, he spotted a photo. Ray picked the picture up, holding it at the edges as if it were evidence, and tilted it toward the light. Two towheaded kids, a boy and a girl, stood with a dark-haired girl and a woman who looked like Kate. He squinted, trying to bring their faces in sharper, but the photo was old and fading. Turning it over, he saw someone had written something on the back, but he could only make out a capital N with a lowercase i next to it along with "1963."

He recognized Kate because he'd seen a few photos from her childhood. And the grown woman by her had to be her mother. The resemblance was strong. But he had no idea who the two blond kids were.

He wondered why she would have hidden the picture. After one long last look, he tucked it back underneath her diaphragm bag. Things were bad enough between them without her finding out he'd been snooping.

When he turned to leave, Maggie growled at him from her stance just outside the bathroom. He stood in the doorway, arguing with himself. Losing the fight, he went back to the drawer. He pulled out the little bag, unzipped it, and extracted the plastic container. Feeling like some kind of pervert, he opened it and looked with relief at the thin beige rubber ring. He hurriedly replaced everything again and went back to the kitchen.

Maggie stalked him, barking the whole time as if she'd never met him before. *What the hell. When Kate sees the cat is out, she'll know I was here.* He opened a can of tuna and filled the pug's food dish. She stopped barking and began gobbling the food. He tossed the tuna can in the trash and left the house.

———◈———

KATE WAS WASHING HER dirty dishes the next morning when the phone rang. Drying her hands, she answered, expecting Ray with some version of an interrogation.

"Good morning. I wanted to be sure you were fine on this bright new day," Morgan said. "I followed you home last night to be sure you arrived safely but didn't want to intrude further."

"Thank you." She was surprised at the chivalry, and then she wasn't. He'd always been a perfect gentleman with her. But so had Ray. She waited to see why Morgan was calling. She really hadn't expected to hear from him again after she made it clear last night that they would not be lovers.

"You may set the terms, but I would like to see you again. I enjoy your company." Morgan paused as if waiting for a reply.

Kate straightened, gripping the phone tightly. Maggie the cat sidled up to her, and outside in the yard, a blue jay screamed.

After a moment of silence, he said, "Join me for dinner again. Tonight. I promise you a wonderful meal, some good wine, and no pressure."

She wondered if she should believe him and go. She thought of Ray. But then she imagined the distraction, the pleasure of someone catering to her, and the way Morgan made her feel beautiful and special. "That would be fine."

"Good. I've got some work on the sailboat this afternoon, so why don't I come by and pick you up around six? That way, I don't have to worry about you driving home alone."

A sudden tension flared in her. She did not want to be trapped at his house without her car and no easy way to escape. "No, I'll drive. No reason for you to have to go so far out of the way."

He agreed after some protests, they made their goodbyes, and she hung up the phone. After she finished the dishes, she took two aspirin and tried to nap. When she couldn't sleep, she got up and walked Maggie the pug, paid some bills, and went outside to half-heartedly water her begonias and periwinkles, which were crinkling from the drought. She had just finished putting away the hose when Lilliana drove up in her driveway, LB leaning out the open window on the passenger side with his head in the wind like a puppy.

Lilliana leaped out of the car and slammed the door. LB followed, keeping a pace back from Lilliana. Kate was struck with how much both of Luke's children looked like him as she watched them approach.

"That shithead husband of mine's taken my baby and run off to his momma's house. He's been drinking, and I got to go get my baby. So help me God, if Stevie hurts that little boy, I'll kill his ass." Lilliana panted, swinging her arms and staring at Kate. "I got to go. Right now."

Kate nodded. "Of course. What can I do?"

"Mom and Dad are off together and won't be home till around eight tonight. I'm supposed to babysit LB and—"

"You're not babysitting me. You're just supposed to carry me over—"

"Can you keep him till Mom and Dad come home? I'm real sorry to ask, but I don't want him getting around Stevie if he's drunk. And I don't think I should just leave him alone at the house for such a long time."

"Go on. I'll take care of LB. If you need me, give me a call. Ray's around, too, if you need that kind of help."

"Thanks!" Lilliana shouted, already jumping back in her car. "I owe you one," she yelled out the window as she backed down the driveway.

LB stared after her. "She wasn't babysitting me. She was just supposed to pick me up at baseball practice and then take me to get pizza."

"Of course. I know." Kate smiled. "You're much too old for a babysitter. She was probably too upset to explain it properly." She led him onto the porch and opened the door. "Come on in. I'm all by myself this afternoon, so I'm pleased to have you stay and keep me company. Did you finish your baseball practice?"

"Yeah."

"Then let's get you cleaned up, and you can catch me up on what's happening with you. We'll go for pizza a little later, okay?"

"That's all right with me."

She sent LB to wash his face and hands, then she went to pour them some juice. It was three thirty in the afternoon, so she figured she would need to call Morgan and cancel dinner. She wondered if she should call Ray and ask him to check on Lilliana. Kate didn't have any idea where Stevie's parents lived, but Ray could probably find out.

After LB finished his juice, he played with Maggie the pug, both of them rolling around on the floor and growling at each other like puppies. Kate tried Morgan's phone several times and got no answer. Oddly, he didn't have an answering service. She called Ray's phone and got a recording. She left a brief message telling him that Lilliana might need his help and for him to call her or Lilliana.

After her calls, she went and sat with LB. He bubbled over with talk about his science project, his baseball teammates, and how nobody was supposed to know about it, but Stevie was drinking a lot and getting hard for Lilliana to handle.

An hour later, she called Ray and left another message. She tried Morgan again with the same result.

She looked up Stevie's last name in the phone book and found three listings, one of them a Stephen, which she figured could be Stevie's father. After calling the number and getting no answer, she decided to drive by there. Once she got LB in the car, it only took about twenty minutes to get there. No one answered the doorbell when she rang, so she got back in her car and sat for a moment. "Let's go home," she finally said.

Just as she started the engine, she remembered Morgan saying he'd be working on his boat that afternoon. Since she couldn't get him on the phone, she figured she might as well go over there and cancel their plans in person.

A few minutes later, she turned onto Bayside Drive where Morgan lived then pulled into his long driveway. As soon as she stopped the car, LB jumped out and ran toward the sailboat. Morgan was on the deck, working in the hot late-afternoon sun. Kate could barely see him for the glare in her eyes.

LB shouted, "Wow, man! What a boat."

Morgan climbed down as she reached the dock. He wore khaki pants and a sleeveless white T-shirt, and she couldn't help but notice his muscular arms. She'd only barely spoken his name when he leaned in and gave her cheek a quick kiss. LB made a little huffing noise.

"And who is your friend here?" Morgan asked, looking at LB.

"My name is Luke Latham, Junior, but everybody calls me LB."

"LB? Well, that's a distinctive name, isn't it?" Morgan offered his hand. "I'm pleased to meet you. My name is Morgan McKay."

LB shook Morgan's hand. "Please to meet you, Mr. McKay."

"Please, just call me Morgan."

"Okay, Mr. Morgan." But LB's eyes were already back on the sailboat.

"I couldn't get you on the phone." Kate felt a flush rise on her face and hoped neither LB nor Morgan noticed. "LB's parents are out for the day, and his sister had to drop him off with me while she took care of a family situation. Anyway, I can't make it tonight, and I—"

"She's going to take me out for pizza in a little bit. But I'd sure like to see your boat. My daddy has one, but it's just a little ol' skiff, nothing like this."

"Come on, then. I would be delighted to show you around." Morgan grinned at LB and stepped toward the boat, the boy scampering by his side.

Kate stretched out in a chair on the patio and let Morgan and LB tour the boat without her. Even in the shade, she was warm.

After about twenty minutes, LB came running over and skidded to a stop beside her chair. He started chattering a mile a minute in a buzz that Kate couldn't quite follow.

Morgan knelt beside her and kissed her on the mouth. Kate kept her lips closed then jerked back. Beside her, LB gasped.

"I'm not giving up on you," Morgan whispered.

She scrunched back farther in the chair. "I'm still going to fight Antheus Mining."

"Of course." He offered her his hand. "Come on. Let's go to the house. I promised LB I would show him my album on the sailboat, the before and after pictures. A good friend of mine and I restored it. A fine old wooden sailboat like this—"

"And then he's going to call out for pizza," LB finished.

Kate didn't think that was a good idea, but Morgan and LB were already racing ahead with LB talking as if nobody had listened to him all day. Morgan laughed several times. He seemed to like kids, which somehow surprised her. Maybe it would be okay to hang out and have some pizza.

Kate followed them into the house. When Morgan started showing LB the photo album, she asked if she could use his phone. After Morgan pointed it out to her in the next room, she excused herself and called Lilliana then Ray. Nobody answered at either house. She couldn't just sit around eating pizza when Lilliana might be in trouble.

She returned to the living room. "We need to go," she told LB. "I need to find your sister."

"But we're going to get pizza, and—"

"LB, this is important. I've got to find out about Lilliana. We'll get your pizza, but first, let's find your sister."

"If you need to, you can leave him here with me, and I'll take care of him." Morgan eyed Kate, something like a grin playing on his face. "LB and I are fast friends by now, aren't we?"

"Yeah, man."

"No, thank you. It's a kind invitation, but I need to have LB with me. There's... there are some family problems."

"All right." Morgan patted LB on the shoulder but kept his eyes on Kate. "Call me tonight, then, will you? Or sooner. Let me know if I can help."

"Yes."

LB waved at Morgan. "Thanks for the tour. The pictures are really cool."

"Sure. Have Kate bring you back any time. Maybe we can go for a sail."

As Kate walked out to her car, LB by her side, she realized with a sudden clarity that she didn't know a thing about Morgan. She'd all but forgotten about Antheus Mining Company and had ignored that he was the man who wanted to mine phosphate in the watershed of the Calusa River. She didn't know if he had a wife in Bartow or an ex-wife and kids somewhere. She didn't know where he'd gone to college or what his politics might be. He seemed to like LB, and he'd certainly been good with him, but that didn't tell her much.

LB tugged at Kate's arm. "Don't worry, Kate. Lilliana'll be fine. She's a whole bunch smarter than most folks give her credit for, and she's not going to let anybody hurt that baby."

Kate was amazed how much LB sounded like his father. On the way home, she drove by Lilliana's house and was relieved to see her and Ray's vehicles in the driveway. She pulled in and parked behind Ray's car. LB jumped out and ran into the house without knocking, and Kate followed.

In the living room, Lilliana was holding her baby and crying, a bright red spot on her cheek and a bruise beginning around her left eye. Ray glanced up at Kate and motioned for her to take LB out.

Kate went over to Lilliana and kissed her cheek. "I'll take LB and get him some pizza."

On the way out the door, she heard Ray talking about Stevie's arrest and how Lilliana needed to see a lawyer and start proceedings for an injunction to keep him away from her and the baby.

———⊶❖⊷———

KATE HAD ALREADY SHOWERED and crawled into bed with a book she couldn't concentrate on when the doorbell rang. She peeked out her window and saw Ray's car. Pulling on a robe, she went to answer the door.

"We need to talk," he said.

"Does it have to be tonight? I'm exhausted."

"Yes. Right now."

"Fine." She went to the living room and collapsed into a chair.

Ray followed but did not sit. Towering over her, he asked, "What's going on with you and this Morgan guy?"

Kate glanced away. She figured LB had told him something about the afternoon. "I really don't know."

"Is he your lover?"

She shook her head. "No."

"But he kissed you. And you've gone out with him?"

"Yes."

"How long has this been going on?"

"Not long. I'm not sure anything is really going on. He's just…" *Just what?* She didn't know how she could explain it to Ray when she didn't understand it herself. Morgan was just the one who didn't ask questions or make judgments and whose hands on her skin made her forget what she didn't want to answer or be judged about.

"Is it about money? Is that it, that this phosphate guy has money and I don't? That he's got the big house and the big sailboat, and I don't have any chance of ever having that?"

She sighed. LB must have had a mouthful to tell Ray, and she'd never even bothered to ask him not to do so. "No. It isn't money." *Is it? Is wealth the missing factor?* She'd grown up poor, and it wouldn't be the first time a woman without any money got swept away by a man who had plenty of it.

Money. Maybe that was why she'd sat back quietly and without any objection while Tank and Nicky smuggled drugs. And she'd never tried to stop them. And she'd taken the drug money when she ran to Georgia. *Is it about money after all?*

She looked up at Ray's angry face. She thought of the bruise on Lilliana's cheek and realized how easy it would be for Ray to strike out at her. Off in the other room, Maggie the dog snored, the sound clear in the sudden silence.

She crumpled the cuff of her flannel robe. "I don't know what it is, exactly. He's just… attentive."

"Damn you," Ray said, his voice harsh and gravelly. "To hell with it all." He turned to leave.

"Ray, I love you. I want to marry you. Please ask me again when you're not so mad."

He slammed the door, and a minute later, she heard his car start.

Kate was not at all certain that what she had just said was true. Maybe she didn't love him. Maybe he'd just been a persistent habit.

Morgan thrilled her in a way Ray didn't. She had to face that. Whether it was money or something else, Morgan intrigued and enthralled her. Whatever that something was, it would have to run its course.

Chapter Thirty-Four

Tuesday morning, Luke contemplated a fourth cup of coffee, weighing the energy boost against the heartburn that was trying to gurgle up in his throat. Dayton ran into the office and sprinted over to Luke's desk, clutching a handful of papers and grinning.

"So, Dayton, what's up?"

"You know how I finally got those records from the phone company this morning?"

"Yep." *You mean* we *finally got those records with more than a little help from Miriam and Judge Goddard and a warrant.* "Phone company acted like it was the White House and we were after the Nixon tapes."

Dayton gave him a blank look.

"You know, the Watergate tapes?" Then Luke realized Dayton would have been in grade school during that time.

"Oh. Yeah, whatever. Anyway, you're not going to believe what I found in what we got."

Luke waited. When Dayton just grinned and waited back, Luke started to jump on him for wasting time building it up. Then he thought how many times he'd done the same thing, using what Ray called his "dramatic pause." *Give the rookie his time. Let him tell it.*

Finally, Dayton thrust a list of tiny numbers at him that Luke couldn't read without his bifocals. "Look here." He pointed. "The night of Weaver's murder, he called this number twice."

"And?"

"Right here." Dayton pulled out another sheet of paper. "Greenstreet called the *same number* three times in the week before he was murdered."

Luke sat up straight, put on his bifocals, and peered at the two sheets.

"I looked up that number in the City Directory, you know the cross-directory part where they put numbers first, and—"

"I know about that, all right," Luke said. He'd taught Dayton that trick himself. "Whose number is it?"

"Guy named Carter Russell." Dayton stepped back as if expecting Luke to jump out of his chair.

"Holy shit. The rattlesnake guy!" Luke drummed his fingers on the desk, enjoying the rising flush of excitement. "Our first real break. By God, that's connecting the dots, for sure. Wait till Ray hears. He always did think something was funny about that Carter guy leaving his car and going out in the swamp instead of staying with the car or on the road. He'll be tickled pink to hear he was right."

"Where is Ray?"

"Over at the courthouse, waiting his turn to testify in that lady realtor's murder. He's the key witness, and Gilroy's not taking any chances on having his testimony discredited or thrown out, so he's got Ray sequestered. Even got him under a gag order, so he's not supposed to talk with anyone except Gilroy himself."

"Gilroy can do that?"

"Sure looks like he can. That way, defense counsel can't claim outside influence or anything. Gilroy's bound to be nervous about the case, especially with him just recently being appointed state attorney."

"Bet Ray's not happy about that," Dayton said. "He sure was a bear yesterday."

"You got that right."

Ray had been so royally pissed off that nobody went near him, not more than once, anyway. Luke had hoped when Ray stomped into the office on Monday in a foul mood that it was just because of the upcoming ordeal at the courthouse. But given what LB had told him about Kate, Luke suspected the problem had to do with more than the trial. However, he hadn't asked Ray about it and hadn't mentioned the man with the big house and sailboat, who had kissed Kate on the mouth in front of LB.

"You know how it goes," Luke said. "He'll sit there most of the morning in that tiny witness room, drinking bad coffee and messing up his gut. Gilroy won't even let him in the courtroom in case Ray hears somebody else testify to the same thing he's going to talk about and defense can claim he was influenced by that. Like Ray ever got influenced by anything outside his own head." He pulled open a desk drawer and fished out his police-car keys. "For now, I'll obey Gilroy's ordering Ray not to talk to any of us. But I reckon I better go have a word with the dead man's widow, Mrs. Russell, and see if she has any idea why the state attorney would be calling her husband the night they both died." Luke didn't look forward to it, and he didn't think it was fair to go without Ray, but he didn't want to put it off.

"Want me to go with you?" Dayton looked all puppy-dog eager.

"Yep." Dayton wasn't Ray, but he was good with women, and Luke figured maybe he could help.

Dayton grabbed his coat and practically danced over to the door. "Wish we could take Ray."

Luke grunted and started pulling on his sports jacket.

"I hate testifying." Dayton held the door for Luke, then they stepped out into the morning sunlight and heat. "I mean, like you said, you sit around all day, wasting time, then the state attorney puts you on the stand for about ten minutes and won't even let you say what you meant to say, and then the defense attorney takes an hour to make you look like a liar or a fool or both." He shook his head. "Man, I hate it."

"Let's see, you hate testifying, and you hate looking at dead bodies," Luke said, remembering Dayton's dismay at Weaver's funeral. "Exactly what do you like about this job?"

Dayton grinned. "Figuring it out. Yes, sir, figuring it out and busting the bad guys."

"Right," Luke said, thinking he'd been at it so long that he'd forgotten the thrill of "figuring it out," like they were just on the brink of doing right then. With Carter as the connection between the two dead lawyers, Luke was confident it was just a matter of time before he and Dayton figured out the rest of the picture—and Ray, too, once they got him back from James Gilroy. Luke smiled at Dayton. "Well, come on. Let's go see the widow woman."

Dayton stopped and shook his head. "There's something else you need to know."

"What?" Luke slowed his pace but kept walking toward his unmarked police car.

"The night he was killed, Weaver also called Miriam. Twice."

Luke let that sink in as he unlocked the car and opened the door. Miriam had told them all that the last she'd seen or heard from Weaver that night was when she left the office right after five. "What times?"

"Six thirty and then again at twenty-six minutes before eight."

"Damn, probably right before he got shot." Luke leaned against the car as the captured heat from inside the vehicle rolled over him. "What time did Weaver call the snake guy's house?"

"About ten minutes before each of his calls to Miriam."

"Damn." Luke looked at Dayton and let the sadness in the young man's face register before he spoke. "Look, Dayton, I'm sorry, but you know we got to go talk to her again."

"Sure. I know. But would you let me?"

"How about I go with you right after we see the widow? I'll just sit there and let you talk? Then if..." *Then if you screw it up, maybe I can fix it?*

As if he had read Luke's mind, Dayton shook his head. "Look, you got to trust me with it alone sometimes, you know?"

Luke blinked at the brightness of the sun as his jacket pressed down on his body like a lead blanket. He had the urge to put his arm around the younger man's shoulders and say, "Why sure, son, you go right on." But even he and Ray double-teamed when possible, and Dayton was still so green. Worse, Dayton had a sweet spot for Miriam that would get in the way, and that was reason enough not to let him talk to her alone.

Luke felt something shift inside his head as if he'd heard the first clank of the changing of the guard. "All right. You go talk to Miriam. Take her out for coffee so y'all are alone. You go on now, and I'll see the widow."

Luke watched Dayton jog off toward his own car, then he shrugged and got inside the hot police vehicle.

Chapter Thirty-Five

Kate's worry reached a peak she couldn't deny any longer. She needed to see CeCe, and she couldn't wait until that evening after work. Instead, she told her coworkers that she felt ill and left early on Tuesday afternoon.

Even with her sense of urgency, Kate dreaded the visit. She drove slowly, negotiating the traffic, and refused to even look at the turnoff to Dolphin Cove. The bay waters on both sides of the causeway glistened with sunlight. Sooner than she wanted to, she crossed the bridge to the island and turned onto the narrow road toward CeCe's B and B. Once she had loved the slow, meandering drive with its silver-green Australian pines and cypress houses on the bay side. On the northern end of the island, the spectral ruin of an unfinished hotel had guarded the point during Kate's childhood, the half-built resort a casualty of the collapse of Florida's land boom of the twenties. For over forty years, the ruin had stood like some sentinel against further development on the island.

By the time Kate graduated from high school in 1971, development on the islands had boomed. Nothing checked the exponentially expanding condominiums, resort hotels, and timeshares that sprang up, bribed past violations of zoning, common sense, and coastal-land-use plans. They were thrown together as quickly as possible by stoned boys who'd quit high school to grow their hair and work construction while chugging beer and listening to the Allman Brothers and Pink Floyd. Open beaches and funky cypress houses had long since given way to the fake pink stucco and white latticework of the new buildings that choked the island. Like most of the natives, Kate sometimes thought a hurricane that leveled it all would not be such a bad thing. She didn't even see many of the landmarks of her childhood anymore because the landscape was so altered by development.

But even the occasional passes where the open beaches and blue Gulf were still visible from the road didn't cheer her up. By the time she knocked on the back door at CeCe's, Kate actually did feel sick like she'd told them at the library.

CeCe, wearing an apron over her jeans and cotton camp shirt, answered and motioned her into the kitchen without speaking. Rail thin like she'd been as a kid, she still wore her blond hair long, and the same freckles crossed her straight nose and cheeks.

"You look just the same," Kate said. That was mostly true, though crow's feet crowded CeCe's eyes and parallel lines marked her forehead.

CeCe went back to the counter where she was kneading bread. The kitchen was big and smelled of nutmeg and cinnamon. A yellow cat rubbed against Kate's leg and purred when she petted it, then it ambled out of the kitchen.

"You have a beautiful place here."

CeCe punched the bread, her hand a hard fist in the dough, and didn't reply.

"I've driven by it. I always wanted to stop and see you, but... well, you know. It was hard."

"Did you see Nicky?" CeCe asked.

"Yes."

"What do you need from me, then?"

"I don't want it to be like this."

CeCe put the bread in a greased bowl and placed a towel over it. She washed her hands, looked at Kate, and sighed. She pulled open a cabinet, grabbed a coffee container, and loaded the coffee maker. "It's fresh. I get the beans from that store on Main Street and grind them myself. You want cream? Sugar?"

"Both."

"Come on. While the coffee's brewing, let me show you the place."

They wandered from room to room, Kate admiring the tasteful charm of the inn and CeCe explaining bits and pieces about the place. When the coffee maker beeped, they went back to the kitchen and struggled at small talk until the coffee was mostly drunk.

"Now then, what is it you need?" CeCe's voice had a softness that hadn't been there the first time she'd asked.

"I need to know if you have any idea where Bobby or Jimmy or any of them are now. Or who they really were. I mean, you and I didn't know them, except Jimmy. I hardly saw any of them except Polky." Kate thought of the time Polky had come to Tank's, frantic over his missing brother, and she'd made him show her the way to the farmhouse where she'd seen Bobby stripping out of his bloody clothes.

"And Dave," CeCe said. "You saw Dave a time or two. He came to church and sat with us."

"Yes, Dave." Kate remembered the tall, lanky man who'd had a crush on CeCe, who wouldn't give him the time of day. "But I'm not sure I ever laid eyes on that other one. Bobby's bodyguard, I guess he was. Rock was what Nicky called him."

CeCe nodded. For a moment, Kate wondered what Nicky had told her—that was, if he'd told her anything—about what had happened at Bald Point and later at the farmhouse.

"Do you know where Jimmy is?" Kate asked.

"No. He got arrested again. In '81 or '82, I think it was. And he skipped out on the bail. I don't know anybody that's heard about him since then."

"What about any of the rest of them? Anything you might know or remember."

CeCe raised her cup as if to take a sip, then looked at it, seeming surprised that it was empty, and put it down again. "No." She got up and filled the coffee maker again with water and the ground beans.

When CeCe turned back around, she was crying. Kate rose from her chair and took CeCe in her arms. This was the woman she had loved as her best friend from the time they were toddlers until Tank and Nicky's drug running split them up. Whenever anyone spoke of best friends, CeCe was the person Kate thought about. Perhaps the friends one made in adulthood were never the same as those you opened your heart and life to as children and as teenagers, but no friend would ever mean as much to Kate as CeCe had.

"I'm sorry," Kate whispered into CeCe's hair.

After CeCe dried her eyes, she backed out of the embrace and slipped off her apron. "Let's go walk on the beach."

Walking down the fine white sand, they went to the edge of the water, took their sandals off, and let the Gulf nip at their feet and ankles like tourists. The water was like a warm bath thick with salt. CeCe told Kate about Tank's last days, how Dave had come back and helped her at the end and how, after that, she went to California and worked in a town called Eureka, trying to forget everything. After a while, she'd returned home and put her name in the phone book. That was how Nicky had found her again. By then, he was married, and they had both agreed it was best that he didn't contact Kate.

Kate hated to break the moment, but she had to ask. "Do you know where Dave is now? I mean, you seemed to have kept up with him."

"Why do you need to know?"

Kate told her everything she could about Weaver and Greenstreet and her visit with Nicky, about the van at the bottom of the sinkhole with the two bodies and the kids on the beach. She told CeCe about Ray and how he wanted to marry her, but he was trying to close the case on Weaver and Greenstreet. If he ever did that, he would know her father had been running drugs and her lover had been knee-deep in the dead people on Bald Point and in the sink-hole. And somehow, in ways she didn't understand, those bodies had led to Weaver and Greenstreet's murders.

"I can't tell Ray what I know," Kate said. "I can't go to the police."

"Why not? Just leave Nicky out of it. Or give him a fake name if you can't keep him out of it. But damn it, don't tell anybody about Nicky, not the cops or anybody."

"No, I know. I won't, ever. Not about Nicky. But even just with Tank... I mean, there's no way to explain it without putting me in the middle of it."

"But you weren't in the middle of it. Wouldn't Ray understand that?"

"I don't want him to know about Tank. I don't want him to think... to think about my part in it. I knew what they were doing, and it was my van they used more than once. I knew Nicky was using it for drugs."

"Come on. Ray can't blame you for what your father and your boyfriend did."

Kate looked up at CeCe and tried to read her expression. "You did."

CeCe stopped walking and turned to face Kate. Her eyes were narrow in the sunlight. "Yes, I did. I thought you could have made them stop."

Kate wondered if she could have. She'd never really tried to make them quit, though.

"Jimmy gave me money." CeCe spoke slowly in a faraway-sounding voice. "A lot of money. For taking care of Tank... and for keeping my mouth shut. That's what I used for a down payment on the inn, Jimmy's drug money."

That explains it. Kate had wondered how CeCe managed to buy the inn. Kate didn't judge. She let the warm water of the Gulf race between her toes and felt the sand bunch then wash away under her feet. She thought of the money she had taken with her when she fled Tallahassee. Tank and Nicky's drug money had gotten her started on a new life in Georgia and helped her through college.

"None of us are clean of it, are we?" CeCe asked.

"No."

"Then let it go."

Kate studied the worn look on CeCe's face and understood that finally, after all this time, CeCe forgave her.

They walked back to the inn without talking. At her car, Kate knocked the wet sand off her feet before sliding her sandals back on. She hoped they might stay in touch, but she doubted that would happen.

As Kate crawled into her car, she spotted the grocery sack holding the framed photo of the men Nicky had identified as Bobby and Rock. She realized CeCe had never answered her question about Dave. She pulled the photo out of the bag. "Take a look. The bearded one is Bobby, and the other one is Rock. Do they look like anybody you see around here?"

CeCe took the picture and studied it. "No." She tilted it as if to catch better light on the image. "Maybe if you take off the frame and mat, we could see it better."

Kate had cleaned the glass and not seen any improvement, but maybe CeCe had a point. She took the photo, broke open the cardboard back, and pulled it out of the frame. When she saw their feet, she stared, shocked. Bobby wore what looked to be standard Sperry topsiders without socks. But the man next to him wore military-style camouflage boots.

Like the man in her house for the meeting she'd held to stop the phosphate.

No, that doesn't mean anything. Lots of people probably wore those kinds of boots back in '72. But her heart was thrumming, and her mouth suddenly dried as if her body knew that the man in the picture was the same one who had been at her house.

Kate studied the man's face in the photo: his broad nose, thick arms, and a kind of cowlick in the hair over his wide forehead. He wasn't young—not like Bobby appeared to be anyway, but his weathered face was bold with strong features like Bobby's.

She closed her eyes and tried to remember the details of the face of the man in her living room. He'd been muscular, too, and the right age. Of that much, she was sure. The more she dug at her memory, the more she could see in her mind that the man in her house had the same broad nose and cowlick. She hadn't noticed the resemblance before, but she now realized they were probably the same person.

Her eyes popped open. She couldn't breathe. Rock had been in her house, watching her.

"Kitty? You okay?" CeCe put an arm around her. "You look—"

Kate inhaled with something like a gasp. "Scared." Rock knew who she was and where she lived. She wondered if he knew she'd gone to Tallahassee and if she'd led him to Nicky.

"What?" CeCe demanded. "What's wrong?"

Kate pointed at the image of Rock. "He was in my house. The boots... it's hard to explain, but this man had the same boots. And now that I think about it, I can tell the man's face is similar, even the hair... I mean that weird cowlick. He looks older, sure, but he still has the bulk, you know, the muscles."

"Why was he in your house?"

"I held a meeting about stopping phosphate mining. I advertised the meeting in the newspaper. God, that was so stupid!"

"Did you... did you talk with him? Say anything like—"

"What? Like... don't I know you from somewhere?" Kate put the photo down. She couldn't bear to look at it anymore. "No. I grinned at him and said something like 'Thanks for coming.' Maybe... no, that's all I said."

"Good. Then he has no reason to think you know who he is." CeCe straightened and stared out at the water, her expression grim. "Unless he followed you to Nicky's."

"No. I'm sure of it. I stopped a lot on the way there, and nobody followed me. They couldn't have." She remembered how Nicky had looked up and down the street when he first recognized her. There hadn't been a car in sight. But that didn't mean Rock hadn't been skulking around the corner.

CeCe turned to look at Kate. "There's something else you need to know. I know what happened to Dave." She lowered her eyes and softened her voice. "David James was just a made-up name he used with Bobby. He went back to his real name, and he got straight and made something of himself with a little handyman business. I had him fix a dozen or more things at the B and B, and sometimes... sometimes he just came around to see me. Thing is, we ended up being pretty good friends. I even went to his wedding." CeCe's voice faltered. "He's dead now. Just recently. You might have read about it, the guy who ran off the road out by the Calusa River. He wandered away from his car and got snakebit. His real name was Carter Russell."

"Jesus," Kate said, uttering the blasphemy she had chided Nicky, Ray, and Luke all against. She felt dizzy with the thought of what Dave's death must mean. Panic rose in her throat, nearly choking her. She felt a fear as righteous as what she'd experienced the night at the farmhouse when Nicky pushed her out the window and told her to run. "I've got to go."

Kate spun around and hurried to her car. Going to the cops with what she knew didn't feel right, but she was scared and out of options. Rock had sat in her own living room, and she couldn't deny that he had to know who she was. Dave had been at Bald Point, and he was dead now. Nicky was there, and she knew what had happened there, so maybe they were next on somebody's list. CeCe might even be at risk. If Kate could find out where Bobby or Polky were, maybe she would have another choice, but that wasn't the case. She couldn't wait for Nicky or CeCe or herself to be killed. She had to go to the cops.

Still, calling in law enforcement was counter to everything in her upbringing. Tank always said not to call in the police or any government officials, no matter what. But she'd been trying to rise above those teachings. Anyway, going to Luke was going to a friend, not the cops exactly.

Once she made up her mind to talk to Luke, Kate practiced her story as she drove. She rehearsed a version that left Nicky out of it. There was no statute of limitations on murder, and his role in all of it added up to felony murder as she understood it. She also kept her role to that of an innocent bystander because she wasn't sure how much trouble she'd be in for keeping her mouth shut for twenty years and for owning the van in which the bodies were buried. Her altered story made it Tank's van instead of hers. She felt guilty about that, but Tank was dead and couldn't go to jail.

The biggest problem, though, was that she couldn't tell Luke she'd seen Bobby at the farmhouse in his bloody shirt without putting herself smack in the middle of it. After some thought, she decided to say she'd seen Bobby at Jimmy's fish house. That made sense, and it kept her and Nicky in the clear. Even telling Luke that much was risky, but she had to do something to try to stop the killings.

At the police department, she parked and made her way to the detective division, her body aching as if she had the flu. She clutched the photo, still out of its frame but wrapped in the plastic grocery bag.

Kate wasn't much for praying, but she offered a quick word and asked that she be able to tell the story without getting Nicky or herself in trouble. She also prayed that Ray wouldn't be there because she didn't think she could go through with it if he was.

Chapter Thirty-Six

Luke hadn't learned a thing from Carter Russell's widow. He couldn't help being queasy about trusting Dayton with Miriam. He hated that Ray was still apparently sequestered by James Gilroy because of the dead realtor lady's trial. All his frustrations burned in his gut, and he reached for the pack of Tums he kept in his desk drawer.

As the chalky lozenge dissolved in his mouth, he thought maybe he'd walk over to the courthouse and find Ray no matter what Gilroy said. But just as Luke was making up his mind to do just that, Kate came in. He started to ask her to come back later until he saw her expression and realized she didn't look very good.

He motioned toward the chair beside his desk. "Have a seat."

"No. Look, is there some place we can go to talk privately?"

"Sure. Want to walk over to that place on Main, the French bakery with the chocolate croissants? Ever I saw somebody needed a chocolate croissant, that'd be you. This time o' day, won't be anybody much there."

It took them less than ten minutes to walk there. Kate hadn't said a word beyond "okay" when he'd warned her to be careful of an oncoming car she hadn't seen. Her purse was slung over her shoulder, and she held a grocery bag in her other hand, clutching it tightly as if it contained something important.

In the bakery, Kate took a seat in a booth at the back, far away from the only other couple in there. Luke went to the counter and ordered two chocolate croissants and two coffees.

After putting the items on the table, he slipped into the seat across from her. He sipped from his coffee and waited for her to talk. Kate and Ray had probably had a fight, especially since LB had blabbed. Luke figured she wanted to talk it out with him, even if he was Ray's best friend and, by definition, on Ray's side.

Kate pushed the coffee to one side and broke off a piece of the croissant but left it on her plate. "Is Lilliana okay?"

"Doing just fine. She's a trooper, you know. Like her mom. She and the baby are back at the house with us till the dust settles. Moved right back into her old room. Thanks for helping out."

"I didn't do much."

"You did just fine. You did what Lilliana needed for you to do."

As she stared at the croissant, Luke studied her in the harsh light of the bakery. He recognized the fatigue that comes from not sleeping, and he wanted to help her and Ray get back together. He didn't care what LB said about the other man who'd kissed her on the mouth. Kate was a great lady, and if Ray had a chance at all of making a relationship work, she was probably about his last shot.

"Kate?"

She looked up at him. "I need your help."

Here it comes. The other guy and the story and how to get Ray back. Would Ray take her back if she'd been with another man?

"Luke, I need your help. Please."

Luke realized he must have paused too long. Ashamed she'd had to ask him twice, he responded, "Of course."

"Please don't tell Ray about this. Okay?"

Thinking Kate was just going to explain about the rich man, Luke nodded, though he didn't feel right about doing so. "Sure."

She took a deep breath. "I don't know who killed Weaver and that other lawyer, but I know why. And that guy who died from the snakebite, Carter Russell, he was tied into it all."

Luke nearly dropped his coffee. "What?"

In a long stumbling story, Kate spit it out for him. He felt a surge of adrenaline when she mentioned that Carter used to go by the name David James. There was a dead girl and young man on the beach too that fit into it all. She told him that a guy named Bobby used Tank's van, but the last time he borrowed it, he put it, along with a couple of bodies, in a sinkhole somewhere near Perry.

At the sinkhole reference, Luke let out a little sound almost like a growl, deep in his throat. *How did we not know any of this?*

She insisted Tank hadn't been the one who killed the men in the van. She said she'd only seen Bobby once, at a fish house where she worked.

Kate talked in a halting way, and he realized she was weighing her words to keep from saying the wrong thing. He'd been around too many suspects trying to tell only half of the story not to know that something was left out of Kate's version.

Luke tried to imagine coaxing or badgering Kate to tell him everything. But he remembered that wholly aside from Ray, she was his friend, a friend of his wife's, and a woman who cared for his children. He couldn't pressure her for more than what she was able to tell him. Later, he would have to, but for now, he'd let her tell it her way.

He reached over the table and tapped the grocery sack. "This relevant?"

"Yes. It's a photo of Rock and Bobby back in the seventies."

He grabbed the bag and pulled out the picture. He studied it, feeling disappointment ripple up inside him. The guys could have been almost anybody, at least anybody who dressed like they were in a rock band or running dope.

"The boots." Kate pointed a shaking finger at the guy on the left. "A man wearing boots just like that was at my house during that phosphate meeting. It's more than the boots. That man had the same broad nose and wide forehead, even had the same cowlick. Ray was there, and he saw him, too, but..." She looked away.

Luke felt a kick of fear for Kate in his gut. He understood, perhaps more than she did, what it meant that the man from the killings on the beach had been in her house. "I've got to tell Ray."

"No. You promised."

"Kate, you are in danger. And this is an official police investigation, one that involves at the very least three current murders and probably a hit-and-run attempted murder. I might not be much else, but I'm a cop and a damned good detective. I can't be holding back information like this from my partner or from the investigation."

"Ray and I had a fight. He's mad at me, and he has good reason. But he'll get past it, I think. Did you know he asked me to marry him?"

"No. He didn't say." *But that's Ray, isn't it? Keep it all in, good or bad.*

"He did. But you know how self-righteous he is. If he finds out that I let them use my van in a drug deal tha—" Kate stopped and shifted her eyes to the left of Luke. "I mean... that is... it was Tank's van, but I sometimes used it." She sat perfectly still, and he thought she might even be holding her breath.

"Kate, don't lie to me. You have to tell me the truth here no matter what. Do you understand that?" Luke kept the anger out of his tone, but he felt it rising in his chest. She was lying, and he knew it.

She started picking at the croissant. Finally, as if she'd made up her mind, she met his eyes. "I am sorry. I'm just so... afraid."

"Was it your van?"

"Yes."

Luke pushed back in his chair and resisted the urge to reprimand her. But the fact that she would lie to him meant that he could no longer trust her, not completely, and that he was going to have to figure out if she were more involved in the current murders too.

Kate as a suspect didn't feel right, rather Kate as a kind of hostile witness was closer. On the other hand, maybe it was just Ray she was worried about. She was right about him. Ray would never understand if she'd knowingly let drug smugglers use her van for illegal purposes. No more than Ray had understood that Cindy Lu's gambling was an addiction, an illness, and not some inherent evilness in her soul. Good people sometimes did bad things—a basic concept Ray's strict religious upbringing never seemed to let him accept.

"All right. I'm going to hold off telling him but just for now." That was an easy promise since Ray would still be under orders not to talk with anyone but James Gilroy. "You and me, we got to figure this out. But"—he didn't try to hide his anger this time—"you can't be lying to me again."

Kate nodded. "Somehow Weaver and that other lawyer found something out about what happened back then. So whoever is behind the murders, he—or *they*—must be trying to cover it up. It's got to be Bobby, Polky, or Rock. It's probably Rock—you know, because of the boots—but he was Bobby's right-hand man. Kind of his... pit bull."

"What about that Jimmy Chukenears?"

"He wasn't that involved, not in the murders. I mean he was arrested, but the charges were dropped. But Bobby, Polky, and Rock are the ones with the most to lose."

"Jeez, Kate, you're making me scared for you. You got to be real careful here. You ought to get Ray to stay over, or you come stay with me, and—"

"I know how to look out for myself."

"No, you don't. With all due respect. Who you are," Luke said, staring right at her to be sure she understood, "is probably the only person in the country who might be able to identify the man who killed the state attorney."

"Rock."

"Yes. Rock. And the other two, Bobby and Polky. You don't know real names, I guess. Can you identify them, though?"

"I can identify the man who was in my house, the one with the boots. But not the others. Like I told you, I barely ever saw Bobby. I might recognize Polky because he hung around Tank more, but everybody was young and had beards and long hair. I don't even look the same."

All true, but would the killer know that? Luke shifted and stretched his neck, but it didn't help with the knot of tension building up. That Rock character might have gone—or been sent—to her house to see if she would recognize him. Maybe since she hadn't, they still had time, and she wasn't in immediate danger.

If she could just identify Bobby or Polky. He wondered if he would recognize somebody from twenty years ago that he'd barely met. He thought about his high school reunion, where he hadn't recognized one of his friends. But the man had gained weight and gone bald. But Bobby and Polky could've gotten fat and lost their hair too.

"Let me take the photo, okay?"

Kate slid it over to him. "Keep it. I've about got it memorized." She frowned. "One more thing, though I'm not sure how it helps, Bobby had a scar on his right side. It was a bad one, real jagged and big. You could see it from a pretty good way off."

Luke cut his eyes up at her, wondering how she knew that. She hadn't mentioned seeing the man without a shirt on. Once again, he had that feeling she was keeping something from him.

"Tank told me," she added as if reading Luke's mind. "I only saw Bobby once at the fish house."

He fingered his coffee cup. Pushing her too hard now might break what trust she did have in him. "Well, you might be surprised what you could remember given a fair chance."

He sure would like to have her look at Ledbetter and Constantia and see if she thought either of them might be Polky or Bobby. Ledbetter was the closest thing they had to a suspect in Greenstreet's murder. He had the urge to drive her out to Ledbetter's and see if she thought he was Bobby or Polky. *Damn catch-22.* He couldn't get Ledbetter in for a lineup without more, and he couldn't drive Kate out for a look at him without tainting any identification she might make. He had the mug shot from Ledbetter's arrest for setting the dogs on them and could do a photo lineup. *Better than nothing.*

"Let's go back to the station. I want you to look at some photos."

Back in the detective squad's office, Luke went to a filing cabinet and pulled out several mug shots, including Ledbetter's. He spread the photos on the desk in front of Kate. "See if you recognize anybody."

Leaning over, she stared at each photo for a long time. Finally, she pointed at one. "That could be Polky, but none of these seem right for Bobby."

The photo she'd selected wasn't Ledbetter's mug shot. Luke resisted the urge to cuss. He debated having her take a look at a picture of Constantia that had run in the newspaper. Kate had probably already seen it, but that would have been before she saw the old photograph of Bobby and Polky. Constantia wasn't exactly a suspect, so a suggestive ID wasn't so much of a problem, but he didn't want to take Kate to see him. If Constantia were involved in all this, Luke didn't want to be poking the bear and letting him know that Kate had come to the police.

He wished he had a good mug shot of Constantia to show her. Ray and Luke both had the nagging idea that Karma Guy knew something, and maybe somebody had tried to kill him because of what he knew. Getting an ID on him as Bobby or Polky could move the investigation and interrogation along. He remembered the scars on Constantia's chest when he'd seen him in the hospital. Maybe he had another scar on his stomach on the right side.

"Kate, I got some other photos for you to look at. Sit tight a minute while I line them up."

Her chin moved a tiny fraction, and Luke took that for a nod.

Luke had trouble finding the photo of Constantia that he had carefully clipped out of the newspaper during the early coverage of Weaver's death. A newspaper photographer had snapped it as Constantia was leaving the courthouse, but it was a good, tight shot that showed his face and enough of his body to give Kate an idea of his size. After finally locating the clipping, he had to dig up a couple more newspaper photos so it would be closer to a real photo lineup. When he got the pictures all together, he put them on his desk in front of her.

Kate studied each for a few seconds then picked up the one of Constantia. "I remember seeing this in the paper. He's the guy that found Weaver, isn't he?"

"Yep."

"He definitely could be Bobby. He's got the prominent nose and looks about the right size. The scar would be proof, but I don't imagine we can get him to take his shirt off."

Luke shook his head. "We could ask, but I don't see him going for it."

"I can't say for sure, but it looks like he's the right age." Kate shook her head. "You know, the dark hair and the nose, maybe. But that's not—"

"Enough," Luke finished. He would have to go through everything all over again, dig a lot deeper, and see what they might have missed on Constantia. Ray would have to be in on it, too, once he got loose from Gilroy.

Luke sighed and looked at his watch. All that took time, and he wasn't sure Kate had much of that to spare. The scar Kate mentioned could be the key, but he didn't know how he was going to get the man to take his shirt off.

And if Constantia was Bobby, then that would mean Rock or Polky was trying to kill him. If someone was trying to kill everyone who knew what happened on the beach with those dead kids, Constantia should be eager to talk and cut some kind of deal for his own safety. But he wasn't.

Luke thought about Dayton and his charm and big blue eyes. Women trusted and confided in him. Maybe Dayton could sweet talk one of the nurses who had seen Constantia at the hospital to find out if he had an old scar on his right side. It wasn't by the book, and they wouldn't be able to use it in a court of law, but Kate's life might be on the line. He figured it was worth a try. In the meantime, he had to keep Kate safe.

"Come on. You need to come home with me. You can stay with us till this is all over."

"I can't do that, not with Lilliana and the baby there. That's just too much for Aleyna and you to deal with."

"Naw, there's room." But she was right. There wasn't. He would have to put her on a cot in Lilliana's small bedroom, which already had Lilliana and the baby.

"I'll be all right, really. I've got the gun Ray gave me. I know how to use it. And Ray installed those locks on all my doors and windows."

And if anyone wanted you dead, you'd be dead by now. "All right," Luke said. "I'm not happy about it, but I can't force you. At least let me walk you to your car."

They left and walked back out to where she'd parked her car on the street. As Luke held the car door for Kate, he saw Miriam standing on the sidewalk outside the courthouse. *What a good-looking woman.*

A black Lincoln Continental pulled up, and Miriam's husband got out to come around and open the passenger-side door. Miriam slid into the car, and her husband walked back to his side and got in. The car drove off.

A big, black car. The hit-and-run driver had been in a big black car.

"Son of a bitch," Luke blurted.

Startled, Kate spun around and stared at him. "What's wrong?"

He was too tired to explain. "Look," he said, "I still think you should come stay with me, but I'm at least going to follow you home and make sure you get inside safe and sound."

"Isn't Aleyna expecting you by now for supper?"

Luke shook his head. "She learned a long time ago not to put supper on the table until she heard my car in the driveway."

Chapter Thirty-Seven

When Luke got back to the office, he saw no signs that Ray had been there. He figured his partner hadn't testified yet, and that meant Luke was going to have to drive to the man's house. This wasn't the kind of story to drop on him over the phone.

After seeing Miriam's husband's car, he wanted a closer look at the vehicle. He figured it was probably best to do it when Miriam wouldn't be there, which meant he would have to wait until the next day.

Given his fatigue and hunger, Luke decided to go home before going to Ray's. When he pulled into his driveway, Dayton's car was already there.

He went into the house and found his wife in the kitchen. Aleyna kissed him distractedly. Lilliana, LB, the baby, and the puppy all sort of hurled themselves at him in a loud circus of chatter he did his best to decipher. He pulled out of the clutter of his family when Aleyna waved to get his attention.

"Dayton's waiting in the den and wants to speak to you. I'm guessing he's staying for dinner. Is that okay?"

Luke nodded and went to the den. Dayton was slumped in Luke's favorite chair. The younger man looked so beat, with that hurt puppy-dog quality he had at times, that Luke didn't even mind he was in his chair.

"Hey," Luke said.

Dayton glanced up and grimaced. "I'm sorry, Luke. I kind of lied to you about something."

Luke sat down on the couch across from Dayton. "About what?"

"You know how I told you Miriam didn't tell me anything new?"

"Yes?"

"Well, she did. And I didn't tell you because... because I didn't think it mattered. Not to Weaver's murder. But maybe it does."

"What'd she tell you?" Luke tried to keep his voice calm, but anger at Dayton and hope that the missing information might matter made him speak a bit sharply.

"Her and Weaver. The reason he called her. She was supposed to meet him at the office that night. He called her to tell her he was going to meet somebody and she should come a little later than they'd planned. Then he called back to say the man he was going to meet hadn't showed up, but he was still waiting. She was real clear that Weaver didn't tell her who he was supposed to be meeting, and she didn't have any idea. I made sure of that. But it was important enough, whoever it was, that Weaver sort of canceled their plans of getting together."

"Getting together?"

"Yeah. Like, ah, you know, hooking up."

Luke closed his eyes for a minute. When he opened them again, he asked, "You sure?"

"I'm sure. They've been getting together on Fridays for a long time. Seems like that's the reason, or one of the reasons, she went to work for him. They met at some country club and started playing tennis and golf together, right after she moved down here, I think. And it all kind of, well, you know."

"She's a good ten years, maybe more, older than him."

Dayton rubbed his hands on his pants and shifted his weight in the chair. "Age don't... doesn't matter that much when there's a real connection. And I get the feeling this wasn't some... it wasn't just some cheap little thing." He shook his head. "That poor woman, what all she's been through."

"Yep." Luke thought about how she must have felt that night he and Ray had gone to her condo, blathering on about the murder, with her husband prowling around, and her having to hide her grief. "God makes women tougher than us, Dayton, and don't you ever let any macho cop BS convince you otherwise. You understand me?"

"Yes, sir. I do. I reckon she really loved him. Weaver, I mean. But I guess it would've been too difficult for them to get married or something."

"I think Weaver probably liked being single, and Miriam probably liked being married to her husband."

The two men sat without speaking while Luke tried to put it all back together. Because of the phone records, they knew Weaver had called Carter Russell twice. Apparently, those calls were right before he'd called Miriam.

As if he were reading Luke's mind, Dayton said, "I reckon it was that rattlesnake guy that he was supposed to be meeting that night."

That would do it. Connect the dots. Carter must have been meeting with Weaver to spill his guts about the killings twenty years ago on the beach that Kate had told him about. But Luke didn't get why this would all happen after so many years had passed. Maybe Carter had gone to Greenstreet for some reason and told him about the murders on Bald Point or told Greenstreet who was behind it. But that didn't make sense. Carter had no need to go to Greenstreet with a criminal matter. Still, something about Bald Point had gotten all three of them killed.

Damn, that means Kate's in real danger too. He should never have let her go home by herself. "We can't be screwing around now. We got to figure this out and quick."

"I know."

"One thing you got to do. Get over to the hospital and find a nurse or somebody who saw Constantia without his shirt on. Find out if the man has a scar on his right side."

"You know they aren't supposed to tell stuff like that."

"That's why you're going to do it. I'm too damned irritable to charm anybody into telling me anything, and Gilroy has Ray under house arrest, so that leaves you to go romance some cute nurse's aide or whoever."

Luke was glad Dayton didn't ask what a scar had to do with anything. Luke wasn't ready to tell him much, certainly not about Kate's role in it, not until he talked to Ray. "Did the Karma guy know about this? I mean about Miriam and Weaver?"

"You mean Constantia? I don't know. I'll go by his apartment on the way home tonight and ask him if you want me to."

Some part of Luke's tired brain understood that this was an important moment between him and Dayton. He looked over at the younger man with a weary grin. "He's invoked his right to silence for now. Maybe you can question him later, or if things change, I'll send you in. Now, let's have supper. Eat quick then get over to the hospital and see if you can find out anything."

Dayton looked satisfied, and Luke realized he was beginning to trust the young detective.

"You go on in there and see if you can set the table or something. I got to call Kate a minute." *Tell her what? Watch your back. Don't open the door to strangers. Be careful. There's somebody out there killing people. That the world is a dark and evil place at times.*

Dayton left the room, and Luke dialed Kate's number. "Hell fire," he said as he listened to her phone ring and ring. Finally, she picked up. They chatted until he felt comfortable that no one was there holding a gun on her, and he hung up.

"Daddy, dinner's ready," Lilliana said, balancing the baby on her hip and smiling at him from the doorway. Her black eye was already healing.

"Coming, baby sister," he said, using her childhood nickname for the first time in years.

In the kitchen, Dayton was setting the table and talking to LB, but when Lilliana walked into the room, he stopped and smiled at her. Then he pulled back her chair for her to sit.

After supper, Luke drove over to check on Kate and inspect her locks and windows. He volunteered to sit out in his car all night and watch the place, but she said no. He begged her to come sleep over at his house, but she refused. In the end, they settled for her agreeing to sleep with her snub-nosed .38 on her nightstand and to call him first thing in the morning.

Weary almost beyond his endurance, Luke went to Ray's house next, only to find it dark. When no one answered the door, Luke drove by Ray's old hangouts, looking for his partner's car. He didn't want to find him drinking, but he did want to find him.

An hour later, Luke pulled into his own driveway. Wherever Ray was, he wasn't easy to find, and if Luke didn't sleep soon, he would pass out.

THE NEXT MORNING, LUKE called the state attorney's office. Gilroy's assistant explained that Ray had been subpoenaed by the defense to testify again, and Gilroy still didn't want Ray talking to anybody else but him. Gilroy was so serious about it that he'd made Ray stay in a hotel last night.

Luke had never heard of such a thing, but Gilroy had to be under a ton of pressure so was probably overreacting. Or maybe the attorney just didn't trust Ray.

"Well, I reckon that a night in a hotel will improve his charming disposition about one hundred percent," Luke said sarcastically. He hung up and turned to Dayton, who had just walked over to his desk. "What'd you find out last night at the hospital?"

"Nothing." Dayton grinned. "*Yet*, that is. See, there's a CNA who was helping out with Constantia, and she's on duty this evening, and I'm going to try again with her."

"All right. You can't talk to Constantia, but you can sure question folks around him at the state attorney's office." Of course, Luke and Ray had already done that, two or three times in fact, but maybe somebody had something new to tell Dayton. "See if you can find anything out, suspicious or otherwise, about that man. What's he hiding that somebody'd want to kill him over it?"

They split up, with Dayton heading to the state attorney's office and Luke to check out Miriam's husband's car. Luke made up his mind that if Gilroy didn't cut Ray loose soon, he'd just have to bust into the courtroom and grab him. But first, he was going to find out what Miriam's husband and that big black car had to do with anything.

Miriam's husband answered the door, dressed in a lime-green polo shirt and beige pants. With his thin white hair carefully pushed into place and his face rosy colored and smooth, he had the look of the well-groomed retired executive. He introduced himself as Gordon.

"Getting ready for a golf game?" Luke asked.

"No. I play on Mondays and Fridays." Gordon stood in a way that blocked the doorway to his condo. "Miriam's not home. She's at work."

"I know. Actually, I came to see you."

"Yes?"

All right, we can do it in the hallway of your fancy high-rise if you want to. "I'd like to look at your car. I hope you don't mind, and I'd really appreciate it if you won't ask me why."

Gordon didn't move or speak for a long enough time that Luke began to get fidgety. "I seriously doubt you have probable cause for a warrant."

Luke put on his best just-among-friends smile. "Sir, I'd like to keep this between you and me for the time being. If you could see your way clear—"

The man turned and went back into the condo, leaving the front door cracked. A minute later, he returned with a set of keys. He walked out the door and locked it behind him then started down the hallway toward the elevator. Luke followed him, and the two of them did not say a word as they went into the garage. Gordon turned on the light.

Luke peered at the front of the car. He walked around it and studied it at all angles. "Would you mind pulling it out in the bright sunlight and letting me get a better look?"

"I would mind having my neighbors see a police officer examining my automobile."

"Then how about I drive it down the beach to a private spot?" Luke was thinking he'd drive it down to Hali Beach, to the spot where Constantia had been hit. He could see if he got any kind of rise out of the man at the site of the accident.

"If that's what it will take to satisfy you. But I'll drive."

Luke was surprised Gordon agreed. He'd already been trying to figure out how to pitch it to Judge Goddard to get a warrant. But like the man had said, Luke didn't really have probable cause. "If you'd just go down to the entrance to Hali, the one—"

"I know where you want me to go. To where that man was hit on his bicycle."

They drove in the same, strained silence in which they had walked down the hallway. After Gordon parked, Luke got out and looked at the car in the strong daylight. He poked and prodded until even he became restless with the search. He didn't see any evidence of damage or recent repairs, but he wanted the techs to look it over. Those forensic science guys could find things he couldn't see. When he asked if the technicians could come and examine the car, Gordon said no, that enough was enough.

On the way back to the condominium, Gordon said, "I know you're thinking that I hit that man to keep him from telling you about Miriam and Weaver, but I didn't. I don't even think he knew about them, and if he did, he seemed content to keep his peace. So whatever you're thinking, I don't have a motive, and I'd appreciate you not telling Miriam about any of this. She's suffered enough."

The guy kept surprising Luke. So Gordon didn't want Miriam to know he knew she had been having an affair with Weaver. That meant Gordon needed Luke to keep his secret. *Okay, we can deal then.* "Sir, I'll make sure the techs examine the car while Miriam is at work. And I give you my word of honor that if the techs say that car is clean, I'll never say a word about this to Miriam."

Gordon shook his head. "It seems I don't have much choice."

"I'll make the arrangements and let you know when to expect them."

———— ◉ ————

WHEN LUKE GOT BACK to the office, Dayton was on the phone at his desk.

Cupping the receiver with his hand, Dayton said, "Those folks at the state attorney's office didn't have anything real helpful to say about Constantia. I'll tell you more in a minute." Then he went back to his call, nodding and saying "yes, sir" at regular intervals.

Easing into his desk chair, Luke made a mental list: Get the techs to examine Miriam's husband's car. Call Kate at the library, even though she'd called him at six that morning to report she was safe. Reignite looking into Ledbetter's and Constantia's backgrounds. Track down Jimmy Chukenears. Call the DEA and the Franklin County Sheriff's Office and reopen the case for Bald Point murders. And tell Ray everything that was going on.

Gonna be a helluva day. He picked up the phone to get started.

Kate wasn't at the library when he called, but before he became too worried, he reached her at home. She told him she was taking the day off to think. He didn't like her being alone, but he couldn't spare Dayton, Ray was trapped at the courthouse, and Luke had enough work for two men. In the end, he settled for her promise to keep the doors and windows locked and to not go out.

He cornered a uniformed officer and told him to drive by Kate's house every hour, if not more often. He told the officer that if he saw another car or anything even vaguely amiss, he was to knock on the door and check on her.

Luke had to hope that would be enough.

Chapter Thirty-Eight

Kate couldn't sit still. After talking to Luke, she paced. Both Maggie the cat and Maggie the dog had been fed and were napping. She envied their sleep.

Finally, she called Nicky. The phone rang for a long time, and nobody answered. If she could just get some kind of lead on all this mess, maybe Luke wouldn't have to tell Ray all of her and Tank's parts.

Ignoring Luke's warning and her promise to stay put, Kate got into her car and, with a feeling of dread, drove to the fishing village where she'd grown up. CeCe and Nicky's parents were long dead, but if she could find some of Jimmy's family, they might know something helpful about him or even about Bobby. Finding Jimmy himself wouldn't be easy, though, if he was on the run from a warrant. Jimmy's people, the Chukenears, weren't listed in the phone book, but that didn't mean some of them couldn't still be around. They'd once been a big family in Dolphin Cove, and maybe somebody was left in the village.

She drove the narrow streets of Dolphin Cove Village and looked at the houses, most of them small with jalousie windows and screened-in porches on the fronts or the sides. Lush vegetation grew wild, with sprays of bougainvillea draping over the houses and hibiscus bushes forming erratic hedges.

She parked the car on a side street then got out and walked through the neighborhood. She read the names on the mailboxes that had them—most only had numbers—but none were familiar, and she didn't find any Chukenears. A few children were playing outside. Laundry hung in side- and backyards, and the jetsam of boats, nets, and fishing gear was piled in drifts about the yards.

At the marina, she walked out on a dock and peered at the boats. A shrimp trawler caught her eye, and she eased over to check the name on the boat.

"Can I help you?" a man asked, trotting out of the door of the marina office.

Kate studied his face for some sign of familiarity and saw none. "Yes." She smiled, though she didn't feel like doing so. "I used to live here. My father was Tank Pettus."

The man just stared at her, his expression neutral.

Kate forced a little laugh. "See, I'm looking for an old boyfriend of mine. Name of Jimmy Chukenears. He used to fish out of here."

The man shook his head. "Nobody by that name's been around here for years."

"He had a trawler, *The Jackpot*, and I wonder if I could just look at the boats. Closer." Though what in the world she thought she'd see, even Kate didn't know. *Ghosts maybe?*

"These docks and boats are private property. You want to charter a boat, I can help. You want to buy some seafood—"

"Sorry. I didn't mean to trespass." She hurried off, imagining the man staring at her back until she was gone from the marina.

Before she went back to her car, she walked to the house Tank had once owned. She stopped and stared at it, trying to remember the exact layout.

A young woman stuck her head out the door. "Something you want, lady?"

"I used to live here," Kate said. "Just looking around."

The woman nodded but continued looking at Kate.

"I'm looking for an old boyfriend, actually. Jimmy Chukenears."

"Nope, I don't know him. I haven't lived here long, though." From inside the house, a baby cried, and the woman turned back to look.

"Thank you. Sorry to have disturbed you." Kate walked away, fighting the urge to cry.

She left Dolphin Cove, crossed the bridge over to the island, drove up to the northern end, and parked. Ignoring the no trespassing and no access signs, she cut through a yard to get to the beach.

When she was younger, that end of the island had been open, and beach access had been easy. People just walked through the sand spurs and the sea oats until they came to the shore. Now the people who'd bought all the property didn't want the public on the beaches they fancied were their backyards, though state law proclaimed the shoreline itself remain public. But if people couldn't get access to the beach, it didn't matter what a statute in a book on a shelf in a law library said. Not many people would walk the miles from the public access at the center of the island to get to the tip, where the riptides made it unsafe to swim anyway.

So the people in the big pink and yellow stucco houses with the manicured lawns on which they wasted water and money perfecting grass and scrubs that had no natural business growing in salt spray on a sandy key had won. The public beaches were their own private backyards, and government taxes went to shore up the beaches and keep the natural erosion at bay so the rich people could keep their corner of paradise to themselves against nature and the public, no matter what damage the sand dredges did in replenishing the shorelines designed by nature to ebb and flow like the tides or what it cost in taxpayer dollars.

Sometimes it's hard to stay in this part of Florida. Kate knocked over the no trespassing sign she walked past. *So let them arrest me. They probably will be soon anyway.* She sat on the sand and stared off in the distance at the hazy span of the long suspension bridge over the bay.

A troublesome thought burst out of her subconscious. *Could Morgan be Bobby?* At first, she couldn't really think of a reason to wonder that other than he was near the right age. But the more she thought about it, the more the idea took hold. Dave had been killed because he knew what had happened on the beach, and he'd also been involved in fighting the phosphate mines. Morgan was front and center with the mines.

The only way to find out for sure was to check for the scar. She figured given the way he'd pursued her, getting his shirt off shouldn't be hard.

When she got home, she dialed his number.

Chapter Thirty-Nine

When Kate pulled up at Morgan's house, he was waiting to help her out of the car. Though the gesture was gentlemanly, it was also a bit irritating. She could get out of a car by herself. Still, she rested her hand on his arm and smiled up at him in what she hoped was a flirtatious way. In the fading light of sunset, she studied him while thinking of the photograph and trying to see if he could be Bobby.

Morgan was solid, almost chunky, and Bobby had been stick thin. Nicky said Bobby's nose had been broken, and Morgan's straight nose didn't show any sign of that. But she was there, so she might as well follow through.

The wind whipping in off the bay blew her hair in her face, and she tugged it back with her hand. "Let's go sit on your deck and watch the sun go down," she said.

What she wanted was to see Morgan in sunglasses, the way Bobby was in the old photo. Getting his shirt off would have to wait.

They sat side by side, with Morgan pressing close so that his leg rubbed against hers. He put on a pair of sunglasses, not aviator like Bobby's in the picture but still big, and he poured a couple of glasses of wine. *Good wine.* She could appreciate the difference between what he served her and what she bought at the grocery store.

She sipped slowly, letting him lead the conversation and eyeing him as often as she thought she could without seeming rude or too curious. But even with the sunglasses, she still couldn't put Bobby's face into Morgan's. He seemed too smooth, too educated for Bobby.

However, she was glad to have the snub-nosed .38 in her purse. She still intended to see his stomach and look for the scar.

"Let's go inside," he said. "I have another bottle of sauvignon blanc chilling. I remembered that you like it."

She followed him in and looked around, marveling again at the elegant grays, blues, and beiges and the newness of his home. She wondered if his sense of style was really that good or if he'd hired a decorator.

He led her to the couch and poured her another glass of cold wine. Sitting next to him, Kate felt shabby and unsure. *Why am I even here? If I find a scar, would that really mean Luke didn't have to tell Ray about me and my father all those years ago? Can't the police find a way to get his shirt off?*

She wondered if she should excuse herself, get in her car, and go home. She could call Ray and see if he was still mad at her. But she hadn't slept in days. Her defenses were down, and the wine was perfect. She couldn't summon the energy to leave.

When the bottle of wine was gone and a second bottle opened, he fed her fresh grouper, lightly broiled in herbs and butter. She ate without tasting, though she did wonder if he had a chef or did his own cooking.

When he led her into his bedroom, holding her hand lightly in his own, she sat on his bed. She couldn't remember what they had talked about. Though it was still early in the evening, she couldn't recall a single topic of conversation.

Morgan sat beside her and took her hand again. "You look beautiful." He leaned over to kiss her.

She moved into his embrace, returning the kiss, though it was more automatic than passionate. Her fatigued mind, dulled by wine, summoned no plan beyond seeing if he had that scar. She needed to get his shirt off, look, then leave.

Either way, she had to leave.

AT A QUARTER AFTER five, Luke was about to hike over to the courthouse and grab Ray even if it meant being charged with contempt of court. But as he pushed back his chair to leave, Miriam came into the station. He stood up to greet her.

She gestured for him to sit. "Please, no need to stand."

They exchanged pleasantries after she took the chair opposite his desk, then she said, "Dayton explained to me that he... that he left out some information that I told him. I want to make sure you're not mad at him. He was trying to protect me and my reputation. He's got a kind of old-fashioned gallantry about him."

He just nodded at her.

"My husband pretends that my Friday nights out are with just the girls. He is a very fine man, and he's a good husband. I've been very unfair to him."

Luke didn't want to hear her confession. He wanted to find Ray, check on Kate, and maybe get home before dark. But he didn't know how to tell Miriam to shut up, so he let her talk.

"I'm not sure why I want to explain this to you. I loved Weaver. I love my husband, too, but he's a boring man, not at all like Weaver. I don't fault him for being boring. It's just the way he is, steady, reliable, and boring. Decent."

Luke nodded again, wondering how he could stop the conversation.

"Maybe we're just born with these character traits. Like you. Maybe you were born droll. And maybe your friend Ray was born with no sense of humor, and Weaver... Weaver was born exciting. And I was born—" She stopped as a blush crept across her tanned skin.

He thought back to the Saturday after Weaver's murder. When she had tried to answer their questions about Weaver's private life, she had blushed and stammered. She was ashamed.

Aren't we all, one way or the other?

He wanted to make her feel better. "Yes, I reckon so. Like Dayton's born with that goofy—"

"He's not goofy. He's just enthusiastic. I've known you and Ray, worked with you both, for years now. You can't help it in a job like you have, but you've lost that enthusiasm. Dayton hasn't. He will. But until he does, you shouldn't fault him. And you shouldn't blame him for wanting to protect me."

"No, ma'am, I do not fault him for that. He's just being himself."

"He's not in any kind of trouble, then? With you, I mean?"

"No."

She rose and offered him her hand. "Thank you. I appreciate your listening to me."

He took her hand, thinking again that she was a true lady.

"One last thing and I intend never to bother you with my personal life again." She stared into Luke's eyes as if she were about to make another confession. "I would be grateful if you never mention this conversation to my husband. It will be better for us both if he never understands that I know that he is aware of... things. And I assure you, the technicians won't find anything on his car to indicate it was involved in a hit-and-run. He simply is not that kind of man." She turned and left.

Damn Dayton. He must have told her about the techs and the car. Gallant or not, he had a mouth on him like a girl. As Luke fumed, the phone rang. He snatched it up.

"Hey, got something for you," Dayton said proudly.

Luke started to read him the riot act for blabbing to Miriam, but something told him to be quiet and listen. "What's that?"

"This CNA at the hospital, she says she saw a scar on Constantia. His right side. She's sure of that. I mean, right side and all."

Luke inhaled sharply, a kick of adrenaline hitting him.

"Want me to go pick him up?"

"No. He already said he's not talking with us."

"Then what?"

"Do this," Luke said, thinking fast. "You follow him. Stay on him like a tick. He makes any move even vaguely toward Kate, you call me and don't let him out of your sight."

"Okay." Dayton still spoke in his happy, excited voice.

Pretty impressive for a man who'd already been shot on the job once.

"I'll get Ray, call Kate, and start working on what we tell our new state attorney about all this. Maybe ask Gilroy to tell Constantia he's going to subpoena him to a grand jury and, following that, give him a Garrity order to submit to an administrative interview." Such an interview would be inadmissible in a criminal proceeding against him, but Luke figured it would be helpful to him and Ray. That, and maybe he'd just flat-out ask Constantia to let them look at him with his shirt off.

"You got the hard part, then," Dayton said. "Let me go get in place and make sure I can follow Constantia after he leaves work."

"Be careful, Dayton."

"Always."

Luke hung up, grabbed his coat, and sprinted for the courthouse. He and Ray needed to talk.

Chapter Forty

Ray braked so suddenly in front of the ABC Liquor store that the car behind him honked and swerved into the next lane. Without even looking at the irate driver, Ray tightened his grip on the steering wheel and cut in sharp to a parking space directly in front of the store. Half an hour earlier, he'd practically run out of the courtroom, so steamed he couldn't see straight, let alone think about catching up to Luke or Dayton.

He jumped out of the car, but by the time he reached the door, he'd slowed down. *What are you doing?*

A storm was exploding in his gut, and his head hurt. *All fucking day wasted, sitting in the courthouse waiting to be called, and nothing. Nothing.* He had to do it again tomorrow. It was almost as if James Gilroy wanted him out of the game, out of the Alton Weaver investigation.

No. You're being paranoid. Besides, the defense attorney was the one who'd been playing hell with him that day.

Reining in his frustration and anger, Ray held open the door for an older woman coming out with two packages. She smiled and thanked him, and he eased into the store, the heavy AC hitting him like a slap.

Go see Kate.

Call Luke.

Work out.

Go drive along the beach.

Do anything but what you're about to do.

He shook it all off and went straight to the whiskey aisle. He picked up a bottle of Jack Daniel's, not just a little pint but a fifth. At the register, he paid cash while ignoring the woman in line behind him who tried to flirt with him. Bottle tucked under his arm, he went out, slammed into his car, and fought the urge to open the bottle right then and there.

Fifteen minutes later, he pulled into his own driveway and, booze in one hand, leapt out of the car. Inside, he flung off his jacket, yanked his tie off so hard it cut into his neck, and took off his dress shirt. Down to just his pants and a white undershirt, Ray poured a jigger of Jack into a glass then sat down and stared at it.

Why now? But he knew. It wasn't the case. It wasn't wasting the day at the courthouse. It was Kate.

Go see her. Now. Get it straightened out.

"I'll do just that." He threw back the whiskey with one quick jerk of his hand. It burned as it went down, and a warning light flared in the back of his mind. *Stop. Now. One's not so bad.*

He poured a second jigger. He stared down at the amber liquid. When he'd stopped with the hard stuff, he hadn't gone to AA or to counseling and hadn't read any self-help books. *Maybe I should have.*

Go see Kate. Don't let this go bad.

Ray gave the jigger another hard look before he headed to his bedroom. He changed into jeans and, as was his habit, put his holster on his belt then slipped his service revolver into it. Then he pulled a chambray work shirt over the gun and started for the front door. Snatching up his keys where he'd dropped them before, he caught sight of the Jack Daniel's bottle out of the corner of his eye. *Leave it. Go see Kate.*

He stepped back and downed the jigger of whiskey. He left the bottle and went out to his car.

When he pulled into Kate's driveway, he exhaled until he'd emptied his lungs. Her car wasn't in the carport, and no lights were on, but he got out of his car anyway. On the front porch, he rang her doorbell. After a minute, he knocked and waited again. Another thirty seconds passed, then he pulled out his key and went in.

Ray searched her house carefully, looking for any clue as to where she might be, but he figured he knew. Fighting his better instincts, he finally gave up and checked in her bathroom. Her diaphragm was in its container.

But does that really prove anything? The guy had kissed her. On the mouth. LB had said so.

Though ashamed of his jealousy, Ray couldn't stop imagining what else they might have done after she'd gotten LB home. After confronting Kate about the man, Ray had driven by Morgan McKay's house twice, and he'd noted the expensive neighborhood, the dock behind the property, and the sailboat he could see from the road. The man was rich. Ray couldn't compete with that. But Morgan was also a phosphate champion. *How could Kate stand to touch him?*

He grabbed a beer from her fridge and took a long swallow. After another quick look around, he headed back to his car. He drove half a block away and parked in the shadow of a giant live oak. Nursing the beer to make it last, he stared at her house. His car would be half hidden, and there wasn't much traffic on the short street where Kate lived. He'd wait and see her when she got home.

Half an hour later, his beer long consumed, Ray stretched out on the narrow front seat of his car. He kept thinking about the bottle of Jack still sitting on the counter at his house. And how much his hip ached. Too much sitting. He needed a walk. Or a workout. Or a couple of aspirin. Or a couple, three, four jiggers of Tennessee's best whiskey.

Lights from a car down the road hit him through the windshield, and he slumped down, though he doubted anyone could see him in the cover of the live oak. The vehicle was traveling slowly and nearly stopped once or twice, as if the driver might be looking for something. Suddenly alert, Ray watched as it passed him, the driver no more than a dark shadow. The car pulled into Kate's driveway.

Leaning forward and squinting, Ray could just make out that the person getting out of the car was a tall, thin female who looked to have long pale hair. She knocked on the door, waited, then walked through the carport and knocked on the other door. After a few seconds, she circled around to the back as if checking windows or looking for another door.

Ray eased out of his car then, keeping to the shadows, moved quickly toward Kate's house. The woman reappeared, got back in her car, and left the way she had come.

Ray raced back to his car and jumped in. He started the engine and followed her. The woman drove a gold-colored Toyota, like about half the people in Concordia, and he had to pay careful attention not to lose her in the evening traffic. After about twenty minutes and several turns, he had a nagging feeling he knew where she was going.

The next time she turned, they were on the street where the late Carter Russell had lived. She pulled into Russell's driveway. Ray slowed and drove past the house. In the rearview mirror, he saw the woman head to the front door and step inside without knocking. In the light over the stoop, her long hair looked white.

After parking a couple of houses down, Ray stepped out and headed toward the Russells' house. He knew he should call Luke, but he was in his own car, and he didn't have a police radio.

As he approached, he heard voices. Eavesdropping through the closed door, he couldn't make out many words. He was sure there were only women talking, but he didn't hear Kate's voice. One woman said something like "Nicky's gone," but the other voice was too muffled for him to hear the reply.

He stepped to the side, intending to press his ear to the door, and tripped over a potted geranium. Though he didn't think the noise had been that loud, the door swung open, and the blonde glared at him.

"What are you doing?" She didn't sound scared, but she also didn't sound friendly. The blondest hair he'd ever seen flowed around her face and draped past her shoulders.

"Police. Detective." He pulled out his badge and held it up.

She stared at the badge as if memorizing it before looking back at him. "You followed me from Kate's." She wasn't asking, and he wondered if she had noticed him following her or just guessed.

Recognition tugged at him. He knew that face. No, not the face, the white-blond hair. That was what was familiar. She glared back at him as if she knew him too.

Mrs. Russell appeared behind the blonde. When she didn't slam the door on him, he tried to remember her first name. Mrs. Russell put a hand on the blonde's shoulder, and they both backed up a step.

Ray remembered Kate's hidden photo with the 1963 date on the back. "You're Kate's friend. From Dolphin Cove, when you were children." He remembered the N and i in the faint writing, the only legible letters. "Who's Nicky?" he blurted.

"My cat. He ran away."

The blond woman lied as smoothly as anyone he'd heard, but he knew that wasn't who Nicky was. She gestured toward the living room. "You might as well come in."

"Where's Kate?"

"I don't know." She was already walking away with her back to him, her hair swinging with the movement.

"I don't think this is a good idea," Mrs. Russell said, edging in front of Ray as if to block him.

"Gayle, let him in. People are dying. It's time we told the truth to somebody."

Gayle looked up as if seeing him for the first time. "You came here with that woman... Kate, for Carter's phosphate stuff."

"Yes, ma'am."

They all stared awkwardly at each other for a strained moment in the pale light of the entry hall until Gayle spoke. "All right then," she said, glancing briefly at the blonde. Her expression somewhere between angry and afraid, she said, "Marijuana. That's what killed him. Killed them all."

"Marijuana?" Ray shook his head, trying to clear his mind from the dizzy whirl of whiskey, beer, and fatigue.

"I've lied for a long time," Gayle Russell said, her tone as flat as if she were speaking of the weather. "But CeCe seems to believe it's time to own up to it all."

The blonde snapped on another light in the living room and gestured toward a chair. "Come in and have a seat, Detective. It's a long story."

Chapter Forty-One

Kate's objective—to get that shirt off Morgan and check for a scar—evaporated out of her mind as Morgan's hands and lips conspired with the wine. Her blouse was unbuttoned, revealing her sheer white bra, and she lay on his bed with him against her. She arched her back as he traced her neck and chest with his lips and tongue. Through the fabric of his pants, his hardness pushed against her stomach.

Pressing a hand against his chest, she shoved him away and sat up as she tried to collect herself. Things were going too far, too fast. She should never have come into his bedroom in the first place. *What in heaven's name was I thinking?*

The room spun a bit. That was it—she hadn't been thinking. She'd let the wine and Morgan's seductive voice lull her past any semblance of rudimentary common sense.

"Too much wine," she said. "I'm dizzy."

For a moment, Morgan didn't move or speak. She tensed, waiting for him to grab her or threaten or complain.

Then in a soft voice, he said, "Lay back, rest. I'll get you some ginger ale."

He got up and left the room. She turned so she was sitting on the edge of the bed. Wondering if she should try to snoop, she looked around, but before she could even get up, he returned and handed her a glass. She took a cautious sip. It was definitely the promised ginger ale, which was her mother's favorite cure-all, though drinking it only made her feel sad.

"I think it's over with Ray," she blurted, though she'd had no intention of saying anything like that.

"The fiancé?"

"Yes."

He put his arm around her and pulled her closer to him in a half-sided hug. Gentle. Not like a killer. She rested her head against his shoulder.

He took the glass and put it on the bedside table. "Do you want me to drive you home?"

Yes. But first, she had to be sure that he wasn't Bobby.

"No. Not just yet." She reached over to unbutton his shirt. About halfway down the row of buttons, she slipped her hand in and splayed her fingers across his chest, weaving through the mat of hair and easing downward.

━━━━◆━━━━

RAY SAT BEHIND THE wheel of his car, the dullness from the whiskey and beer flushed out of his system by adrenaline. *Where is Kate?* Their relationship seemed to be over, though he couldn't understand why or even how they had dissolved. Still, he was going to find her and save her.

But first he had to connect the dots in his head.

Gayle had told quite a story. She had spoken in a resigned monologue, and some of the tale was confusing, but he got the basic idea. Kate's father, Carter Russell, a guy named Polky, some local thug named Bobby, and a guy who went by Rock had been smuggling in marijuana. Kate's cousin Jimmy Chukenears had spearheaded the whole operation at first, but Bobby ended up running the main show. One night, something went wrong, and one of them killed two kids and left them on the beach.

For some inexplicable reason, after twenty years, Carter had decided to come clean. That was why he'd had an appointment with Weaver on Friday night. But Ray didn't understand why Carter had first contacted the other lawyer, Wyman Greenstreet.

CeCe had stated the obvious. Somebody from that night on the beach didn't want Carter talking and had taken out Carter and the two lawyers. Neither of the women had mentioned anybody named Nicky in the telling, but Ray didn't believe for one second that Nicky was CeCe's cat. He figured Nicky was the towheaded boy in that old photo, the one that Kate had hidden. The boy she never mentioned.

He couldn't quite wrap his mind around the fact that Kate knew about the connection. But CeCe had told him in that dry, exhausted voice that Kate knew Weaver and Greenstreet had both looked at newspaper stories about the dead kids on the beach. One of them had even photocopied the microfiche, so Kate knew that was what they were looking at.

Damn Kate. She couldn't even trust him with that information. They were beyond trust and sharing secrets now. But she was in danger, and he still had no idea which one of the men from the beach that night was killing people to keep the story buried. Kate's father was long dead. That left Jimmy, Polky, Bobby, and Rock.

He also needed to know why Carter had decided to rat out his friends—or his fellow smugglers—and put himself in line for a long jail sentence or even on death row after two decades of keeping his mouth shut.

Ray looked back at the house. It was older but a nice, big house on a giant lot. He'd thought before that it seemed a bit grander than a handyman's income would have bought, especially with a wife who didn't have an outside job. So Carter had no doubt come out of the drug smuggling with some cash.

Drug-smuggling money would be the perfect way to explain Ledbetter's cash purchase of his land in east county. It could also have funded Constantia's business in Tallahassee and his three expensive years in law school.

But why in hell would Carter go to Weaver with his story? What would Carter have gained that he'd trade his freedom for it?

Maybe Carter had some kind of deal with Weaver to give evidence in exchange for a lighter sentence or even immunity. It had happened. Ray saw it a lot in criminal conspiracy cases—the first one to rat out the others could make a sweetheart deal. That might explain Carter going to Greenstreet, to use him as a middleman or for help in negotiating a deal with Weaver. *Except Greenstreet didn't practice criminal law.*

Ray wanted to pound his head against the steering wheel. Instead, he decided to get Luke so they could brainstorm it out.

Ray was almost at Luke's house when he remembered the little ad in the newspaper where Greenstreet announced he would be handling environmental issues as well as real estate. Ray played with that for about half a minute, until the answer sucker punched him in the gut. *Phosphate.*

Carter hated the mines. Carter's wife had said that Carter was obsessed with it. He blamed the mines for killing his parents and would do anything to stop them. *Anything.*

The murders had something to do with Carter trying to stop the phosphate mine in Concordia. Poor, stupid Carter Russell must have known somebody with the mine was also on that beach the night the kids got killed, and he must have tried to leverage that into some kind of deal. Or he just hoped the arrest would be bad enough publicity to bring down the mining company.

If that was the game plan, whoever Carter tried to take down to stop the mine was somebody big in the phosphate company.

Morgan McKay.

Ray made a U-turn so sharp he almost lost control of the car, then he hit the gas and sped toward the bayside, where Morgan lived. As if he'd seen a photograph to prove it, he knew that was where Kate was.

Chapter Forty-Two

L uke had suffered a frustrating day even for a police detective, where careers typically consisted of running down dead-end leads, blind alleys, grabbing at straws, and making wild last-ditch guesses. Ray and Kate were both in the wind somewhere, neither at home nor answering their phones. Maybe it was time they all looked into getting those newfangled cellular phones, but until they did, he was stuck with just leaving messages asking them to call him. Hopefully, they were together, making up. At least Kate was safe for the time being because Dayton had Constantia under surveillance.

Eyelids drooping after dinner, Luke sucked on a cup of coffee at the kitchen table, hoping for a second wind while pretending to listen as Aleyna chattered. What Luke was doing, really, was just waiting—for Ray to return a call, for Dayton to check in, and for Kate to get in touch.

LB came running up the hallway from where he'd been hanging out with Lilliana and the baby. "Lilliana and me was thinking..."

"Lilliana and I were thinking," Aleyna corrected.

LB cut his eyes at her but nodded. "Lilliana and *I* were thinking that we'd take the baby and go up to Busch Gardens tomorrow."

"Why take a baby to Busch Gardens?" Luke asked, but he was already trying to remember how much cash he had in the drawer in the den. It would be good for Lilliana and LB to have a day for just the two of them, playing like in the old days.

"I'll keep the baby," Aleyna said.

"That'd be good," LB said.

Luke smiled, knowing LB and Lilliana had already figured that out. "All right, let me go see if I got the money to buy y'all's tickets and some lunch money."

LB followed him into the den, and Luke pulled open the drawer where he and Aleyna kept the household cash. Looking at the pile of fives, tens, and ones, he wondered if a day at the beach, which was still free—at least for the time being—wouldn't do just as well.

LB picked up the photograph Kate had stolen in Apalachicola, the photo of Bobby and Rock standing on a pier in front of a fishing boat. "What's this?"

"Just an old photo I've been studying. For a case."

"Wow, look at those boots! I want me a pair like that."

"Now, where in the world are you going to wear camouflage boots? School? Fishing? They'd be hot as hell." *And probably costly, too, judging from the thick soles, certainly too expensive for a boy who grew a size a month.*

"That guy who works on the boat with Kate's new fella, he wears them. Must not be too hot for him."

Luke stopped counting the money in his hand. "Say that again, son."

"I want me a pair of boots like that."

"No, the part about the man who works on the boat."

"Morgan—that's Kate's new friend's name—he showed me a bunch of pictures of when him and his buddy were fixing up their sailboat. In one of them, the friend is sawing stuff in the yard, and he's got on boots like those."

"You sure?"

"I'm sure. You can't miss the camouflage." LB said it like he thought Luke was accusing him of something. "It's what hunters and soldiers wear."

Luke studied the photograph again then looked back at LB. "Say it again, son. One more time."

LB frowned at him and sighed. "The guy in the photo had camouflage boots on, big heavy things with the thick bottoms. Just like those." He jabbed a finger at the image of Rock.

The caffeine and the adrenaline hit Luke straight on, and his heart rate jumped. "Did Kate see that photo? The one you're talking about?"

LB frowned as though he was thinking hard. "Naw. Mr. Morgan pulled it out of a drawer to show it to me, but she wasn't there 'cause she was off making a phone call. He was real proud of the way they'd fixed up the boat themselves."

"Tell me exactly what Kate's friend's name is again and where he lives, son."

"Morgan McKay. He lives over on that fancy street on the Bay—you know, the one by the museum—in that row of big houses with docks and things."

By God, he's got a cop's memory for detail. Luke was proud of LB and scared for Kate at the same time.

If Rock was working with this Morgan guy, Morgan could be Polky. Or Bobby, even. Or maybe Rock was stalking Kate. Whatever the details might prove to be, Luke feared Kate was in immediate trouble if she was hanging out at Morgan's again.

He reached for the phone with one hand and handed LB the whole wad of money, uncounted, with the other. "You and Lilliana be careful, you hear me? And don't eat so much you puke on the roller coaster."

LB took the money, shouted, "Wow!" at the size of the wad, and ran out of the den.

Luke listened to Kate's phone ring until the machine kicked in. "Luke here. Call me the minute you come in. Don't go out unless it's to come over here. Aleyna will be here if I'm not."

He called Ray next. No answer.

"Damn it to hell!" he shouted while waiting for the answering machine to come on. When it did, he said, "Call dispatch the second you get this."

He hung up and looked up Morgan McKay in the phone book. Relieved when he found a listing with a Bayshore Drive address, he called the dispatcher and asked her to send a patrol car to meet him at Morgan's house. "No sirens. And keep calling for Ray and tell him to get to that address as soon as he can."

He started to ask for Dayton, but he didn't want Constantia running loose, and there wasn't time to arrange a substitute. Dayton was more important where he was. If they couldn't find Ray, Luke would have to go in with just the patrol officers.

Luke went upstairs and strapped on his holster. After checking his police-issued .357 revolver, he slipped it into the holster. He put a second gun, his own snub-nosed .38, in his boot.

———◦———

KATE STROKED THE FURROWS of the scar low on Morgan's stomach. *Don't flinch. If he knows I remember, he'll kill me. Right here. Now.*

He moved her hand off the scar. Kate made herself reach up and trace her fingers down his chest as if nothing were wrong, as if she didn't realize she was in bed with a killer. *Fake it. You have to pretend.*

Morgan cupped her breasts and squeezed lightly. Kate shivered and hoped he would think it was from excitement. She kept picturing the scar on Bobby's side after he had stripped out of the bloody clothes. He had pounded Polky while she screamed as blood splattered against her face.

She stopped moving, realizing she could not fake this. "I need to go," she said, pushing to get out of his embrace. "The wine. Sorry. Feel. Sick."

But he pushed her back down in the bed. "It's not that easy anymore, Kitty." He sounded harder, almost like a different man.

Kate's heart seemed to stop, and her mouth went dry. Morgan stretched over her, pulling up her loose cotton skirt and yanking down her panties in one fierce move. She kicked and struggled, but his weight and strength kept her smashed underneath him as he unzipped his pants. His thrusts came coarse and hard and painful inside her.

Kate's gut roiled, and she screamed, even knowing no one would hear her. Morgan rammed into her for what felt like hours but was probably only minutes. He finally came with a series of grunts.

He rolled off and lay beside her. "I've wanted that for a long, long time. Since I first saw you at Jimmy's fish house."

She bit back a sob.

"I damn sure don't have to pretend anymore. I fucking deserve an award for all that acting, don't you think?"

She slid away from him, toward the edge of the bed. As she tried to sit up, nausea overcame her, and she bent over the side and vomited on the floor.

"Well, damn. I reckon you *did* have too much wine." Morgan squeezed her shoulder. "Go clean yourself up in the bathroom."

She lurched off the bed, careful to step around the mess she'd made, and scrambled into the bathroom. Once she slammed the door and locked it, she looked for a window or some way out, but there was no other exit. Her hands shook as she searched the cabinets for something, *anything*, she could use as a weapon. There wasn't even a pair of tweezers.

After tearing off her clothes, she turned the shower on as hot as she could stand it. In the corner of the stall, she pressed her back against the tiles as the burning water ran down her face. She vomited again then again until she was down to the dry heaves. She stood there while the shower washed it all away, then she soaped herself twice. Rinsing off, she knew she had to go out and try hard not to be killed.

She dressed then unlocked the door and stepped out of the bathroom. He'd put his pants and shirt back on and was holding what looked like her snub-nosed .38 in his right hand.

"I helped myself to your purse. You had to be suspicious already. You never brought a gun before."

"No, I just..." She couldn't think of any excuse. She wondered if she could pretend she still wanted him, even after what had just happened, so he wouldn't kill her. She made herself smile. "Too much wine, but I feel... better now." She stepped toward the door and pulled her hair down over her eye, glancing at him and trying to look coy instead of terrified and disgusted.

"Don't humiliate yourself, Kitty."

She jumped for the door, but he grabbed her before she got more than a few feet. He held her for a moment then shoved her back toward the bed. She stumbled but caught herself and stood, damp and shivering in her rumpled clothes. She scanned the room, looking for a way out or a weapon.

"So you did remember the scar. Too bad. I had some plans for us, good plans."

"Why?" Kate wrapped her arms around herself but still couldn't stop shaking. "Why kill all those people?" She didn't even know which ones she meant.

"Come on." Gesturing with the gun, Morgan motioned Kate in front of him.

With him prodding her, she walked down the long hallway into a den that seemed to serve as a home office.

"Sit. Be cool." He shoved her into a hard-bottomed chair and went to a credenza, still holding the gun at his side.

As soon as his back was turned, Kate jumped out of the chair and ran toward the door. He swung back, catching her easily, and knocked her to the floor.

He dropped down on top of her and, straddling her waist, brought the gun up to her face. "What a fucking waste. We could have had something sweet together right here. Now I guess we'll go sailing. To Mexico."

He was going to kill her—she could see it in his expression. And the best way would be out in the Gulf, where he could shoot her and dump her body. That had to be what he meant by "We'll go sailing."

For a second, she didn't really mind. Ray, Nicky, CeCe, and her own father were gone from her life, and she'd just been raped by a killer. Getting shot and tossed into the Gulf might be what she deserved, payback for keeping her mouth shut for twenty years and contributing to the recent murders. Then she realized Bobby would probably rape her again before he killed her. She had to get away. Or she had to kill him first.

"It's unraveling, isn't it?" He seemed to be genuinely asking, but she didn't know how to answer in a way that might save her.

He lowered the gun, moving it away from her face, and stood. "If you've figured it out, somebody else will too. I can't take the chance on staying here now, so I'm going to run. I've got a briefcase full of unmarked, untraceable bills right in that safe." He pointed at the credenza. "I'm always ready, Kitty. Always. Nobody's ever going to mess me up again like at Bald Point. And I've got more money stashed away in Texas and Jamaica. You wouldn't believe how much money. But you... well, you're a problem now, aren't you?"

"I'm the only one who knows." She didn't flinch as she stared him in the eyes. "And I can't tell unless I want my ass in a jail too. I know about felony murder charges and conspiracy, how I could be found just as guilty as you or Nicky because it was my van and all. I'm not ready for prison." She paused, studying him and wondering how far she should push it. "Just leave me here. I know how to keep my mouth shut. Haven't I proven that already?"

"Get up slow, and don't do anything stupid." Watching her carefully, he kicked an antique chair with lion-claw feet out of his way and reached over to pick up a necktie lying on a drum table. He put the gun down and stretched the maroon silk between his hands. "Turn around and put your hands behind your back."

Kate eyed the gun. As long as he was standing that close to the table, she'd never get the gun before he did. But if he was going to tie her arms, he'd have to move away from the gun. She turned a little sideways and put her hands behind her back.

When she felt his hand on hers, she pivoted and lunged for the weapon. Her hand slid out of his, but she stumbled over his foot. Grabbing her hair from behind with his right hand, he wrapped his left arm around her neck and pulled her away from the table. She kicked out behind her and hit his leg, but the angle didn't allow much force. He jerked her back and held her tightly against him, almost choking her with his arm around her neck.

Bobby reached over and picked up the gun. He pressed the nose of the barrel into the soft spot at the base of her skull. She kicked at his feet and swung her right fist up, but he tightened his hand around her neck till she couldn't breathe.

"You don't want to keep this up. You'll lose, and you'll make it messy."

Kate went limp. He let go, and she gasped air into her lungs as he shoved her hard to the floor facedown. He put a knee in her back and yanked her arms behind her and tied her wrists together.

He got up, and she almost cried from the relief when he lifted his knee from her spine. Using the tie around her hands, he pulled her to her feet, wrenching her shoulders so much she cried out. After shoving her into a chair, he picked up the gun and went over to the telephone, keeping the weapon aimed at her.

"Rock, get your butt over here. Bring your money, passport, and a change of clothes." Bobby paused, as if listening. "No. Forget that, but grab your arsenal too. We're sailing to Mexico."

He hung up, headed back to the credenza, and opened it to reveal a safe. Kate tested the bonds, pulling and tugging on them. She cast her eyes around the room again, seeking some escape, something she could do to stop what was happening. But her hands were tied tightly, and he could easily shoot her or stop her if she tried to run.

He pulled a briefcase out of the safe and put it on the table in front of her. "I'm taking you with me on the boat. We can have a little party on the way to Mexico." He grinned in a way that made her wonder how she'd ever thought him attractive.

He set the gun on the table and started pulling off his belt. Kate pushed her feet into the floor, scooting the chair backward.

"Relax. I'm just going to tie your feet. But so help me, if you try to kick me again, I'll hurt you." He bent over her in the chair as if to wrap his belt around her ankles.

She couldn't let him put her on that boat and rape her again. It would be better to risk getting shot right in his den. Pushing her feet hard on the floor, she tried to stand but ended up shifting her weight to the side, almost tipping over the chair.

"Damn it, Kitty." He swung his arm, slashing the belt down hard across her chest, then he raised it again and whipped her across the face. He pointed the gun at her left knee. "Stop it, or I will shoot you in the knee."

With pain shooting through her face and body, she glared up at him but stopped struggling. With a satisfied grunt, he laid the gun on the table, bent, and tied her ankles together with the belt.

"I'm going to throw some things in a suitcase. Be right back." Picking up the gun, he winked, and her stomach roiled.

As soon as Bobby left, she started pulling at the tie around her wrists behind her back. When the knot wouldn't give, she struggled to get her hands in front of her. By rolling and lifting her hips off the chair, she managed to slip her bound hands under her buttocks and behind her knees. But as she was bringing them under and over her feet, she lost her balance and slipped off the chair.

Sitting on the floor, she used her teeth to pull at the silk around her wrists. The knot had just begun to give way when Bobby came back into the den, carrying a small overnight bag.

He snickered. "Smart girl. And spunky. I always did like that about you."

She lowered her hands to her lap and scooted back from him, her butt bouncing on the hard floor. He stepped closer, the gun gripped in his right hand so hard his knuckles were white.

Trapped on the floor in front of him, Kate sucked air into her lungs, hoping her pounding heart didn't burst. Her mouth was so dry she could barely talk. She licked her lips and said, "Just leave me here. I'm no good to you. You know I can't tell anybody anything without bringing Nicky or me into it. I'm not going to talk, so there's no reason to kill me."

"No, there isn't. But I'm not leaving you. Who knows? You might like living on a sailboat in Mexico."

Maybe he wasn't going to kill her but just keep her as his captive. At the thought of him raping her over and over, Kate gagged and started dry heaving.

"That wine really did get to you, didn't it?" But he chuckled as though he knew the wine wasn't the problem.

When she stopped gagging, he bent and stroked her face, almost tenderly running his fingers down the welts from where he'd slashed her with his belt. "No reason to kill you at all. Unless you give me one. Like Greenstreet did. Son of a bitch tried to blackmail me. But it was that stupid damn Carter—we knew him as David James back then—who fucked it all up. He wanted to stop the mine. You didn't know him all that well, but he was always harping about how the mines dug up his home county and gave his mom and dad cancer. He blamed the mines for all the sinkholes and had some fancy notion he could stop progress. He came to me first."

Keep him talking. If he was talking, he wasn't hurting her. "He knew who you were?"

"Sure, the old gang kept tabs on each other. Like coyotes around carrion. We all settled in and around Concordia. I told you the truth. I grew up here. Dave was chasing that blond woman, so he came back when she did. And Jimmy had his crew and his family here. Jimmy set us all up, right in your old backyard. He and Dave were big buds by then. Dave ran coke with Jimmy and me for a while."

"Where's Jimmy now?" Kate wondered if Jimmy was involved in all this somehow. She wouldn't put it past him.

"Long dead. A Mariel Cuban shot him in a turf war."

With a grin, he tapped her leg with the toe of his shoe, but he didn't loosen his grasp on the gun. "That's why I decided to go straight, Jimmy getting gunned down like that."

She nodded, surprised to feel a touch of grief. Jimmy and Tank had been close, first cousins, and she remembered what CeCe had said about Jimmy helping Tank at the end and financing CeCe's B and B.

"Yes, sir, after Jimmy got his ass killed and thrown in the ocean, Dave and me decided we'd go legit. But Dave developed a righteous streak, sort of an attitude like maybe he was better than me. When this mining project in the east county came up, he wanted to deal. He had this cockeyed notion that I could stop the mining company from its plans to dig in Concordia, and in exchange, he'd keep the peace. He didn't believe me when I told him it wasn't my decision. He didn't get that I was just a figurehead for AMCI, not a real executive. I couldn't stop it."

"So you killed him?"

"Not right then. I probably should have, though. But I didn't think I needed to kill him. I'd seen him shoot Polky point blank. Of course if he hadn't, I would have, the way Polky screwed us all up. But good old Dave, a smug little bastard even then, had to have the honor of plugging his childhood buddy. Then he hid Polky's body on *The Jackpot* when we scuttled it with me standing there watching. I guess we both figured that balanced it out so that we had to trust each other."

Kate grunted and pushed her feet against the belt, testing its hold.

Bobby kept talking, apparently enjoying telling his story. "But Dave saw some stupid ad in the paper and went to Greenstreet to see if he could come up with some kind of legal deal to stop the mines. Greenstreet wasn't much help, so Dave threatened to expose me if I didn't stop the mine. But he didn't know how to turn me in without putting himself in the electric chair too. You can kind of feel sorry for him, that little catch-22 he was in."

"That's why he went to Weaver," Kate said, beginning to understand.

"Yeah, he and Weaver had started talking, only Greenstreet didn't know that. Then Greenstreet got greedy with what Dave told him and tried to blackmail me."

He knelt in front of her. "That's why I started paying better attention and learned some of the details, what was going on. I got a guy at the state attorney's office—I reckon you know who. I ran some coke with him back in the day. He told me what was going on, what my old buddy Dave was planning to do. He was gonna turn state's evidence in exchange for a light jail sentence. He figured me getting busted would kill the phosphate company."

"Who killed Weaver?"

"Me." Morgan sounded proud. "I killed Weaver."

"How'd you get in the building?"

"Constantia. He had the access code and let me in."

Bobby pushed his face so close to Kate's she could see the faint hint of sweat above his lips. "Course I might still need to take Constantia out since that little hit-and-run didn't actually kill him, but it damn sure reminded him who's in charge."

So Constantia was part of it, too, though that info wouldn't do Kate much good at the moment.

"Stupid, stupid plan." He rocked back on his heels and stood up, swinging the gun as if he might be thinking of using it right there. "AMCI wouldn't give a shit about me. They'd just put somebody else in my office and keep right on mining. But nobody ever thought Dave was gonna get a Nobel Prize for brains."

Bobby tossed the gun onto the drum table, where it skittered toward the center of the surface. He grabbed her, one strong hand on each arm, and yanked her up off the floor. "They were working out the terms of a deal and were going to meet that Friday night in Weaver's office to settle it. So I sent Rock after Dave. The snake thing was just plain old blind luck, but you sure don't kick a winner in the teeth, do you?"

"Rock?" Kitty felt a fresh wave of panic. She'd never get away from two of them. Whatever she was going to do, she had to do it soon.

As he spoke, Bobby eased the pressure of his hands on her. "Yes, Rock. You met him at that meeting at your house. He's a lot more useful and loyal than Dave or your stupid Nicky."

Kate jerked her head back. Her feet and hands were still tied, but the knots around her wrists were loose now. She squirmed, trying to free herself from Bobby's hands.

Bobby shook her. "Stop it. You can't get away."

A trickle of pee ran down Kate's legs. *Keep him talking.* That was all she could think of doing. "Why phosphate?"

"To launder the money. That's how it started. I got the idea from Dave. He was ranting one night about this one phosphate company going under. They were broke, and he was glad because it would be one less phosphate company digging up his precious Florida. So I made an approach to the right man, and next thing you know, my money's coming out clean, and I'm a vice president of an up-and-coming business. Pissed old Dave off royally. Of course, I'm just a figurehead, something Dave didn't get. The company never lets me run things, not even after I got my nose fixed and took some speech and acting lessons, made myself all slick for my new role. But I didn't care that I didn't have any real power. I got to look and act like a legitimate businessman, and they let me do enough to keep me amused and to keep my money clean."

As he spoke, Kate studied him, waiting for a break in his attention, her heart thrumming so violently in her chest she could hardly breathe.

"Well, that's our little chat. Now come on, it's time to get. If Rock doesn't show up in the next minute or so, he'll just have to catch up with us later."

Once more, she jerked away from him, this time with more force. Her arms came loose, and she stumbled and fell back on the floor, hitting her hip hard against the foot of the antique chair. She grunted with the sudden pain.

Bobby yanked her up again.

She tried to pull free but stumbled and fell again. "I can't walk. You tied my feet together."

"I'm sure as hell not carrying you to the boat. Now behave, damn it."

Kate looked up at Bobby. The fight was suddenly out of her. This was going to happen. He was going to keep her on the boat, raping her until he got tired of that, then he would kill her.

Bobby leaned over her. "Be cool, and I'll untie your feet. You can walk onto the boat. You try anything else, and I'll shoot you in the gut and toss you out for the sharks. You understand me?"

Kate nodded. She believed him. All that gentlemanly stuff earlier had been an act. A good one to be sure, but just as fake as a Halloween mask. He untied the belt around her ankles and pulled her to her feet.

"Thank you," Kate said, trying to appear complacent.

He smiled. "See? It's easier if we just get along, isn't it?"

She didn't have the energy to reply. She took a couple of small steps, her legs tingling as she moved them.

Bobby walked beside her, still talking as if he had some point he hadn't yet made. "I'd been clean for twelve years when Dave screwed it up. Phosphate was my going legit at a time the Cubans and Colombians were killing off all the old Florida cracker dope runners like Jimmy. Not many Florida natives in that line of work anymore, not with the coke anyway."

Kate glanced over at where the gun lay in the middle of the drum table.

Bobby's eyes followed hers. "Don't screw up this late in the game. I'm thinking we might still find that sweet thing if you don't get stupid."

"I've been stupid all along." Kate's shoulders sagged, and she looked away from the gun.

Bobby turned back to the drum table as if to once more grab the gun. As Kate watched him move, panic choked her. With her hands tied, there was nothing she could do. *My God, I might as well have let him kill me back in the farmhouse for all that it matters now.*

Yet over the pounding of her heart and the ringing in her ears, she heard Tank, his voice as strong and clear as it had been before his illness. "Butt him with your head," Tank said.

Bobby was a few steps away from the gun on the table, his body sideways in front of her, but his head was turned so he could watch her. He would have to practically turn his back to her to reach the gun. Kate hunched up, ready to throw herself at his back to knock him off balance or maybe knock the gun to the floor and kick it out of play if she was lucky and fast enough.

Her whole body hummed with raw energy. She felt Tank's strength, the physical power he'd had before his illness, permeate her. Bobby was not going to kill her. Or if he did, he was going to have to fight hard to do it.

He turned, putting his back to her so he could reach for the gun. She leapt forward and head-butted him right between his shoulder blades as hard as she could. A sharp stab of pain cracked through her neck and into her shoulders, and she fell on her back at his feet.

Bobby slammed forward against the table but was able to grab the gun. Kate jerked her knees up to her chest, wincing with pain from the quick movement. With both feet, she kicked the backs of Bobby's legs, making solid contact with his knees, which gave under the force of her strike. He yelped as they buckled, then collapsed on the floor next to her, facing her.

⸻ ◉ ⸻

RAY PRESSED THE GAS pedal harder, even though he was already speeding beyond what was legal or safe.

If Ray had figured it out about Morgan, Kate would have, too, and that meant Morgan had to kill her. Ray's heart pounded at the thought. He wished he had his police radio with him because he didn't want to take the time to find a telephone booth that might actually work. All he could do was get to Morgan's house as fast as he could.

As he turned on to Morgan's street, he switched off his headlights. He parked in front of the house next door to maintain the element of surprise. Jumping out of the car, he pulled his revolver from the holster. Sticking to the shadows as much as possible, he rushed to the front door. He stood beside it and checked the knob. Unlocked. He slowly turned the knob and eased the door open.

When he heard a thud and yelp from Kate, he gave up all pretense of stealth and charged toward the sounds. He entered a den just as Morgan fell to the floor beside Kate. A gun lay between them, inches from Morgan's hand but also inches from Kate's.

Ray swung his revolver down to aim at Morgan's back, his finger tightening on the trigger. But Morgan was too close to Kate. They could suddenly move, and there was the risk that the bullet would go through Morgan and into Kate's body.

"Freeze, or I'll put you in hell!" Ray shouted as he ran around, hoping he could somehow get between them or get a clear line of fire.

KATE COILED ON THE floor, her eyes even with Bobby's. His face glistened with sweat, and he gave off an animal scent. She stared into the blackness of his pupils and into the cold pit behind them. He moaned, and his eyes closed in a kind of slow motion.

The gun was right there on the floor between them, where the force of his fall had knocked it from his grasp. Her hands, still tied, were in front of her, just an inch or so from the gun.

Bobby's head rested where it had bounced off the edge of one of the extended lion's claw feet of the antique chair, which he'd apparently hit when he fell. Kate inched her hands forward until she could pick up the gun with her fingers.

"Roll away!" Ray shouted at her.

"Kill the son-a-bitch. Kill him!" Tank shouted in her ear.

It was Tank's voice she obeyed.

Kate squeezed the trigger slowly as she exhaled, just like Tank had taught her.

Chapter Forty-Three

Luke explained to anyone who asked that Kate's shooting Bobby was self-defense. That was how Luke had seen it.

He had arrived about two minutes behind Ray. He ran into the den in time to point his own weapon at the man on the floor as Ray circled, looking for a safe angle to fire. But it was Kate who got off the killing shot. She had pointed the gun, with her wrists still bound, and shot the man who had tied her up. *Self-defense.*

Luke had untied her and held her while she sobbed. Then he had carried her outside and propped her against her car before he called 911. He had them send an ambulance for Bobby, even though he knew it was pointless.

Neither Luke nor Ray questioned self-defense as Kate stammered through a long explanation once they got her to the station. She tried to explain how Tank was somehow in the room and had given her strength. She said Morgan, who they had discovered was Bobby, had raped her. When she'd told them that, Ray flinched and left the room. Luke hadn't gone after him.

In the days that followed the shooting, no one questioned self-defense when they closed the file. They were never going to know how Ledbetter got that money in 1973, but it didn't matter. "He's just a butt-headed redneck, and it's none of our business anymore," Luke told Dayton.

Constantia was a different story. Yes, he had a scar, a tidy little appendectomy scar nothing like the deep, jagged one on Bobby.

Luke, Dayton, and Ray were all over Constantia about letting Bobby into Weaver's office and for leaking information to him, and all his protests didn't matter. All they had was hearsay, what Kate said that Bobby said. But if corroborating evidence existed, the detectives were going to find it. In the meantime, since Gilroy fired Constantia before Bobby's body was cold then reported the matter to the Florida Bar, that man's career as a lawyer was effectively over. Luke figured that Constantia had come out ahead in an odd way because he was still alive and safe from Bobby.

Constantia probably saw it differently, since James Gilroy was preparing an indictment to charge him with conspiracy to commit murder and first-degree murder under the felony murder statute. The way Gilroy saw it, Constantia was just as guilty as Bobby in the murder of Weaver, Gilroy's friend and mentor.

Regardless of what the detectives dug up, the new state attorney was not going to let Constantia walk. While a defense attorney might angle to keep Kate's testimony out as hearsay, Gilroy assured Luke that he could get Kate's statements about what Bobby had said in a trial as an admission against interest or even as an excited utterance or spontaneous statement.

All in all, Gilroy was shaping up to be a fine state attorney. Arrogant, yes. Obnoxious, sure. But effective. So it wasn't over yet.

The night Kate killed Bobby, Rock had come speeding up to Bobby's house, saw the cop cars, spun a U-turn, and hauled ass, but with two patrol cars on his tail. When he lost control and flipped his car, they had him. After he got out of the hospital, he spilled his guts to make a deal. He put it all on Bobby. He said he wasn't even on the beach the night of the killings and nowhere near that sinkhole in '72. That meant he didn't pull Kate or her father into it at all. Luke didn't believe any of that story, but at Rock's age, that twenty-year sentence he plea bargained for would be close enough to a life one.

All that time, with all the loose ends falling into place, Luke hadn't questioned that what he'd seen that night had been a righteous shoot.

In a news conference, AMCI's public relations people maneuvered to dissociate the phosphate company from its vice president in charge of development, trying and failing to put distance between themselves and a man who had built his fortune on the murder of four people twenty years ago in the panhandle of Florida then murdered two lawyers and his own colleague to cover it up.

Luke sat in his chair, thinking about Kate killing Bobby, then tried to make himself not think about it. As he listened to the phosphate public relations people deny the federal charges that the business had been financed by cocaine and money laundering, he realized AMCI wouldn't go away. Even if it did, some other phosphate company would take its place. Rich Northerners were eating up the beaches on the west side of the city, and phosphate mines were going to eat up the eastern edge of the county, and the whole state was just about out of water. Dayton was probably going to be his son-in-law, and that was fine, except he didn't want to work in the same department as his daughter's new husband. Maybe it was time to get out of Dodge and see if he could find an orange grove that Disney or the developers had left standing. He pushed back in his chair and shut his eyes.

And he saw it then as clear as if a movie projector was beaming it into his brain. Bobby's eyes were closed. He wasn't moving. When he fell, he had busted his head on the lion-claw foot of that antique chair. The blow to the head may not have been enough to kill him, but it had knocked him out. He hadn't been reaching for the gun when Kate fired. She had shot him as calmly as if she were at target practice, aiming at a piece of paper with the black outline of a man on it.

Maybe Ray hadn't seen it, being in the thick of things as he was. But Luke had. He had seen Kate shoot an unconscious man.

Luke figured he could go to his grave with his mouth shut on that one, but the plain truth was that Kate had executed that man.

KATE CALLED NICKY'S number repeatedly. She wanted to tell him it was over. Bobby was dead. Rock was in jail. Nicky was safe. But he never answered. After two weeks of hearing the phone ring and ring, she got a recording that the phone had been disconnected.

CeCe said she didn't know where Nicky had gone. He'd called CeCe to say goodbye, but he said he wasn't going to tell her where he was going because he'd figured out CeCe had told Kate once before. Nicky had left his daughter behind for nothing. He lost everything—his house, job, and family—by running.

Trying to push the thoughts of Nicky out of her mind, Kate walked into her bedroom and pulled out the box with Ray's engagement ring. She put the ring on her finger and looked at it. After a few seconds, she took it off and put it back in the box, thinking she needed to return it. Ray didn't have money to throw away on jewelry.

The Franklin County Sheriff's Department in north Florida closed the case on the two kids killed at the Bald Point beach end of Alligator Point. When the Dixie County officials pulled the van out of the sinkhole, the vehicle was long past being traceable back to Kate, and Luke never mentioned Kate's connection to the van to anyone. The bodies inside were put to rest.

Kate thought about all that as she stared at the jeweler's box, which held what should have been her engagement ring. She thought how nice it would be to sleep through the night. She thought about forgiveness. *Why is it so hard to forgive someone?* Now that it didn't matter, she'd finally forgiven Nicky.

Surely her father would have forgiven her, too, for running out on him. After all, he'd ordered her to take the money and leave long before Bobby killed those kids on the beach.

Over it all, though, she wondered if Ray would wait until it didn't matter anymore before he forgave her.

Maggie scratched on the outside screen of the bedroom window, and Kate went to the front door to let the cat inside. While she was standing there with the door open, Ray's car came down her street and slowed in front of her house. She waited to see if he would pull into her driveway.

Acknowledgments

A s book lovers surely know, it takes a dedicated and talented team to produce a good book. I am fortunate to have some of the best people on my team.

First and foremost, I want to acknowledge the generous and knowledgeable help of my brother, William D. Hamner. I am more grateful than I can fully express to him. He is a law enforcement officer of forty-eight years and counting, who shared his expertise on police procedures, forensics, cop talk and comradery, the criminal mind, investigative techniques, weapons, and autopsies. He is a fine writer to boot and authored some of the dialogue between Ray and Luke as well as a few of the fight scenes. Any screwups are mine, as he has a distinguished service record and absolutely knows his stuff.

I have been blessed for years by the talents and generosity of two amazing writers who offer support, free editing, and advice, and I can trust them to tell me the truth. For Donna Meredith and Marina Brown, I am most appreciative.

My good friend Mike Lehner and my husband, Bill, also deserve praise and thanks for their understanding, patience, and support as well as all those free grammar edits, help with Spanish translations, and those long, weird brainstorming sessions. Mike has been a tireless alpha and beta reader for more manuscripts than either of us want to count. And when I told Bill years ago I was going to quit my day job and write a novel, he built me a room of my own to do so in.

My agent, Liza Fleissig, has amazing energy, insight, and dedication, and I thank you, Liza, for finding such a great home for *The Smuggler's Daughter* at Red Adept Publishing.

The owner of my publishing house, Lynn McNamee, who took time from her own busy life to edit *The Smuggler's Daughter*, deserves a big round of applause for her attention to details, her wit, her talents, and her patience with the raw manuscript. She has a wicked eye for the right word and an astute sense of pacing and organization, all of which tremendously improved *Smuggler's Daughter*. Thank you, Lynn, for whipping it all into shape and teaching me more than a few tricks along the way. You were a whole lot of fun to work with.

Thank you to all the authors and the team at Red Adept Publishing who shared support, ideas, memes, and fun things, especially Karissa Laurel (aka Karissa Sluss), my Red Adept mentor by assignment, and Russ Hall and Erica Lucke Dean, mentors by proxy. And thank you to Streetlight Graphics for the bold, beautiful cover.

James O. Born, a former state law enforcement officer who began his career in police work as a US drug agent, helped me with a tricky part in the drug-smuggling sequences and, in the process, gave me a great line to use. Jim is an excellent author of many crime thrillers himself. Thank you, Jim.

Thank you to the generous, helpful people at the Florida Archives in Tallahassee, who pulled out the many volumes of the capital murder trial transcripts in the case that loosely inspired this whole story. Day after day, someone at the archives rolled out those transcripts for me to study and take notes on so that I could learn such pertinent facts as how much a bale of marijuana weighs and what went down on an isolated beach in the Florida panhandle that led to what became known as the sinkhole/Sandy Creek murders.

A final word about cities, rivers, and places used in this story: Some of the names are fictional, including Dolphin Cove Fishing Village, the Calusa River, Cattleguard Creek, and the city of Concordia. However, Alligator Point, Perry, Old Town, the Suwannee River park, Bald Point, Carrabelle, Steinhatchee, the Ochlockonee River, Tallahassee, and Apalachicola are very real places, though adapted here for fiction.

About the Author

Claire Hamner Matturro was raised on tales of errant, unhinged kith and kin, whiskey making, ghosts, and the War Between the States—in other words, classic Southern Gothic tales befitting her Alabama and Florida Gulf Coast roots. Inspired by such stories, she wanted to be a novelist, but pursued more gainful and steady employment first. Which is to say, she has been a newspaper reporter, a lawyer, and taught at Florida State University College of Law and as a visiting professor of legal writing at the University of Oregon School of Law. Claire and her husband Bill also own an organic blueberry farm in Georgia, where they lived for many years.

After the lawyering years, Claire returned to her love of storytelling and began writing fiction. Her big break came when a vice-president at HarperCollins took a chance on Claire's comedic legal thriller set on the Gulf Coast of Florida. The resulting Lilly Belle Cleary series of books won several awards. These days Claire is writing more serious fiction, but still with an eye toward the Florida

Gulf Coast, where she, her husband, and their rescue cat now thrive. Claire remains active in writers' groups, environmental groups, and, as an avid reader and reviewer, regularly contributes to *Southern Literary Review* and *Compulsive Reader*.

Read more at www.clairematturro.com.

About the Publisher

Dear Reader,

We hope you enjoyed this book. Please consider leaving a review on your favorite book site.

Visit https://RedAdeptPublishing.com to see our entire catalogue.

Don't forget to subscribe to our monthly newsletter to be notified of future releases and special sales.

Printed in Great Britain
by Amazon